Lady Macbeth's Daughter

ALSO BY LISA KLEIN

Ophelia

Two Girls of Gettysburg

Lady Macbeth's Daughter

LISA KLEIN

BLOOMSBURY

NEW YORK BERLIN LONDON

Published by Bloomsbury U.S.A. Children's Books
175 Fifth Avenue, New York, New York 10010

Library of Congress Cataloging-in-Publication Data
Klein, Lisa M.
Lady Macbeth's daughter / by Lisa Klein. — 1st U.S. ed.
p.   cm.
Summary: In alternating chapters, ambitious Lady Macbeth tries to bear a son
and win the throne of Scotland for her husband, and Albia, their daughter, who was
banished at birth and raised by three weird sisters, falls in love, learns of her parentage,
and seeks to free Scotland from tyranny in this tale based on Shakespeare's *Macbeth*.
ISBN-13: 978-1-59990-347-7 • ISBN-10: 1-59990-347-4
1. Gruoch, Queen, consort of Macbeth, King of Scotland—Juvenile fiction. 2. Macbeth,
King of Scotland, 11th cent.—Juvenile fiction. [1. Gruoch, Queen, consort of Macbeth,
King of Scotland—Fiction. 2. Macbeth, King of Scotland, 11th cent.—Fiction. 3. Kings,
queens, rulers, etc.—Fiction. 4. People with disabilities—Fiction. 5. Witchcraft—Fiction.
6. Murder—Fiction. 7. Scotland—History—To 1057—Fiction.]
I. Shakespeare, William, 1564–1616. Macbeth. II. Title.
PZ7.K678342Lad 2009   [Fic]—dc22   2009006717

First U.S. Edition 2009
Typeset by Westchester Book Composition
Printed in the U.S.A. by Quebecor World Fairfield
2   4   6   8   10   9   7   5   3   1

To my sisters,
Marilou, Jeanne, and Barb

"... I have given suck, and know
How tender 'tis to love the babe that milks me."
                    —LADY MACBETH (1.7.54–55)

"Bring forth men-children only!"
                    —MACBETH (1.7.72)

Cast of Characters

Names or descriptions in boldface denote characters also in Shakespeare's Macbeth.

MACBETH, thane of Moray, later king of Scotland
GRELACH, his wife (**LADY MACBETH**)
ALBIA, their daughter
LUOCH, Grelach's son by her first husband

RHUVEN, Grelach's servant
HELWAIN, a soothsayer   } **THE WYRD SISTERS**
GEILLIS, known as Albia's mother

MURDO, a farmer
COLUM, his son, a shepherd   } Albia's friends
CAORA, a shepherdess

BANQUO, Macbeth's general, Albia's foster father
BREDA, his wife
FLEANCE, their son and Albia's love

DUNCAN, king of Scotland killed by Macbeth
MALCOLM, his son

MACDUFF, thane of Fife, leader of the rebels against Macbeth

FIONA, his wife (**LADY MACDUFF**)

WEE DUFF, **their son**, one of several children

ROSS
ANGUS } thanes and allies of Macduff

EADULF, **murderer**, servant to Macbeth who turns against him

SEYTON, servant to Macbeth

Lady Macbeth's Daughter

Prologue

Wychelm Wood, Scotland. A.D. 1032

The nameless baby lay on the cold ground, wrapped in a woolen cloth. An owl hovered overhead and seemed to clutch a shred of cloud in its talons, drawing it across the moon like a blanket. In the darkness, two figures struggled against the stone walls of Dun Inverness. Groaning, the man stumbled away. The woman, Rhuven, wrapped herself in a cloak and picked up the baby. She set out in haste over the scrubby, open heath, now and then looking over her shoulder to be sure she was not being followed.

Across the blasted heath Rhuven ran, entering an ancient forest, the Wychelm Wood. Murk rose from the ground and dripped from the branches overhead. Unseen creatures with shining eyes watched her. She passed into a grove of young birches, their white bark shining in the moonlight. Beyond them in a clearing loomed twelve tall stones in a wide circle, Stravenock Henge. Nearby a wolf howled and Rhuven thought she saw its shadowy shape among the stones. She clutched the baby tighter.

Just ahead she saw Pitdarroch, the great oak tree whose gnarled roots grasped the boulders from which it grew. From its branches the owl uttered its shuddering call, summoning Rhuven onward, deeper into the pathless Wychelm Wood.

In an ancient roundhouse deep in the wood, a woman with wild graying hair sat on the hearth, stroking her chin with knobby fingers. The smoldering peat fire cast a faint light on the soot-blackened walls.

"Someone comes this way, Geillis," she said. "I feel it."

The woman sleeping on a rush mat stirred and lifted her head. Her face had few lines and her hair was brown and sleek.

At the door Rhuven called, "Sisters, let me in!"

Geillis, more nimble than Helwain, leaped up and lifted the latch. She gasped at the sight of Rhuven with a child.

"It is my lady's babe, not mine," she said with a frown. "My lord has ordered her to be killed. Having no other hope, I brought her here."

"But why?" asked Geillis, horrified.

"Her leg is misshapen. Otherwise she is perfect."

"So it is a girl," Helwain mused.

Rhuven turned to her. "Why did you promise Macbeth sons?" she asked sharply.

"He came to me for a cure once. He desired to know when he would have a son." Helwain shrugged. "I told him what he wanted to hear."

"Now he believes you cursed him, and my mistress and this poor child suffer for it," said Rhuven accusingly.

Geillis wrapped a scrap of cloth around her finger and dipped it in sheep's milk. The baby sucked it with an eager mouth.

"What do you expect me to do?" demanded Helwain.

"Keep his daughter alive," said Rhuven, her eyes keen and narrow. "And heal her crippled leg."

"Do you know what you ask?" Helwain's voice shook with controlled anger. "He slew our kinsman Gillam and drove Geillis and me from our land into this wilderness."

"Do it for the sake of the child," Rhuven pleaded. "She is not guilty of her father's wrongs."

"We are poor and have no means to raise her," Helwain objected.

Rhuven held up an armband made of gold with a stone as red as blood. It glowed in the faint firelight. "This was my lady's."

Helwain nodded. "It should fetch a good sum."

"No! It belongs to the child now!" Geillis seized the jewel from her sister. "*My* child. I will raise her as my own daughter."

Rhuven sighed and whispered her gratitude.

"But how did *you* get the babe?" Geillis asked gently.

Rhuven's eyes filled with tears. "I followed my lord's man and pleaded for the bairn's life. He refused. In the end I had to . . . to *buy* her from the filthy skellum." She looked away from her sisters in shame. "I must go now. Only give the child a name to thwart misfortune, and she will be well."

At the door, Rhuven turned again to her sisters.

"Above all, I beg you, keep her life a secret. If my lord knew that she lived, we would all be in grave danger."

❧

The full moon spilled its light onto the surface of the wide loch. Geillis and Helwain crouched on the shore beneath a rowan tree, its berries orange-red as embers. Helwain dipped her fingers into a small leather pouch, then rubbed the baby's head and the soles of her feet with ashes of oak and elder for strength and luck. She crushed juniper berries, releasing the sharp scent of pine.

"For protection from all enemies and harmful spirits," she murmured while Geillis held the child over the water.

A swan glided from the still reeds, her feathers white in the light of the full moon. The bird made barely a ripple in the water.

"Let us name the babe Albia," said Geillis. "She, too, is innocence sprung from darkness."

Helwain nodded. She cupped her hands and poured water over the silent child. A few drops splashed into her eyes and Geillis hastily wiped them away.

"We don't want her to be plagued with the sight of ghosts!" she said.

"She is already destined to have a troubled life," said Helwain. "But a babe that doesn't cry at its naming will have but a short life in which to suffer." She pinched the baby's left foot, the one that turned oddly inward.

Albia flinched, then began to wail.

Chapter 1

Dun Inverness

Grelach

I feel as weak as a child. I can barely rise from my bed, though Rhuven urges me every day, brings me food, washes my hair. I am Grelach, granddaughter of Kenneth, who was once Scotland's king, and I will do as I please. Now it pleases me to die, but I haven't the means or the strength to do it. I am sixteen years old and have nothing to live for, now that my baby daughter is dead.

My room is at the top of this tower built upon stones that are older than history, older than grief itself. I would throw myself from the window, but it is too narrow. Below, the River Ness flows into the sea. Gulls screech, the only sound. The wind is damp and smells of the sea.

"Rhuven, am I as wicked as he says I am?"

"Nay, child, there is no evil in you," Rhuven says, her voice soothing.

I look down to where the milk seeps from my breasts, staining the cloth wound tightly around my chest.

"Can you not stop this? Oh, it hurts, it hurts as if it were blood!" I wail. But I do not weep. Not from my eyes.

"I will fetch clean swaddling and a warm posset to calm you," says Rhuven. At the door, she turns to me. "Do not think about what is past and done. That way lies madness." Her eyes are dark with sadness, too.

But I cannot help thinking about the past. Only a few short years ago, I was a child with no cares. Then my father, Ranold, announced that I would be married. I thought, *What does a girl of thirteen winters want with a husband?* If my mother had been alive, she would not have let me marry for at least another year. But a father must be obeyed.

My father had killed many men and I was afraid of him. We are a family of warriors, always fighting, even among ourselves, and taking revenge on our enemies. My grandfather the king was slain by his own cousin, Malcolm, who became king and declared that his grandson Duncan would inherit the throne. I will never forget how this angered my father.

"It is the tradition to share power among kin. But now Malcolm has shut out my family from the succession! He shall pay dearly for this," he threatened.

But I was the one who paid. Ranold married me to Gillam, a cruel warrior more than twice my age who became thane of Moray by killing the prior thane.

"Moray is its own kingdom within Scotland. By marrying the thane, you bring power into our family," my father explained, gripping my arm so hard he left a bruise. "Obey

Gillam and bear him sons. Remember you are descended of kings, but always keep your ambitions hidden. That is the key to survival."

I took my father's words to heart. I was afraid of what he would do to me if I forgot them.

I was even more afraid of Gillam the first time he put his wet and foul-smelling mouth against mine and thrust his hand under my skirt. I called out for Rhuven, but the ugsome thane smothered my cries and forced me to lie with him. Soon I was with child, but being only thirteen, I was ignorant about my body. It was Rhuven who noticed my growing belly. Months later came the terrible pains that left me gasping and groaning. I thought I had been poisoned and was about to die. Rhuven summoned the midwife, who pulled from me a black-haired boy covered in wax and blood.

"What a foul creature!" I cried. "Is it a monster?"

"Not unless you have lain with the devil," said the midwife.

My husband is *the devil,* I thought.

The midwife shoved the wailing boy into my unwilling arms. He suckled me until my nipples bled. At the touch of his hungry mouth, I gritted my teeth. When I put him from me, he screamed like the banshee.

"I wish you had not been born!" I screamed back. I felt like I was chained to a stone.

We named the boy Luoch. Even then, I couldn't love him.

One day Gillam left to lay siege to a town, and soon word came that he had been burned to death by flaming pitch. I smiled for the first time in months.

The man who had killed Gillam won his lands and titles. Within a month, my father forced me to marry the new thane. His name was Macbeth.

I knew what marriage meant, so at the wedding I refused to speak. My father slapped me, causing me to cry out, which the priest took for "Aye." Thus for the second time I was married against my will. My new husband gave me a gift, an armband made of gold and set with a large gem. When the jewel caught the light, it gleamed bloodred. I had never owned such a treasure, and it softened me just a little.

Macbeth was only ten years older than I. His most remarkable feature was the carrot-colored hair that fell to his shoulders and glistened on his mighty forearms. He did not seem to be cruel like Gillam. But we had nothing to talk about. We ate in silence and he spent the evening with his warriors. He slept in a chamber next to mine and did not try to force himself on me.

Soon I grew curious about this unusual man. I put my ear to the door of his room and reported to Rhuven that he did not snore or grunt in his sleep. Then I spied on him, with Rhuven beside me in the shadows, as Macbeth and his companions sat before the fire drinking.

"She is barely out of childhood and already mother to a son," said one man. "Be a man, and beget an heir on her at once!"

"The oracle said I should father many sons," came Macbeth's reply. "I would not be in too much haste and overleap my good fortune."

I whispered to Rhuven, "I wish I knew everything the oracle promised him, for it would touch my future as well."

I decided it was time to make my new husband notice me. At dinner I would stare at him until he looked at me, then I would smile and glance down. I brushed his arm while serving him and felt him start at the touch. A shiver ran through me as well. Then I spoke to him directly for the first time, saying, "My lord, will you have some wine?" My voice was high and nervous.

"Indeed, I desire it," he replied. His eyes met mine. They were deep-set and as black as a raven's wing.

That night he came to my bed and I let him touch me where he pleased. He was not rough as Gillam had been. I began to look forward to lying with him in the darkness. Soon I sensed that I was with child again. As my breasts and belly grew large, I marveled at my power. The granddaughter of a king, I carried a king in my womb! Though I could not choose my own husband, I could bear a son who would fulfill his ambitions, and in so doing lift me as high as the stars.

When my pains began, Macbeth was away on a sea journey. I pushed until I had no strength left, but the child would not be born. Even Rhuven looked afraid. Finally the midwife reached in to seize it by the feet. I screamed in agony, feeling myself tear apart, and fell into blackness.

When I opened my eyes again, Rhuven was holding a tightly swaddled baby. A gold fuzz covered its head, not the black tufts Luoch had been born with.

"How can he be mine?" I asked, fingering my own black hair.

"It is doubtless Macbeth's child," Rhuven replied. "Will you hold her now?"

"Her?" I asked.

"The babe is a girl," Rhuven said softly.

"My lord will be unhappy," I said, turning away. "Let me sleep now."

"No, my lady, you must look at her."

The urgency in Rhuven's voice made me sit up. She removed the baby's swaddling. An amazed cry escaped me to see the naked, pink-skinned girl with wide blue eyes. She waved her tiny fists and one leg kicked the air. Then I noticed that the other leg barely moved. Its foot pointed inward.

"Is it a changeling?" I heard my voice rising. "The faeries took my baby and left this one in her place!"

"Nay," said Rhuven, frowning. "This is the bairn you bore and none other, for I have not closed my eyes since she came from you."

"O Rhuven, what have I done wrong?" I wailed. "Everyone knows it is a mother's fault if she bears a deformed child!"

"Nothing, my lady. Perhaps it was the midwife's fault. Or a weakness in your husband's seed—" She broke off and threw me a fearful look.

My heart began to pound at the thought of Macbeth.

"We must keep it from him," I said in a rush.

Rhuven nodded. "You can trust me to be silent."

A month passed. I nursed the baby and watched her become

fatter. She did not bite and torment me as Luoch had. And with each swallow of milk she drew from me, affection flowed into me like waves lapping at a shoreline. There was no reason to love her, for being a girl, she could bring me no gain. But I loved her anyway. It did not matter to me that she was not perfect. I longed to give her a name, but until Macbeth returned she could not be properly baptized.

Two more months went by. Every day I scanned the sea, and when I finally saw Macbeth's ships approaching the harbor, I almost fainted with dread. Rhuven took control. She dressed me in my best gown and told me to wear Macbeth's gift, the gold armlet.

I picked up my daughter and held her close. Then I changed my mind and put her back in the cradle. I greeted Macbeth alone, placing his hands on my milk-swollen breasts to distract him.

"My dear heart, my sweet chuck," he murmured, kissing me hungrily. "I don't want to leave you again for so long."

I sighed with relief. All would be well!

"Now show me my son."

"In good time, my lord," I said, reaching for another kiss.

He would not be deterred. "Rhuven! Bring in the child."

Her eyes downcast, Rhuven carried my daughter into the room.

"Now that you are back, let us choose a name and have the baptism," I said, disguising my dread with false cheer.

Macbeth did not reply. He fumbled with the baby's swaddling, then let out a groan of dismay.

"Great warriors must have daughters to give in marriage to their allies," I said.

He stared at her. "Does the oracle deceive me?" he asked, bewildered.

"The next one will be a boy, I promise." I took the baby from Rhuven, intending to cover her again, when my lord seized her. The blanket fell from her and all her little limbs began to writhe—except for the leg that hung limp, its foot turned inward.

"This cannot be my child!" Macbeth cried, and fixed his black, mistrustful eyes on me. "With whom—or what—have you lain?"

"With no one but you, my lord," I said, fear rising in me. "Look, she has your fair hair and skin."

"She has the bones of some weak, creeping villain," he growled. "Who is the father?"

"You accuse me wrongly!" I said, indignant. "We are innocent."

"The oracle does not lie!" Macbeth shouted, his face red with anger. "She said I would have sons. Strong sons. Not weak and deformed daughters."

He shouted for his men, and the burly Eadulf appeared.

"O you fates that meddle in mortals' lives," intoned Macbeth, staring overhead. "Witness that I hereby renounce this unnatural child of a wicked mother."

"I do not deserve this!" I protested, clutching my daughter until she began to cry. "It is you who should be punished. You slew my husband and took his lands and titles. And you stole me, too. I never wanted you."

Fury gathered in his black eyes. He took the child from me and thrust her at Eadulf.

"No! I am the granddaughter of a king, and she belongs to me!" I threw myself at Eadulf, but Macbeth blocked my way. I grabbed his forearms and groveled to him. "I am sorry to offend you, my lord. I will do anything you desire, only give me my daughter."

He shook off my hands. "You will forget her." To Eadulf he said, "Take the spawn of evil to the heath and leave it for the wolves."

Eadulf ducked out of the room, my daughter under his arm. My legs gave way and I fell back onto the bed. I saw Rhuven follow him, heard stumbling on the stairs. Macbeth leaned over me, his breath hot on my cheek

"She shall not live to rebuke your deeds—or mine!" He pressed his body against mine, and I struggled until I felt a roaring in my ears like a sea-storm and blackness engulfed me.

When I awoke on the rumpled bed, I was alone. The cradle was empty. My breasts leaked with longing for my pale-faced daughter, and all my motherly feelings spilled out in cold tears.

⚜

Here I lie, still. Weak and helpless as she was. Dry as dust, with no drop of milk, no tears left to shed ever again.

My hand reaches for the other arm. It is bare.

"Rhuven, where is my jeweled cuff?" My voice sounds dull. "I have not seen it since—" But I cannot bear to speak of that day my daughter was taken from me.

"I don't know, my lady," Rhuven replies, not meeting my eyes.

"I think Macbeth has taken it away to punish me," I say. "Next time I will give him a son, and he will give it back to me."

Chapter 2

Wychelm Wood

Albia

These are my first memories, fragments mostly.

Lying in my mother's arms, looking up at the wychelm tree. Its limbs sway and its leaves tremble. Birds flitting in its branches, a squirrel dashing up the trunk. A longing I have no words to express.

Tumbling with the lambs in the sheepfold. Burying my face in their soft dun fleece, imagining I am one of them.

The smells of peat and lime, heather and damp moss. My hands and legs, dirty from scooting along the ground. Mother coaxing me with a finger coated in honey while I cry in frustration.

A hot, smelly cloth wrapped around my leg. Helwain muttering over me. Mother rubbing my leg. Her look of dismay.

The small horse that hauls peat from the moor. The sledge bouncing along the rocky ground while I hold on with both hands to keep from sliding off.

A bird with a long white neck making ripples in the loch. I reach out to touch it, but the water pulls me in. Cold and terror fill me. Mother's arms lift me out of the water. The bird glides away.

And this, most vivid of all: night, the moon a round face overhead. Being carried in a sling on Mother's back and clinging to her neck. Helwain leaning on an elder staff. A grove of trees with white trunks. Great dark stones jutting from the earth like arms reaching for the sky. A woman who calls my mother and Helwain "sister."

Helwain saying, "I tried to heal her, but my powers are weak from disuse."

My mother explaining, "So we came here, where the spirits are most powerful."

Lying on the damp grass. The stone rising up before me blacker than the sky. Helwain using her staff to draw a circle around me and the stone. The three sisters chanting:

The old sun dies and the new one is born.
Dead souls rise, their graves to scorn.
The spirits come, mankind to warn.

Helwain walking backward around the circle. Her voice wavering like grass in the wind.

Let nature's false knot be torn,
That bound this babe when she was born.

The chants filling my ears. I feel the sound deep in my bones. The spirits whirling on the winds, pushing through the earth, surrounding me.

"Look at her eyes darting dart back and forth," Helwain saying to her sisters. "She sees them."

<hr />

I think that Mother and her sisters and I are the only people in the world until the day I meet Murdo and Colum, who live in a cottage on the edge of the Wychelm Wood. Murdo grows barley and oats and has more sheep than I can count with my fingers and toes. He frightens me at first. His voice rumbles like rocks falling down a hill and his head is as hairless as an egg. He carves two pieces of wood and fixes them to my leg with strips of hide. Mother explains that he is helping my leg grow straight and strong. Like a tree.

Colum is a child like me. He has curly hair and makes me laugh with his silly faces. He can run and jump like the squirrels. I want to do the same, and one day I grasp Colum's arms and pull myself to my feet. I take my first steps. My mother weeps, but somehow I know she is happy.

Walking is so much better than crawling on hands and knees. I walk to the village with Mother to trade wool and baskets for cloth and food. People give me pitying looks, but I am too pleased with myself to care. When I come home my leg aches and Helwain wraps it in hot, smelly cloths. She mutters and complains, yet I know that she, too, is pleased.

I have been to the village often enough to know that my mother and Helwain are not like the folk who live there. Helwain seldom leaves the roundhouse. She sits by the hearth, turning the stone quern, grinding flour. Or she spins, holding the wool under one arm and twisting the strands with the thumb and forefinger of her other hand. The spindle drops to the floor, whirling. It makes me dizzy to watch.

Only at night does Helwain go out, and in the morning she returns with a basket full of leaves and roots. She hangs them from the beams to dry, where they rustle and put out strange smells. Sometimes she brings back the skull of a small animal, a snakeskin, or a lizard from beneath a mossy stone. These are my playthings—until she grinds them into powders and puts them into small pots and forbids me to touch them.

Rhuven, the sister of my mother and Helwain, always brings me a toy when she visits and sometimes a new dress. Her own clothes are made of soft cloth the color of the summer sky or ripe berries. She peers at me with tears in her eyes and says, "How big you are getting!"

Even my leg is growing. I can climb to the top of the Skelpie Stone on the path to the peat bog. It has rings and zigzags where the faeries have worn down the stone with their dancing. The faeries are small enough to fit in my hand. Their skin is the color of buttercups, their speech like the splashing of water or the rattle of tiny stones. At night they sometimes pinch and bite me, and when I wake up I have red marks along my arm. I even play with them in the daytime. We float a cockle shell in a bucket of water, placing tiny pebbles in the shell until it is almost underwater.

"*Now sink little boat; no more shall you float,*" I sing. "Here comes the storm!" And the faeries and I rock the bucket.

"Stop, Albia, you naughty girl!" says Mother, who is watching me play. But the cockle shell and all the little stones have already sunk to the bottom of the bucket.

"I did it, just like I have seen Helwain," I announce.

"You shouldn't listen to Helwain's nonsense."

But I do, even though her stories sometimes frighten me. Helwain says that the moor is haunted by a bogle that leads people to their death. But she claims to have tamed the spirit so that it guides her around the sucking bog and keeps the wolves away.

"What does the bogle look like?" I ask her.

"Sometimes it takes the shape of a doe and sometimes a dog. The doe is the ghost of a lady who disappeared on the moor and the dog is her husband. He went to look for her and his body was found dashed on a rock. It happened before you were born."

Not long after that I dream of a large black dog that leads me onto the moor until a white deer appears and the dog runs away. When I wake up I am sitting beneath a stunted birch tree in the midst of a bog. Everywhere I step, the mire sucks my feet downward. I cry all day until Mother and Helwain find me.

"You must never wander off like that!" scolds Mother.

"I didn't!" I protest, still sniffling. "A black dog led me here."

Helwain examines my arms and legs for bite marks. I cringe from her as if she is the fearsome dog.

"Helwain, don't frighten her again!" Mother says. "We must watch her more closely."

"Indeed I will," says Helwain, staring at me with dark eyes that want to see inside my head.

"It was only a dream, Albia, only a dream," Mother says, her arms around me.

❧

I know my way through the woods to Colum's house. I am not supposed to go there alone, but Mother and Helwain cannot watch me every hour of the day.

One day Colum and I are picking bilberries and eating most of them. From nearby comes the *swish-swash* of a sickle cutting barley. Murdo's bald head bobs along the edge of the field.

All of a sudden Colum asks, "Where is *your* father?"

I look at him, thinking him stupid. "I don't have one," I say.

"But everyone has a da," he says.

"No, I have never had one," I insist. "Mother says I don't need one." I ask him why he does not have a mother.

"She died when my baby brother was born, taking him with her."

"So I have no father, and you have no mother," I say with a shrug. It is just a fact, nothing even to wonder about.

"Shhh!" Colum whispers. He pulls a slingshot from his pocket and fits a stone into the pouch. "I will show you how fast I can let fly with the stone, and there will be rabbit stew for supper."

I see the rabbit hopping through the stubble in the field. I close my eyes and hear the snap of the sling, then a sigh from Colum. He has missed.

"Now you try, Albia. He is afraid now and will not move. It is an easy shot."

I shake my head. I have no wish to harm the rabbit.

"Well, if I don't kill him, Da and I will go hungry."

He aims again and before I can stop him, the rock hits the rabbit. A triumphant Colum runs to examine his prey. Curious yet full of dread, I follow him. The rabbit lies unmoving, its eyes open and glassy. Blood pools on the ground, a lot of blood for so small a creature. I cannot take my eyes off the gleaming flow, a thin dark stream of animal grief.

Chapter 3

Dun Inverness

Grelach

I am mistress of this tower and its furnishings of carved ash and oak, the jewels and finely woven dresses, and the kist of Viking treasure at the foot of my bed. I am mistress of all of Dun Inverness, its servants and livestock, the terraces and garden plots, the defensive ditches revetted with banks of rock. Mine is the town of Inverness, mine the rock-strewn heath that rolls all the way to the mountains. I am mistress of the wave-dashed rocks, the firth where my husband's fleet lies at anchor, and the sea-roads beyond.

I am Lady Macbeth of Moray, whose husband is more powerful than the thanes of Ross, Sutherland, Glamis, or Cawdor. His immense war-galley with its high stem and stern requires seventy-two men just to pull the oars. It skims across the water like a gull through the air, noiseless and swift, scattering the Viking raiders and the Orkney warbands who threaten this northern coast. Yet for all his wealth and the resources he commands, Macbeth remains a loyal servant of King Duncan—that imposter, undeserving and untested, placed on a throne of ease by his grandfather Malcolm!

Duncan may rule Scotland, but Macbeth rules this northern kingdom. Our enemies fear us. I have riches beyond my needs or desires. The royal blood of Kenneth, once Scotland's king, flows in my veins. Yet I am no one, and I have nothing, truly, until I have a son.

My husband strives to beget a child upon me, softening me with gifts and tenderness, then treating me coldly when I fail to conceive. I have knelt in the town kirk and made offerings to the mother of God and the saints. I have run my fingers over the stone cross in the kirkyard, the one carved with rabbits and birds and twining ivy, and prayed for my womb to fill. And it did, twice, but emptied again as soon as I suspected a child growing there.

I think that God in his anger has decided I do not deserve another child. Does he not know how deeply I regret losing my daughter? Afterward I would not let Luoch out of my sight. He was all that I had. As the great-grandson of King Kenneth, he might become king someday. So from the time he was old enough to crawl around, I tied him to my waist or to a post, ignoring his wailing. When Rhuven protested, I said, "Should I let him crawl into the fire, then? Or tumble down the stairs and break his leg?"

Now the boy can escape his tether. He only runs as far as the village huts to play with the children there. But every time I call and he does not answer, I think that he has fallen from the ramparts into a ditch or wandered onto the moors to be snatched by faeries.

Faeries? No, it is the wolves I fear.

⁂

Poor Luoch. He actually loves his unworthy mother. When Macbeth is cold to me or makes me weep, the boy puts his arms around me and lisps words of comfort. I kiss his cheek. Even though I don't love him, the sight rouses my husband to fits of jealousy.

"Get that black imp out of my sight!" he shouts when this scene has played one time too many.

Luoch cringes, while I become like a she-tiger.

"How dare you speak to my son like that!"

"He is not my son. Why should I care for him?" Macbeth's tone is cruel.

"Make him your son," I challenge him. "Give Luoch your name and then you will have an heir."

Macbeth stares at my son's raven-black hair and pale skin.

"You keep me childless that your brat may take precedence over a son of ours," he accuses with barely repressed anger.

"That is not true! I submit to you and pray constantly for a son!"

I do not dare tell him that twice I have miscarried. He might decide that I am cursed too. I look down, avoiding his gaze. But his eyes pry into me.

"I know you want Luoch to be king someday. I suspect that

you use me to advance that ambition," he says. "If he becomes thane of Moray after my death, wouldn't that put him in a fine position to steal the throne?"

He mocks my blood, but I must be silent. I will not admit to such a grand scheme. Still my husband presses me.

"Ranold, your own father, seeks alliances among the thanes that favor your son's ambitions over those of Duncan's heirs. You cannot deny it."

I draw in my breath. To speak or even to think of treason is to row in dangerous waters. I realize Luoch is still in the room, taking everything in with wide eyes. Rhuven is there, too, sitting on a stool in the corner. She is always with me. The woman hears everything that passes between us, but she is as silent and secret as stone. I motion for her to take Luoch away, and she ushers him from the room.

"My lord, what you speak of is my father's business, not mine." I stroke his coppery hair to distract him from these jealous thoughts of sons. "My desires are yours," I murmur, "and yours should encompass the greatness that befits you, the most powerful thane in the land. Think to what heights you can rise."

"Nay, I am content. Duncan esteems me. He has promised me Glamis, and it is only a matter of time until the old thane dies."

"Glamis is nothing. You deserve better, for you outshine Duncan like the sun outshines the moon. Let him once visit here and see our wealth, and the soft, weak king must acknowledge your greater deserving."

"Hide your disdain of the king," he says sharply. "We depend upon his goodwill."

"What if his goodwill should turn? It would be better to depend upon ourselves." I am no longer thinking of Duncan, but of myself. How it rankles, that I must depend upon a man who has the power to take my children from me!

"You must notice, wife, how the other thanes rely upon me," Macbeth replies, his tone growing boastful. "The thanes of Ross and Angus vie for my favor, and their cousin Banquo clamors to be my general. Others offer me their best warriors and galleys. I can raise thousands of men to fight for King Duncan. Without us, he cannot hold Scotland together. So spare me your murmurings, and cool your vain ambitions. I am content."

"How can you bear for such an unworthy one to call himself king?" I persist.

"So, you think your own kin better suited?" Macbeth puts his face within inches of mine. His hair flames; his black eyes consume my face. "Before that brat of yours, *I* will be king."

Utter, breathless silence falls between us and grows pregnant with each passing second.

"So you *do* desire it," I say warily.

"What man does not?" he snaps.

"Why, such a thing could not happen—" I begin.

"Unless Duncan were to die," Macbeth says, finishing my thought.

I look into his black eyes and see the flicker of ambition catch fire there.

"We dare not speak of this," I whisper, putting my hands to his lips.

But something has just been born between us, an offspring for us to nurture, together.

※

By the time Macbeth sails with his seven galleys to raid the Orkneys, he has put another child in my belly. Upon his return, I am as big as a ship with its sail full of wind. Macbeth waits upon me, worships me with eyes full of hope and hungry love. All will be well between us once this son is born and the long-ago promise of the oracle is fulfilled.

My lord has even softened toward Luoch. Perhaps he realizes that once he has his own son, Luoch's existence will no longer rebuke him. He gives my son a dirk taken from a Danish pirate, with gems set in its handle and a sheath made of boar's hide.

Luoch's eyes shine, and he dares to ask his stepfather a question. "You left with seven ships and came back with six. What happened to the other ship?"

The boy is sharper than I realize.

"I will tell you a frightful tale," says my lord, frowning. "We were four days from the farthest Orkneys when a storm struck our fleet. Gales ripped the sails and roiled the waves until their crests foamed like the mouths of wild dogs. You could hear the oars crack as the men strained against the sea. We prayed to Columba and all the saints to save us. Then I saw three ravens in the sky. They circled our ships for an entire day."

Luoch's eyes are as round as berries. Rhuven also listens, holding her breath.

"At last they chose a single heaving mast and settled there. Within minutes the galley and all her crew sank beneath the waves." Macbeth looks at me, traces of fear still in his eyes. "It was no usual storm, I tell you, but some unnatural evil that wrought their doom."

"Don't frighten the boy with superstitious nonsense," I say, suppressing a shiver myself.

~

The babe kicks my womb with such vigor that I know it must be a boy. Macbeth agrees that we will name him Kenneth, for all of Scotland will esteem a man named for such a worthy king. He boasts to his warriors of the lusty boy he will train in the arts of combat. Every important thane has at least one son. Banquo has a boy, Fleance. King Duncan has two sons, the princes Malcolm and Donalbain.

One day I realize that my womb is quiet. I prod my belly, but when my son does not stir, I begin to panic. My stomach feels ill and my bowels contract sharply. I should not worry, Rhuven says. She makes me lie down and drink sweet wine. But nothing calms me. The stabbing pains will not stop. The room whirls about me like a falling spindle.

Then blood begins to seep from between my legs. The drops become a stream. It does not cease, though I press my legs together. Like a wounded animal, I cry out as I feel the child slip from my womb. I hear Rhuven whisper, "No, no!" and look down to see, cradled in her bloody hands, a baby boy, perfectly formed but still and silent as Death.

⁂

My heart is a stone lodged behind my ribs. I am hard all over, as the looking glass shows me. My cheeks are flat, my bones sharp. Strands of silver glisten in my hair, though I am only twenty-three. My eyes are pale and hard, like an ice-covered loch.

I refuse to lay him in the kirkyard, because God and the saints ignored my prayers. We bury him near the castle. Rhuven weeps. The green turf at my feet is beaded with dew as if the earth is weeping. We pile stones atop the grave. My husband shakes with grief.

I remember his cruelty toward our innocent daughter, now long dead. Did he shed a single tear for her? Yet now he mourns a son who never opened his eyes.

"Be a man. Cease your fit of tears," I say, full of resentment.

"I am a man. May not a man show sorrow?" he pleads.

My own despair spills forth in cruel words. "You are no man, for you cannot even beget a living child upon your wife."

"And you are no proper woman! Why do you not weep for our son?"

"I am used to such loss," I say bitterly. "Three times my body has quickened with your sons, and three times it has expelled them before their time—"

I bite my tongue. I meant never to reveal this to him.

"*Three* times?" he exclaims. "When were the other two?" Now he is angry, and I feel as if a storm is about to break, blow me down, and dash me on the rocks below. "Why did you not tell me?" He clenches his hands and steps toward me.

"Because, my lord, I was afraid!" I reach out to touch his cheek slick with rain and tears. I am afraid still—that he will cast me away because I am childless.

Macbeth does not react to my touch. He looks beyond me, frowning so deeply I cannot see his eyes. "Three times," he repeats. "That signifies evil luck."

"But surely I will conceive again. The fourth time always brings good fortune," I say. "Come, let us go inside. Rhuven, prepare my chamber and bring wine." I take Macbeth's arm, but he will not move. His fierce gaze shifts to the grave.

"Was the woman a fiend, who said I would bear sons?" he demands of the mound of rocks. "I must find her again and learn the truth."

Chapter 4

Wychelm Wood and Wanluck Mhor

Albia

Sometimes when Mother and Helwain are both asleep, I slip out into the darkness by myself. I should be afraid, but the moon forbids me. Her white light makes the night almost as bright as the day, so that I cannot lose my way. Helwain goes out at night because she says that plants are more powerful when gathered under the full moon. But I think it is the night itself that draws her out. At night the forest is alive with sounds: the sweet call of the nightingale, the mournful hooting of the owlet, and the croaking of frogs from the riverbank. Sometimes a mist rolls along the ground, envelops the trees, and all around me I hear the patter of dripping water, as if faeries are tapping their tiny feet on the leaves. The faraway howling of a wolf on the moor tells me that some small creature has met its doom. Sometimes I walk as far as Stravenock Henge to see the stone giants hunched in a circle. Nearby, the twisted branches of the great oak tree look like the limbs of a bogle crawling from the earth. I relish the shudder this gives me, then I run back to the safety of the roundhouse.

Now that I live like the owl, I am awake when Rhuven arrives late one night. I hear her tell Mother that the thane and his wife have buried a son who was born too soon. Helwain questions her about her thane. They talk of war. I strain my ears to listen.

"Macbeth and his soldiers have been summoned to battle by King Duncan," Rhuven reports. "The rebel Macdonwald, with his Irish footsoldiers and horsemen armed with axes, marches through the Spey valley toward Duncan's castle."

"A rebellion!" my mother says.

"And where does Macbeth's loyalty lie?" asks Helwain.

"With King Duncan, of course!" says Rhuven in haste. "As he was leaving, he said to my lady that he would bring home the victory and lay it at her feet."

"That may have a double meaning," Helwain muses. "Are you sure he has no greater ambition?"

"He seems content," says Rhuven. "The old thane of Glamis has died, and my lord expects Duncan to grant him Glamis's lands and title. But something else worries me." Rhuven pauses. "The loss of his stillborn son disturbs him deeply. Helwain, Macbeth believes you lied to him. He has vowed to seek you out."

"He will ask in the village, and they will tell him where we live," says my mother, her voice rising. "But he must not come here."

However hard I listen, I do not understand all these matters.

32

"Nay, we will go to him," says Helwain. "Next week, when the moon is full, we three will meet at Wanluck Mhor, and in that wasteland of ill fortune, waylay him."

"What will you tell him, Helwain? You must not promise him any more sons," Rhuven warns.

Helwain shrugs. "I will know by then what to say to him."

⁘

All week Helwain is busy with her powders and potions. She casts bones on the hearth and prods the dust for signs. She searches the skies at night. Mother is silent and tense. On the day they are to leave for the moor, she tries to send me to stay with Murdo and Colum. But I want to see Helwain do her dark mischief, so I cry and beg and cling to Mother until she relents.

We set out for Wanluck Mhor early in the day, with Mother pulling the small sledge laden with blankets, food, and Helwain's kettle. It may take several days to find this lord, she says. Rhuven, coming from Dun Inverness, meets us at the edge of the woods. She frowns when she sees me.

"Why have you brought her?" she says in dismay.

"She is afraid to be left behind. You can understand why," Mother says, putting her arms around me. "Don't worry. She will stay hidden."

But I am not afraid, and I don't understand why I must hide. I am simply excited to be going on a journey and curious about what I will see on the moor.

We climb up and down steep braes where the deer drink

from the rivulets running down the rocks. The rising sun in our eyes makes us blink. Dew lifts from the ground and the long purple shadows fade. The sun is overhead, then at our backs. Gradually we descend to soft earth covered with bearberry bushes, dwarf birches, and heather with white and pink flowers. Helwain prods the ground with her staff to feel where the soft, peaty ground gives way to a sucking bog. We are on Wanluck Mhor. When I ask Mother how the place got its name, she says that no one knows. But I think it must have been a great flood, for I see ruined dwellings covered in lichens and brambles, islands in a shallow, grassy sea.

In the distance, too, there is movement. "Something is coming, Mother!" The sound of hooves thudding on the soft ground grows louder.

Helwain heads for a nearby boulder. Mother drags the sledge off the path and into the bracken. We crouch behind the rock. Now we can hear the jingling of harnesses and war-mail as horsemen converge on the path.

"We hail from the king!" shouts one of the men. "What news from the battlefield?"

"Take this message to Duncan," comes the reply. "Brave Macbeth with his smoking sword has slain the traitor Macdonwald."

A deep-throated shout rises from the first party.

"And you spread this word," orders the king's messenger. "The thane of Cawdor has confessed to aiding the king of Norway, and to punish this treason, Duncan has confiscated all his lands and cut off his head."

My mouth falls open to hear about such killing. Mother puts her fingers against my lips.

"Cursed be Cawdor's soul!" growls the man from the battlefield. "Tell the king how the loyal Macbeth fought. He doubled strokes upon our foes as if he meant to bathe in their blood."

"Be assured Duncan will show his gratitude. Where is Macbeth now?"

"Not far behind us, making his way to the king's castle at Forres."

As the men spur their horses and part company, Helwain rubs her hands together.

"So the war-goddess favors Macbeth. And she leads him into our path. We must hurry!"

Helwain leads the way across the rough moor to a hillock high enough to be seen from all directions. Atop the hill are crumbling rocks, the remains of a half-buried dwelling. Rhuven unloads the sledge and covers it with ferns while Helwain makes a small fire. I watch the sisters put on gray-green robes the color of the lichens that grow on old stones and trees. Rhuven and my mother rub their faces and hands with ashes. Helwain does not wear a disguise. She already looks frightful, with her wild gray hair, her bristly chin, and the shadows under her eyes.

"He must be able to recognize who I am," she says.

Mother leads me down some crumbled steps into the ground, where the last light of day shines a little way into the sunken rooms. Brown grass grows between the collapsed stones. I am too excited to be afraid.

"What is going to happen tonight?" I ask. "What magic will Helwain do?"

"I don't know. But you must stay down here and not make a sound. Try to sleep."

When she leaves I stand on a rock and peer between the stones. I am consumed with curiosity. But my leg aches from the long journey and my eyes grow heavy. I lie down to rest only for a moment. Instead I dream something terrible: a man's head dripping with blood and gore. There is no body, only a head with a mouth gaping in a horrible grin. With a cry, I start up from my sleep. It must be Cawdor, the headless traitor, beside me in this tomb! My heart pounding with panic, I crawl up the steps and emerge on all fours like an animal, looking around for my mother.

In the light of the moon, round and full, I see Helwain, Rhuven, and my mother around the fire. Helwain stirs her kettle while my mother and Rhuven dance. Their shadows waver and leap. The wind whips their robes about them. Mist rises from hidden pools and blows like clouds across the moor.

From somewhere in the fog comes a man's voice: "So foul and fair a day I have not seen!"

Two men on horseback emerge from the fog. One has thick red hair. In the crook of his arm he carries a helmet and the moonlight glints on his sleeveless tunic made from links of metal. His arms, thick as trees, are painted from the shoulder to the wrist with circles and curious markings like those on the Skelpie Stone. His horse, spattered with mud, heaves under him. White foam drips from its mouth.

The sisters stop their dancing, link hands, and face the men.

"What are these withered and wild creatures?" the red-haired man says to his companion. Then to the sisters he shouts, "Speak! Who are you?"

Rhuven calls out in a voice unlike her own, "All hail Macbeth, thane of Moray!"

"All hail Macbeth, thane of Glamis and of Cawdor!" cries my mother.

So this is Rhuven's master, the man we have come to meet! I creep forward to get a closer look, ducking behind a gorse bush.

Helwain throws back her hood.

I hear Macbeth's sharp intake of breath. "Banquo, see, it is the very oracle I seek! The old woman."

Then Helwain speaks, her voice like the grating of stones against each other. "All hail Macbeth, that shall be king hereafter!"

Macbeth starts in his saddle. His horse shies as if struck by an arrow.

"My lord, why do you seem to fear things that sound so fair?" asks his companion, coming forward. "You fantastical creatures, now speak to me!" He laughs, as if this is some jest. "Look into the seeds of time and tell me which grain will grow and which will not."

"Hail Banquo!" Helwain greets him. "Lesser than Macbeth and greater. Not so happy yet much happier. You shall beget kings though you will be none."

Banquo makes a scornful sound in his throat. "They contradict themselves, the old women!" he says.

On a cue from Helwain, Mother and Rhuven begin to back away.

"Stay, you fateful sisters, tell me more!" demands Macbeth. "I know I will be thane of Glamis, for he is dead, but how of Cawdor? The thane of Cawdor lives. And to be king is beyond belief. How do you know this? Speak!"

He tries to spur his horse forward, but the creature will not budge. He curses. I am afraid of being seen. I feel like the little brown rabbit in the open field, sensing the boy with his slingshot.

Now Helwain lifts her hood over her face and turns away. A gust of wind blows a cloud of heavy mist around Macbeth and Banquo. Seizing my chance, I scurry for the hole and retreat into the dark earth. Just behind me Rhuven, Helwain, and my mother stumble down the steps, breathing hard.

Faintly I hear Macbeth shout, "They have melted, Banquo, and vanished like spirits into the air!"

Helwain laughs. "Ha! We gulled the powerful Macbeth."

Rhuven is not so pleased. "Why did we hail him with such lofty titles? If these don't come to pass, he will know that we lie. We were to prophesy strife and trouble, for those are certainties."

"You heard the messengers. Because of his exploits in battle, he is certain to become thane of Glamis and Cawdor, too," explains Helwain. "Then what is left for him but to become king? We merely put his own desires into words."

"As you did when you prophesied sons? Yet that did not come to pass."

"So, perhaps this time he will not believe me. What harm is done?" Helwain says, sounding careless.

"I saw him start, like a guilty man, when you hailed him as king," says Rhuven. She sounds worried.

Helwain snorts. "Do you think he will go to Forres tonight and slay Duncan? He is not a fool."

Now my mother speaks. "Even if he wanted to, he would not find the opportunity, for the king will be surrounded by his loyal warriors."

"Then why feed Macbeth with vain promises and lying prophecies?" Rhuven persists.

"I am an old woman without any power. This gives me some sport."

"Helwain, this is no game!" Rhuven's voice rises with distress. "If my lord commits treason against his king, he will be killed and my lady banished, and I will also be ruined."

"By Morrigan and all the gods!" Helwain bursts out. "We are already lost, because of Macbeth. Have you forgotten that he slew Gillam and drove us from our home? I will play foul with his fate!"

"And with Banquo's, too?" asks Rhuven. "He is an honorable man. Lesser than Macbeth and greater—what does that mean?"

"Banquo is not superstitious," Helwain replies. "My double-talk is meant to twist Macbeth's reason. And how easy that is!"

"Do not overlook my Albia," my mother interjects. "What will be her fate, when Macbeth fulfills his?"

I hear my name mentioned, but I do not understand how I have any connection to the weird events of this night. Nor do I understand why my mother and her sisters have waited for the painted warrior and taunted him with great titles. Perhaps they have eaten some mixture of Helwain's that makes them act so strangely.

In the morning Rhuven is already gone. Helwain and Mother are silent on the way home. I follow them, biting my lip. I know that I am somehow to blame for what happened. They didn't want to bring me. Even Rhuven was not happy to see me. Now they have quarreled and Rhuven has gone away angry. If she never visits again, there will be no more gifts for me, and it will be the punishment I deserve.

I forget to look where my feet are taking me and stumble against a hawthorn tree. A long, sharp thorn breaks off and sticks in my hand. For a moment my mind is somewhere else. A slow, fearful wail rises from my throat. The sound surprises me.

"Be quiet, my head hurts," complains Helwain.

"You hush, Helwain. She has cut herself, my poor child." Mother pulls out the thorn and dabs at the blood welling from my palm.

But it is not the pain or the blood that made me cry out. It was the brief sight of three bodies and a man holding a dagger with blood on its blade. I shake my head to dispel the scene, but when I close my eyes it is still there. I rub my hands together, but it only spreads the blood.

"What are you doing, Albia?" asks Mother.

"She has a strange look," says Helwain excitedly. "What do you see? Tell me." Her face is so close to mine that her features blur, except for the gleam in her eyes that frightens me. "Speak up, girl!"

But I press my lips tightly together and close my eyes. I will not let Helwain see inside me.

Chapter 5

Wychelm Woods

Albia

After that night on Wanluck Mhor, I stay away from Helwain. Mother puts a salve on my cut until it heals, leaving only a tiny scar on my palm. She keeps me close to her. I know she regrets allowing me to go to the moor. I don't think she even suspects that I saw the painted warrior and heard every word that was spoken. But I often catch her gazing at me with a sad and worried expression.

"Why do you look at me that way?" I ask her. We are sitting in a small coracle, fishing in the loch with nets on long poles. A sleek, glittering fish noses my net, then darts away.

"There is so much you don't know," she muses, shaking her head slowly.

"Then tell me!" I tease, wanting to see her usual smile.

"Do you know that your eyes are blue, and yet gray, as when a cloud is reflected in the loch on a sunny day?"

I peer into the water where my reflection is broken up by ripples. It scares me to look where the water is so deep it is black. I sense something lurking there, something as unknowable as the time before I could speak. Mother is right. I know almost nothing. But it is not the color of my eyes I wonder about.

"Tell me where this water comes from, and the creatures who live under it." It is the only question I can put into words just now.

"I will," she agrees. "You are old enough to learn the ancient wisdom."

Mother tells me how, ages and ages ago, the god Guidlicht lay with his wife Neoni, and from her womb the earth and skies rumbled into being, the mountains and valleys, fire and winds and water, and everything that lives, from the humblest creeping bug to the great leviathan of the sea.

"All these creatures, because they sprang from the same source, Neoni, partake of each other. So each person's nature mingles the traits of different plants, animals, and elements."

I feel my mind expand with amazement and wonder. "What makes up my nature?" I ask.

"Alas, Albia, I cannot see it. You must be the one to find it out. All I can advise you is that it is mixed of good and ill, and that you must feed your better traits that they may grow stronger than your worse ones."

I do not understand this, nor do I know how to discover my own nature. Instead I study the nature of others. The eagle that can seize a single mouse from the moor shows keen-sightedness, but in flying so high, it also shows ambition. It is the nature of the spiky hawthorn to protect the birds that nest there and to stab any other creature that strays too near.

What is Helwain's nature? She is like the black, harsh-voiced crow and the bent moor-pine with its rough bark. She is like the elder tree from which her staff is made, for she used its magic to cure my lameness. Once she was generous of heart, like the skies that shed rain, but now she is the dry stalk in the drought, withered by her own unkindness.

My mother, on the contrary, is all good-natured. Being light and strong as the reed, she tolerates hardship. Cheerful as the golden broom-flower, she can love even the ill-natured Helwain. Nurturing as the mother bird who feeds her chicks, she is easy for me to love.

But something begins to change between us when I am about thirteen winters old. In just a few months, I grow until I stand nose to nose with her. I no longer want to sit on her lap. Sometimes I hide in order to be alone or dally behind when we are walking together. I speak rudely to her, then look away so I will not see the hurt in her eyes. If she tries to soothe me with stories, I say that I am tired of her old tales.

Now I see that even Mother's nature is mixed. She is the twining ivy that holds fast to what it grows upon, sometimes choking it. I want to be free of her. But how? Everything in nature depends upon something else. How could I survive on my own?

Thus I am tied to my mother and to Helwain as well. She and I are like two rams butting heads until our horns lock together. She stares at me with hard eyes and demands to know what is in my head. I stare back and refuse to tell her. When Mother is not around, she presses me harder still.

"The warrior with the painted arms we met on the moor. Do you ever see him in your thoughts?"

A noise like a hive of bees fills my ears. I do not want to remember that night. I press my fingers to my eyelids to keep away the dreadful images.

"Why do you ask me? I have nothing to do with him!"

Helwain picks up her heavy scrying stone and sets it on the table before me.

"Look and tell me, what will he do?"

The stone is round, with facets of shining quartz that scatter the light in a thousand directions. I close my eyes.

"I do not care about the future. You cannot make me see it."

But Helwain takes my head, forcing my nose to the stone. "What . . . will . . . he . . . do?" she repeats. Her arms tremble as I push back against them. I am surprised by her strength.

"I don't know!" With a thrust of my hands, I send the scrying stone tumbling into the fire. The ashes and embers scatter and thick smoke billows up.

"Cursed child, spawn of wickedness!" Helwain shouts, slapping me across the face. "Ungrateful wretch!"

"I hate you—you foul witch!" I shout back, coughing on the smoke.

I run from the house and into the sheepfold, where I curl up with the lambs. Their warmth stops my trembling. But I can still hear Helwain screaming.

"She hoards the Sight! She will destroy, when she could save!"

I begin to weep silently. I know my nature now. My heart is colder than the loch-water with hatred of Helwain. I am the cruel mockingbird, the bitter wormwood, the wrathful destroying fire. There is nothing good in me.

❧

"What do I see? A new ewe in the flock!"

The cheerful voice awakens me and I sit up, rubbing my eyes. My cheeks are stiff with dried tears, and flecks of hay fall out of my hair. Colum leans on a staff, regarding me with his head tilted to the side. He wears a tunic cinched with a belt, sheepskin leggings, a pointed cap, and a bundle on his back. A waterskin, a slingshot, a pipe, and a horn hang from a strap across his chest.

"What did you do that your ma made you sleep out here?" he asks.

"No, the question is, why are *you* here?"

"It is Beltane, the first of May, and I am taking your sheep to the summer pasture, remember?"

Scrambling to my feet, I stumble against Colum, for my leg has gone numb. "I'm coming with you," I decide just then.

At the doorway of the roundhouse, Mother looks up; she knows. Without a word she gathers my clothing, a blanket, and food, including a small bag of oats and a honeycomb. Helwain is asleep, snoring like a dragon.

"I will walk with you as far as Pitdarroch," Mother says, putting on her cloak.

Colum, whistling, leads the sheep, all crowding each other

on the path out of the Wychelm Wood. Mother and I follow. I don't know what to say that will not offend her. I wish she would try and persuade me to stay or at least hold my hand. But there is only silence and a space between us. When we come to the oak tree, the sun is rising, tangling us in the long shadows of its gnarled limbs.

"Helwain does not hate you," Mother says in a weary voice. "She is angry at what she cannot change. The feeling is far older than you are. Do not hate her . . . or me."

Her pleading brings tears to my eyes.

"Albia, there is more that I must tell you, if you are to understand her." She pauses. "If you are to know yourself."

"I am listening," I say. My voice sounds hoarse after so long a silence.

"There are four worlds created by Guidlicht and Neoni. We live in the Now-world. In the Under-world live the spirits of the dead, and in the Other-world live faeries, merpeople, and dragons," Mother explains. "The fourth world, the Asyet-world, contains all that has not yet come to pass. It is visible only to those who have the Second Sight." She lifts my chin with her hand. "Helwain believes you have the Sight, that you can see the future."

I turn my head aside, unwilling to admit, even to my mother, what I have already seen.

"It is a dangerous gift, Albia. Those who have it are often tempted to misuse it."

"Mother, why are you trying to burden me?" The words burst from me. "I only want to go away for a while." I press my forehead against the rough bark of the oak tree.

"You may go. But first, listen. This ancient tree—and others like it that are bent by the winds and scorched by lightning—holds the four worlds together by its roots. And there, at Stravenock Henge, when the sunlight pours between the stones four times during the year, the borders between the worlds dissolve, and all their creatures mingle."

In the distance I can see the stones. Their ragged tops are lit by the sun, their bases hidden in the mist.

"I don't doubt that these are magical places, Mother. But what do they have to do with me?" I sigh, weary of her wisdom.

"My sisters and I come here to greet the gods, but we are not gifted. You, Albia, are different." Her voice is low and urgent. "Come back to this place, when you are ready to know the truth and use its power wisely. Daughter, farewell."

She touches my arm. My eyes remain fixed on the stones. When I look away from them, my mother is gone, vanished into the pale shroud of mist.

I hear Colum whistling. He stands on a sunlit hill, waving his arms for me to follow him.

Chapter 6

The Shieling

Albia

We walk for two days, pausing to let the sheep graze and sleeping on ferns in a hollow in the earth. Finally we come to Colum's bothy in the middle of a wide wold, a dwelling of sod and sticks with a ruined roof. I help Colum gather bracken and reeds and watch as he weaves them together and repairs the bothy. He is barely two years older than I am, but he knows how to build a shelter, how to hunt for food, and how to find his way using the sun and stars.

Away from Mother and Helwain and the brooding wychelms, my discontent blows away like smoke on the wind. Around me sheep gambol on the flower-strewn hills. Colum teaches me their names: Binn is the one who gives the sweetest milk; Bard's bleating is like music; Mam's wool is soft as a cloud. Gath will ram anything with his horns. Colum shows me how to use a staff to draw the flock together and what sounds will soothe them.

"You're a natural shepherdess," he says one day as I approach him carrying Binn and Bard, one under each arm. They are not much heavier than Helwain's brindled cat.

"They were wandering too near those rocks. I was afraid they would fall."

"They're sheep, not bairns! They won't fall," Colum says, laughing. "You have a lot to learn after all."

I had been proud of myself for fetching the sheep from danger, and Colum's criticism stings. "Well, you can't even make an oatcake that doesn't taste like dust," I counter.

"Oh, you think not?" Colum grabs his fire-kit, drills a stick into a piece of wood until sparks fly, then blows them into a flame. "We'll each bake a farl and see whose is best."

I mix some oats with Binn's rich milk and secretly add a bit of the honey Mother gave me. Colum and I glare at each other as our cakes cook side by side in the small iron skillet. When he tastes my farl, his eyes widen and he stares at it. I smile in triumph.

"What did you do to it?" He drops it back in the skillet. "You put a spell on it."

Suddenly angry, I kick the pan off the fire, scattering ashes and embers.

"I have nothing to do with Helwain's magic!" Tears burn my eyes, but I hold them back. "That is a simple farl made with milk and honey. You are a fool to think there is any harm in it."

Colum is silent. After a moment, he picks up the oatcake from the ashes, brushes it off, and eats every crumb.

"That is the best farl I ever ate," he says solemnly.

Still trembling, I eat the oatcake Colum made. It disturbs me to think how quickly my anger flared up, how hot my nature is, like a fire.

"This one is good, too," I say meekly.

"If you like the taste of dust," says Colum with a glum smile.

Suddenly we are both laughing. I can't stop, though my sides ache. I think that Colum and I are like two lambs of the same litter. We wrestle, play, and sometimes nip each other, but easily forget our hurts.

While the sheep graze on the green and plentiful grasses, Colum plays on his pipe and teaches me songs. My favorite is about a lad and a lass who meet in a dream. The haunting tune carries the words deep into my mind.

I see you now with the moon in your hair
And the dew on your lips. O nevermore
May I waken to find
That I've left you behind
In the cold dark enchantment of air.

I feel something stir in me, loneliness mixed with a nameless longing. I think of Mother's kisses, but that does not satisfy me. I try to imagine putting my lips to Colum's face and the idea makes me giggle.

When we tire of singing, Colum tells stories. I never knew there were so many goblins, giants, princes, fathers and sons, faeries, and silly fools, more than in all the tales Mother and Helwain have ever told me.

One day a lone shepherdess by the name of Caora wanders by with her flock. Her hair falls in curls as fine as the fleece on her lambs. Her supple limbs remind me of a willow tree. She and her sheep stay with us for most of the summer. One night the three of us recline beside a loch whose islands seem to float in the mists rising from the water. Frogs hidden in the reeds send up their hollow croaking. The hour is late, but on the shieling, a summer night is never entirely black, even when the moon is hidden.

"It's a perfect evening for stories," Caora says. "True ones."

So Colum tells about the Greentooth of the River Nairn, who called his little cousin, a bairn barely able to walk, to the water's edge, pulled her beneath the surface, and devoured her.

"I myself have seen the hag's flowing green hair and her shilpit arms like those of a starveling," says Colum, lifting his arms and wiggling his fingers. "She waits just beneath the water, and no one dares swim in the river or even put in a boat there."

Seeing me shiver, Caora reaches over and squeezes my hand. Her fingers are cold, but I do not pull away. I've never met a girl my own age, and I am eager for her friendship.

"Will you tell a story now?" I ask her.

"I have seen a monster even more fearsome than the Greentooth hag," Caora begins. Her voice is silvery, like a waterfall lit by moonlight. "A horse with fins on his legs, a huge mouth that steams like a kettle, and one fiery eye. Nocklavey is his name. Out of his back grows the body of a man whose huge head rolls from side to side. Most terrifying of all, he has no skin, so that you can see all his sinews and the blood that flows black in his veins."

Caora's eyes glow like golden orbs as she tells of Nocklavey rising from the sea and laying waste to the land.

"The monster seizes men with his great skinless hands and crushes them, and the breath of his terrible horse burns everything in its path."

My heart is thumping as if I have been running hard. "Can anyone stop him?"

"He is afraid of nothing except—which is strange—fresh water."

"I've never heard of this monster," says Colum. "Could it have been a goblin instead?"

Caora does not reply, only draws back the long sleeve from her right arm. From shoulder to wrist the skin is scarred red and white, as if it has been burned away and grown back.

Staring at Caora's disfigured arm, my first thought is that we are alike: crippled once and now healed. Then a colder certainty grips me, that one day I will meet such a monster.

Caora lays her thin hand on my knee. It is as weightless as a stack of feathers.

"Don't be afraid, Albia. See, I survived Nocklavey."

A swan glides out of the reeds at the edge of the water. The movement silences the grunting, gurgling frogs. I gaze at her whiteness and slowly let out my breath.

⤙⤚

At the summer's end I say good-bye to Caora and return to the smoky roundhouse in the woods. Once I am home, I realize how much I have missed my mother. I want to tell her everything about my new friend. But she seems wary of me and sad. She does not try to embrace me. I wonder, doesn't she love me anymore? Then I realize that I am the one who has put the distance between us. I try to make it up to her by hard work. I help her carry peat from the moor and spread it out to dry for the winter's fires. I collect the water lily roots that make Helwain's best black dye, digging in the shallow water until my hands grow numb with cold. During the winter we make clay pots and weave baskets from reeds and grass to sell in the village. We dye wool in a cauldron and the roundhouse reeks of the urine that sets the colors so they will not fade. I do my best not to complain.

By day Colum pastures our sheep in his father's fields, and at night we bring them into the roundhouse for warmth. The winds from the northern seas sweep in like airy sheets of ice. Snow falls, deep and thick, and Colum must wait out the storm at our house. He and I tell stories around the fire while the noises and smells of sheep surround us.

That night I dream of Nocklavey, his huge hanging head, his skinless arms and fiery eye. I wake myself with a cry and find Helwain standing over me.

"Did you call out? What did you see?" she demands.

"I don't know. Nothing," I reply, avoiding her eyes.

"I heard you cry out 'Nocklavey!'" says Colum. "You woke me, too."

"I thought so!" says Helwain, her eyes gleaming. "That monster has not been heard of since the strife-filled days of King Giric. It portends a powerful scourge upon the land."

"I only dreamt it because I was too warm by the fire," I protest, showing her my arms damp with sweat.

Colum's wary gaze shifts between me and Helwain. As soon as the sun rises he leaves, even though the snow is still deep. He says his father needs him, but I think he is afraid of Helwain.

In his absence, the winter's gloom is even greater. It seems unnatural for me to be living in a remote wood with my mother and the foul-tempered Helwain. I long for the winter to end and welcome the trickles of snowmelt and the shoots of green that announce the spring.

Finally it is the feast of Beltane and I can go to the shieling again. I am fourteen and I can build a small bothy and kindle a fire almost as well as Colum. He has taught me to tan hides and to make strong cords from the stems of stinging nettles. I know every sheep in Colum's flock as well as mine, and they follow me as ducklings follow their mother. I can even find my way at night using the stars.

Caora finds us again, and from time to time we join up with other shepherds. The summer is full of singing, wrestling, and games. The sheep grow fat and woolly. All too quickly, however, the eve of August arrives, the flowers fall from the heather, and the green begins to fade from the grasses. That night we build a bonfire to honor the god Lug. Caora and I are dancing with the shepherds when I feel a stabbing pain at the center of my belly. It spreads to my thighs, then down to my left foot. Leaving the others dancing in the firelit circle, I limp away until the sound of their merriment fades.

Then, out of the gray murk steps a deer as white as the moon. She gazes at me with glistening black eyes that seem almost human and inclines her head as if beckoning me. My desire to follow her is like a hunger for sweetness and rest and drink all at once. I wonder if I am dreaming, but the pain stabs my belly again. I feel something wet between my legs, and looking down I see blood on my thigh.

"Will I die out here?" My words seem to waver on my lips and fall into the thick mist. I sink to my hands and knees.

The next thing I know, Caora is at my side.

"You're not dying, my friend. The goddess Banrigh has visited you," she says. She takes moss, wraps it in a strip of cloth, and ties it around my loins to catch the blood.

"Banrigh?" I look around in confusion for the white doe. She seems to have vanished.

"She rules the four aspects of the moon and lights the four worlds: the future, the past, the visible now, and the invisible," explains Caora.

"The four worlds—you know about them!"

Caora nods. "There are many of us who follow the old ways. Now you are a votaress of Banrigh, as I am. With our help she controls Blagdarc, the god who strives to bring darkness to all four worlds. But she cannot destroy him, for she relies upon him to conceal the new moon, keeping the Asyet-world hidden," Caora explains. "We are not meant to see the future."

"Except for those who have the Sight," I say, beginning to understand.

"They walk a dangerous path," says Caora, slowly shaking her head, "for they are Blagdarc's sworn enemies."

I swallow hard. The pain still pulses in my belly. The moon overhead is shaped like an egg. While I wonder if she is waxing or waning, a cloud drifts across her face, and it is as black as night can possibly be on the shieling at the end of summer.

Chapter 7

Dun Inverness

Grelach

I have been patient for so long it wears hard on me. Waiting has not made the foolish and ignoble Duncan a good king. Waiting has not brought my husband the renown he deserves. We are still rulers of this northern kingdom only. And I have all but given up hope of bearing a son.

It has been three years since the day my lord arrived with news of how he defeated the traitor Macdonwald and earned Duncan's praise. He hailed me as his dearest partner of greatness, and I was relieved that he meant to keep me as his wife, not spurn me for my fruitless womb. He spoke of meeting three fateful women on the moor who addressed him as thane of Glamis, thane of Cawdor, and—most exalted of all—king of Scotland! Surely those Wyrd sisters had more than mortal knowledge, for the lands and titles of Glamis and Cawdor soon fell to us. Like the passion of young lovers, our ambitions were aroused and we dreamt of ruling Scotland.

Duncan came to our castle to celebrate the victory. I prayed that some mishap would befall him and my lord would that night become all that was promised him. But the visit passed without incident. The next year, when Duncan visited again, I looked in vain for signs of poor health. I questioned Macbeth but found him unwilling to consider what might happen if the king should die suddenly.

"Duncan has honored me, and I have golden opinions from everyone," he said to me then. "Let us not entertain these dark thoughts."

By his very denial I knew his thoughts, and thus I could not keep silent.

"That crown sits on Duncan's head like a bright confection. It may fall into your lap as easily as Glamis and Cawdor did—if you still wish to be king."

"I will not tarnish my good name!" he shouted in a fury. Then he left with his warriors to slay more foes, loyally serving the undeserving Duncan.

Months went by, and when Macbeth returned he poured into my lap the spoils of battles. Gold and jewels! Silks! I slept with him, prayed to all the saints, and waited for my womb to fill, but it remained empty.

I am only twenty-eight, young enough to bear many sons. But not since my daughter have I brought a child to life. Am I now cursed for letting her perish?

Alas, to dwell in the past is to sink like a stone dropped into the sea. I must think of the future instead. What wife worthy of greatness would stand by, year after year, and let opportunity pass through her husband's open hands? The promise of the fateful sisters must be fulfilled! Will it happen tonight, when Duncan visits our castle again?

♒

The king has brought his sons, the big-headed Malcolm and his younger brother, Donalbain. Macduff, the thane of Fife, arrives with his son, and Banquo with his son, Fleance. The young men wrestle with staves and throw stones to see who is the strongest. Luoch joins in their contests. He is fifteen now, and his face is becoming square and manly, his shoulders wide. Watching him, I am struck by his silent determination to win. Deep-voiced shouts fill the air. Duncan rubs his hands in pleasure.

"Your son has the makings of a warrior," he says to me.

I nod, hiding my scowl. *A warrior? My son has the makings of a king!*

Often I remind Luoch of his royal descent, in order to feed his self-regard. Today I see that he is no longer a skulking, fearful boy, but one who strikes with a strong arm. My father has toughened him.

Now Luoch faces Fleance in a match with swords. Fleance is a fine-looking boy, blue-eyed, sturdy and quick.

"Banquo, your son carries himself with the pride of greatness. I will keep my eye on him," the king says in an approving tone.

I see my husband glance at Banquo, mistrustful.

"We are Your Grace's loyal servants," says Banquo to the king. "But the worthiest on the field are the princes, your own sons."

Anyone can see that Prince Malcolm is a puny boy, despite his huge head, and no match for Fleance or even Luoch. But the self-satisfied Duncan smiles. He demands flattery as his due, like taxes and tribute, and we all must pay.

Now Duncan calls out, "Macbeth! How do you judge these worthy princes?"

My lord stands with his hands clasped behind his back, watching the young men fight. I see the muscles of his jaw tense and I know that he is filled with envy. He does not reply to the king. Is he thinking as I am, that we have waited long enough?

The feast that night is fit for a better king than Duncan. Platters piled high with every kind of fish, fowl, and game crowd the tables. Mead-horns overflow, spilling onto the floor. Rhuven hurries about, overseeing the servants. That would be my task, but I have been ordered to sit on Duncan's left hand, while my lord sits on his right. The king has given me a diamond that glitters against my red gown, a jewel hard enough to cut stone. But he cannot soften me with gifts and pretended honor.

Pipers play and a bard weaves a lay of Duncan's latest victories—battles he would have lost were it not for my Macbeth and his general, Banquo. The king is drunk. He splashes wine into my lord's cup. He praises him and Banquo in equal measures. The young men, their bellies full and their faces ruddy with mead, fall asleep on the ground, not even bothering to go to their chambers. Duncan turns to me, squinting, his eyes barely able to focus.

"My dear Grelach, you must waste no more time!"

Startled, I drop my knife. Can he read my thoughts? "What do you mean, Your Majesty?" I ask guardedly.

"You must give your husband a fine, strong son of his own, for that is your duty as my subject and servant."

I feel anger flood my veins like fire. I will have no such obligation to this paltry king! How dare he tell me what is my duty! How dare he call me his servant!

Duncan lurches from his seat and gestures toward his prone and snoring sons.

"There, my loyal war-leaders," he proclaims in a loud but slurred voice, "asleep with his warband is your future king. To succeed me I have chosen—Prince Malcolm!"

I let out a gasp. My eyes seek out my lord's, who looks to me as if an invisible cord between us were suddenly pulled taut. He, too, looks stunned.

How dare Duncan—whose grandfather shut my kin out of the succession—now try to extend his rule to the next generation! The injustice of it brings my blood to the boiling point.

I stand up, almost knocking over my chair. The wine I have drunk makes my head spin. Without asking the king's permission, I leave the dining hall. Rhuven follows me to my chamber to undress me, but I dismiss her.

"Do not come to me until tomorrow. I would be alone. Send my lord to me."

With an anxious glance backward, she leaves. I pace the room like a tethered lion. How dare Duncan allude to my barrenness! As if I am good for nothing but to bring forth sons. If I were a man my brawn and my brains—not my womb—would grant me power. O that this false king would fall, that a more worthy one might rise! It must happen now.

Craving more wine, the feel of its heat in my veins, I empty the flask on my table, drinking every drop. From under my bed I draw out the bag of herbs Rhuven brought me from her sister and take out a leafy sprig of rowan, also called witchwood. I sweep my cross and beads to the floor. This is no business for God's mother and the saints. I pass the witchwood over the flame of my lamp. Small red berries sizzle in the flame and a sweet smell stings my nose.

"Come to me, you ancient spirits. Come Neoni, who brought everything from her vast empty womb. Thicken my blood that no womanly remorse may flow in my veins."

Angrily I press my breasts beneath my shift. I know how tender it is to love the babe that milks me. But my body has betrayed me, refusing to bring forth any more life. Now it is time to use death as my means.

"Come thick night and hell-smoke, hide the wound this knife will make," I murmur through clenched teeth. My mind swims from the wine. *What knife? I have no knife. Must I slay Duncan?* I hear my lord's footsteps approaching upon the stairs. No, it must be his deed.

Macbeth enters my room with clenched fists. "Duncan has gone to bed," he says, slamming the door shut. "Damn him and both his sons, for he spares no opportunity to insult my manhood! Did you hear him praise Fleance? Does he mean to advance Banquo over me?"

I seize his shoulders. The fumes of burning witchwood envelop us. "This night is *our* opportunity to act. Duncan insults us simply by living."

He does not mistake my meaning. Yet all he says is "Are you drunk?"

"Are *you* drunk, my lord, with fear? Or do you dare to act on your desires?"

"I dare not do more than a man should," he says, not meeting my eyes.

"Think of what the Wyrd sisters promised you, and what you promised me," I remind him. "If you love me, keep your word."

"But what if we should fail?"

"*We'll* not fail, if you screw up *your* courage to the sticking place!" I put my hand on the hilt of the dagger at his waist.

"With your mettle you should bring forth only male children!" Macbeth says with a groan that hints of lust.

"And I will yet, if you show me you are a man," I say in his ear. "Now, is the king alone?"

"Two grooms guard his chamber door."

"Stay here while I drug the wine so the grooms will sleep. Then use their daggers, so that it will look like their deed."

He nods, and I go with the poisoned cups. The grateful grooms drink—unwary fools!—and fall sleep. They look dead. I take out their daggers. Then I open the door to Duncan's bedroom and step inside. The light from the torch in the hall slants across his body. His chest rises and falls. My hand twitches as I imagine putting a dagger to the king's chest, above his heart.

No, perhaps the neck would be easier, the unguarded skin where the pulse beats.

The king lets out a long, rasping breath.

When I was a child, after my mother died, I used to creep into my father's room at night. I would listen for his breath to reassure myself that he still lived. Banish tender thoughts! This is not my father but the unworthy sot Duncan. My hands tighten on the daggers until my arms tremble. Yet he is only a man, sleeping. I cannot do it! I back out of the room, lay the daggers down beside the unconscious grooms, and hurry back to my chamber.

In the hall I pass my husband. His eyes are wide and glittering. He gazes at something beyond me, like one who sleepwalks.

"I see it still . . . a fatal vision. It leads me the way that I was going," he murmurs confusedly. The midnight bell rings. "I go, and it is done!" he says as if awakened by its clanging.

In my chamber, I wait. The night is blacker and longer than any night I can remember. My husband does not return. Has he lost his will? An owl shrieks, waking me from a half sleep.

Finally Macbeth comes, soaked in blood but with a face as pale as a ghost from hell. The deed is done! He speaks without sense, saying that he has murdered sleep, that he cannot pronounce "Amen" even while saying the word over and over. Carrying not one, but three daggers. His own and those of the grooms. My heart knocks against my ribs. Has he ruined everything?

"Take these daggers back!" I hiss. "They must lie next to the grooms."

He shakes his red locks violently. "Nay, I cannot look upon what I have done."

"Then go and wash yourself. Put on your nightgown and get into your bed," I say as if I am talking to a child. I grab the daggers and tiptoe down the hall, cursing Macbeth's cowardice. The blood on them is drying, making my hands sticky.

The scene outside Duncan's bedroom makes the wine in my stomach rise up into my mouth. The throats of the grooms gape open. Bone and sinews show. Their faces are dead white. Blood, enough to fill several bowls, pools on the floor around them. It is all I can do to place the daggers near their hands without fainting into the gory mess myself. Not one, but three dreadful deeds have been done here, never to be undone.

What possessed Macbeth to kill the innocent grooms?

I am afraid of my husband.

⤙

I wash my hands. The water in my basin turns pink, then red. But the blood clots beneath my fingernails and seeps into my palms and will not be rubbed away. I toss the guilty water out the window. It splashes against the rocks below.

The cock crows. I hear the servants rise to begin their work. Soon come the screams and shouts.

"Murder! Help! The king is slain!"

I follow the tumult to the door of Duncan's chamber. I close my eyes, but the metallic smell of the blood brings the whole scene to my mind. I begin to sway, but Rhuven is there, holding me up. I see Banquo on his knees, Macduff standing with a horrified look on his face, and my husband pacing and tearing his hair.

"Who among you, if you loved the king, could have refrained from killing these murderers?" he cries, his face a mask of grief.

Lennox rushes up the stairs. "The princes are gone!" he cries.

"Let suspicion fall upon them!" Macbeth declares. "They must have bribed the guards to do the deed."

"Why would they want to kill their father? It is most unnatural," says Lennox, shaking his head. "Yet they are fled, which proves their guilt."

"Nay, they are afraid for their own lives, and wisely so," murmurs Banquo.

I see him glance at my lord, distrust in his eyes. Then faintness overwhelms me and I lean on Rhuven again.

"You have seen too much of this gruesome sight, my lady," says Rhuven. She leads me to my room, locks the door, and seats me on the bed. I see her glance at the rowan ashes by the lamp.

"What did you have to do with it?" she asks, her voice urgent.

"I did not touch any of them. Don't look at me so." I close my eyes and turn my head away from her.

"Grelach, you must tell me, or I cannot protect you." She grasps my shoulders and shakes me gently.

I rub my hands together, unable to stop myself. "Rhuven, bring me some water to wash with."

"Not until you tell me the entire truth." She takes my face between her hands, forcing me to look in her eyes.

I trust Rhuven. She is my constant companion, my other self.

"I only put the drops of mandrake in their wine to make them sleep. It was not part of the plan to slay them," I whisper. "Only Duncan."

I do not need to say more. I have as much as confessed my husband's crimes—and my part in them—to Rhuven. Now she, too, has reason to fear Macbeth.

Chapter 8

The Shieling

Albia

When I come home from the shieling at the end of the summer, I notice at once my mother's gaunt shape and the shadowy circles beneath her eyes. I ask her if she is ill.

"All of Scotland is sick," she replies.

"What do you mean?" I ask.

"King Duncan is dead, his sons have fled, and Macbeth rules in his stead," replies Helwain in a flat voice, like someone who has tasted of a plant that numbs the brain.

So the painted warrior of Wanluck Mhor is now the king! Helwain should be exulting that her words have proven true. Then again, what does it matter which bloodthirsty thane sits on the throne? Nothing in Scotland changes but the seasons, and they follow one another as predictably as night follows day.

But I am wrong about that. First, my body changes. With Banrigh's monthly visitation, my breasts grow round, my hips flare out, and my emotions reel from one extreme to another. That winter I turn fifteen.

The weather also changes, and with violence. Even before the fall crops are ready to be gathered, icy winds blow from the north and cover every green thing in heavy white rime. Murdo's barley freezes and falls limp in the fields. Mother and I have to walk all the way to Inverness to buy grain, and it is so scarce that we can afford only a little. The winter months bring snow so deep that the sheep cannot reach the ground to graze and so they begin to die.

One day, six wolves threaten our flock even as Colum and I stand watch. Though we draw closer to the fire and throw rocks at them, they creep toward us, their teeth bared and their eyes gleaming with gold fire. I am afraid they will attack me, but instead they seize two sheep—not even the weakest ones—and the pack melts away, their tawny coats blending with the dead, gray-brown grasses. The bleating of the hapless creatures rises to the pitch of a scream before ceasing.

"Albia, did you notice anything unusual about those wolves?" Colum asks into the silence.

"Aye, they were fat. It could not have been hunger that made them so fearless."

"Did you see their eyes? Something evil held those wolves, to be sure," he says in a dire tone.

"Do you think Nocklavey is abroad?" I whisper. "And that is why everything is dead and destroyed?"

But Colum does not answer.

My mother is also in the grip of something unnatural. Her cheeks grow hollow and she shivers her very flesh away even while she sits directly before the fire.

The prowling wolves, the deathly cold, and my mother's illness throw Helwain into distress. She scatters animal bones and mutters over their meaning until the clattering crazes me. I cover my ears until I cannot help shouting at her.

"Throw those damned bones outside. Can't you see my mother is ill? Use your magic to make her well, you old fate-reaper!"

Helwain turns on me. "Fair is foul, and foul is fair. Tell me why!" She grabs me by the throat as if to shake an answer from me.

I push her away and she goes sprawling into the fire. She screams as her hand touches the embers. Mother leaps up from her bed, her feverish eyes burning.

"Albia, never lift your arm against my sister!" she rasps.

I hide my head and shake with tears as Mother spreads Helwain's gnarled hand upon a cold stone to ease the burning. But I still believe that Helwain is mad and that I will also go mad if I have to live with her any longer.

In February, Helwain makes us go with her to Stravenock Henge, where the moon and stars align with the stones to reveal when spring will come. Mother is so weak I must hold her up as we cross the frozen streams and clamber up icy hillsides. Helwain uses two walking staffs to keep from falling.

In the grip of the killing winter, the heath bears no sign of life, not a nighthawk or a raven or even a mouse. The tall stones of Stravenock Henge are slippery with white rime that forms patterns more intricate than those of the most skillful cloth-weavers. As we lean close to admire the icy designs, our breath makes them disappear.

Helwain scans the sky, but the moon stays hidden, and not a single star peeps through the blanket of night. Mother and I huddle together, blowing on our hands to keep them warm. Suddenly a bearlike creature lumbers into the henge, giving us all a fright. It is only Rhuven, covered in furs borrowed from her lady. She opens her arms and wraps Mother and me in her warmth.

Helwain shouts to the black sky, "O moon, show us your face!"

"Listen to her. She is mad," I say to my mother and Rhuven.

"Nay, Albia," says Mother. "For if the moon does not appear, then it means that the god of night has usurped the moon goddess. That is why the seasons fail and nature is out of joint."

"I fear this is my lord and my lady's doing," Rhuven murmurs. "On that terrible night, I overheard her summon the god of night."

"She called upon Blagdarc?" says Helwain in disbelief. "How did she come by such power?"

Rhuven's whispering is lost to my ears. Then Helwain's staff clatters against the stones like a lightning crack.

"By Guidlicht and all the gods! Are you saying that Macbeth and his lady—"

My mother interrupts. "Rhuven, why didn't you stop them?"

"I did not understand, until it was too late!" Her voice trembles with tears.

"Ah, Macbeth was bound to act," Helwain says knowingly. "And now Blagdarc rules through him, wrecking the order of nature."

"Indeed there is nothing but misery with us," Rhuven laments. "Sleep never comes to my lady, and she and my lord abuse each other. Luoch will not be ruled by Macbeth, saying the man is no father to him. The warriors who loved Duncan refuse to serve Macbeth. They drink and fight constantly. Horses thrash about in their stalls until they brain themselves. The lakes are frozen and even the seas are empty of fish."

"What is to become of us all?" Mother murmurs.

The moon never shows her face. We trudge back home and fall asleep. When I wake up, Mother is sitting beside me, red-eyed, as if she has been crying all night.

"It is time to say farewell, my dear."

"Where are you going?" I ask, rubbing my eyes.

Rhuven comes and takes my hands. "Geillis is not going away. You are."

"Then where am *I* going?"

Helwain rears up from the shadows. "Away from here! You were not meant to live and die in the Wychelm Wood." She waves her arms at me. "Go, find your own fate, let me grow old in peace."

Stricken, I turn to my mother. She shakes her head.

"You cannot be happy here, Albia," she says sadly. "Go with Rhuven. She knows a good man and his wife who will foster you in their household. There you will learn the customs of the world and how to find your way in it."

"But how can you send me to live with strangers? I want to go to the shieling with Colum in the summers. I'll miss the sheep!" Tears begin to roll down my face.

"It is for your own good," says Mother, embracing me. "One day you will understand."

I pull away from her and say coldly, "I cannot understand a mother who would send her own daughter away from home."

"There is much that you do not understand," says Helwain, frowning.

"Enough, sister!" Mother warns.

My few clothes are quickly packed on the horse that Rhuven and I will take turns riding. As we set out, I feel a stirring of anticipation, like the first time I went to the shieling. I will live with a real family! I might become friends with their children.

At the edge of the Wychelm Wood, we stop at Murdo's cottage so I can say good-bye to Colum. He greets us with a puzzled look on his face.

"Are you going on a journey? At this time of year?"

"Rhuven is taking me to the town of Dunbeag. I will live in a thane's castle, among all sorts of people. Will you take care of my sheep until I come home?"

"You know I will watch them as if they were mine. But why must you go?" His face clouds over.

I choke back sudden tears. "Don't ask. I will miss you, Colum."

"Dunbeag is only a day's journey. I will visit you, if summer ever comes again."

Rhuven is talking to Murdo, who strokes his beard and nods. I hear her asking him to look after her sisters. I feel a stab of guilt that I didn't even try to persuade Mother that she needed me. Why? Because I want to leave, and for that I feel even worse.

"What is wrong?" says Colum. "What are you thinking?"

"Of my poor mother!" I sigh, then shake my head stubbornly. "But I am not deserting her, for she *sent* me away!"

"Don't be sore. You are a fledged bird now, almost grown. Why, in two years you will be as old as I am now," he says, thrusting out his chest.

"And in two years you will be a man," I say, smiling despite myself. "Is that a beard on your cheeks?" I reach up playfully to touch his face.

He takes my hands in his and with a sudden move spins me around so that I am pinned in his arms. He picks me up and I scream.

"I don't want to wrestle now. Put me down!" I laugh and twist in his arms.

"Albia, my lambkin, don't think you can run away from me! I'll come after you and bring you home to the flock."

The sensation of Colum's arms about me lingers long after he sets me down, and I feel less alone as Rhuven and I follow the glen southward towards Dunbeag. The frozen grass crunches underfoot. I know I will see Colum again, but for now I am leaving behind want and worry and fearsome wolves for something unknown but new and therefore promising. The brisk pace warms me, stirring up hopeful thoughts like brew in a kettle.

Then in my mind I see Mother's worn-looking face and the sadness in her eyes when I did not return her farewell embrace. Regret washes over me. What kind of daughter am I? I should stay by her side, Helwain be damned, and love her to the end, like a good daughter.

Chapter 9

Dunbeag

Albia

Weak winter sun shines on a cluster of turf houses in the valley of the River Findhorn. Thin strands of smoke drift from the roof-holes.

"Why, Rhuven, this is no more than a village!" I say, disappointed.

"Aye, but Dunbeag is important." She points to the top of the hill, where a large timber fort overlooks the huddled houses. "This is the seat of Banquo, chief of the king's army in these northern shires. He is an honest and kindly man who will protect you."

So I am to stay with Banquo, the man I glimpsed with Macbeth on Wanluck Mhor! I hide my surprise, for as far as Rhuven knows, I was asleep while she and her sisters danced and greeted Macbeth, then argued about Helwain's promises to him.

"Protect me from whom?" I ask.

Rhuven ignores my question. "Banquo's wife needs a companion. The advantages of such a position can be great, as you see." She spreads her arms for me to admire her soft woolen gown. "A gift from the queen, whom I have served since she was a mere girl."

"Do Banquo and his wife have children?" I ask.

"A son who is near manhood. Their daughter died lately. She was your age."

Do they expect me to replace her? Anxious, I follow Rhuven up the hill.

Banquo reminds me of a bear with his large hands, short, wide body, and bushy brown beard. His laugh even sounds like a growl, though a friendly one. He welcomes me with a wide smile. His wife Breda, on the other hand, is thin, sharp-featured, and cold. The hand she extends feels limp and damp as it touches mine, and her eyes dart around to avoid meeting mine. I know at once she does not want me in her home.

Rhuven whispers to me, "I will bring you some clothes when I come back. She doesn't seem the generous type." Her parting advice is brief. "Always remember to say 'Aye, my lady' or 'Aye, my lord.'"

Compared to the roundhouse with its low walls and soot-blackened interior, the thane's fort is spacious, clean, and comfortable. Rush mats cover the floors, and heavy woven cloth hangs on the walls to keep in the warmth. The windows have shutters, and the ceilings are made of real timber. At one end of the house stands a wide hearth where the cooking is done, and at the opposite end is a smaller hearth, so that all the rooms in between are warmed.

Breda leads me up the narrow steps to a tiny room with a

single window under the slanting roof. It holds a heather-stuffed mattress and baskets for storage. There I stay for the rest of the day, afraid to come down until I am bidden. I smell fish cooking, and fresh bread, but no one comes to offer me food. I lie down upon my mattress and think of Mother, until I begin to cry from loneliness and hunger. Finally sleep overtakes me.

In the morning I open my eyes to see a surly-faced boy frowning down at me. He nudges my leg with his foot.

"I am no servant, you know," he says. "It's just this one time I'll bring you something to eat."

I sit up and take the plate of cold fish and the flour cake he thrusts at me.

"Then who are you?" I ask.

"Fleance, son of Banquo," he replies with a look that suggests I am stupid not to know him. He does resemble the thane, with his thick brown hair and sturdy build.

"My name is Albia," I offer, trying to smile. But already I dislike this ill-bred carl.

"Our little fosterling," he says with a sneer. "Here to share the family hearth and fill my mother's empty heart. Couldn't my father have chosen a lass who was bonny?"

How do I even reply? I know my dress is rough and my hair untidy. But am I really so plain? Tears start into my eyes. Not all boys are as kind as Colum; this is the first lesson life at Dunbeag teaches me.

A sharp voice sounds from below. "Fleance! Send her down here now."

I scramble to my feet and stumble down the steep stairs. There Breda stands with a look in her ice-blue eyes that makes me feel guilty, though I have done nothing wrong.

"You are to eat with us, pray with us, and at all other times busy yourself with spinning, weaving, cooking, and whatever I shall require of you," she says. Her voice is harsh and her tongue gives the familiar words a strange shape.

"Aye, my lady," I reply as Rhuven advised.

"And you shall call us 'Mother' and 'Father,' for my husband wishes it," she says. Her nostrils flare with dislike.

"Aye, my lady. I mean . . . Mother." I no more want to call her that than she wants to hear it.

"Ha!" Fleance's sudden laugh is like the bark of a hound.

"Away with you!" Breda says to him. "And don't come back without a deer to feed us. Even if you must trespass on the king's land."

Fleance and Banquo leave for the hunt, and my hours with Breda pass with little conversation. I watch her weave on a loom the size of a doorway. The frame leans against a wall and its warp threads are held down with clay weights. With fast fingers she passes the shaft back and forth between the vertical woolen threads.

"I have never seen a loom like that," I finally say.

"I brought it with me from Norway."

I wonder if all people from over the seas have such pale blue eyes and hair the color of ripening wheat.

"Why did you come to Scotland?"

"I was brought here. To be his wife." Breda says no more,

but jerks the weft threads tight. I notice that the cloth she weaves is bordered by a delicate gray band, like a cloud skimming the horizon.

When Banquo and Fleance return from the hunt, the quiet house suddenly rings with noise and life.

"Breda, my wife!" shouts Banquo, striding into the room, his tunic splattered with blood. He kisses her loudly, then turns to me. "And Albia, my girl." With his huge hand he touches my head and I smile for the first time today.

Fleance follows his father, carrying a bow. "Mother, I did as you bade me," he says eagerly. "It was I who brought down the doe even as she ran for the trees. My arrow caught her in the neck."

"That is a good son," she says without smiling.

My heart stirs with pity for the doe. I hate Fleance for being proud of killing such a noble creature.

That venison feast is the first I eat while seated at a table. With Mother and Helwain I am used to eating from a common bowl that rests on our knees. But at Dunbeag we each have our own platter. I am startled by the greed with which Banquo and Fleance devour their food, smacking their lips and cracking bones with their teeth. Banquo's beard is greasy with bits of food. Her lips pressed tightly together, Breda reaches over and wipes it clean with a cloth, and Banquo laughs, making the table shake.

Before retiring at night, Banquo makes everyone in the household kneel while he speaks into his folded hands, calling upon "the Lord God and his only begotten son, Jesus" again and again. The image of a mighty warrior and his son comes to my mind. They must be the same gods that Colum's priest worships. Banquo and his family have probably never heard of Neoni and Guidlicht and the four worlds.

"And Lord God we thank you for bringing into our midst Albia, this daughter for us to foster as you do care for us. Amen."

Surprised to hear my own name, I glance over at the great bear of a man, his face bowed to the earth. A feeling of warmth spreads over me. *Is this what it is like to have a father?*

I lower my head so that no one can see my trembling chin.

❧

Spring comes to Dunbeag reluctant as a wayward child. A pallid sun barely shines, no rain falls, and the plants that poke from the hard ground are more yellow than green. Some trees and bushes do not bloom at all. In the town of Dunbeag, a dozen sheep and goats are stillborn and people are still dying from winter's diseases. Or worse, they kill each other. The stonecutter's wife poisoned her husband to put an end to his beatings, and a crofter stabbed his neighbor in a dispute. Banquo prays to his God for relief, asking that the grip of Satan—who must be the god of their Under-world—be loosened from us.

I overhear Banquo complaining to Breda that King Macbeth has seized more land from his thanes, worsening the people's want. Now it is a crime for anyone in Dunbeag to hunt in the nearby forests as they always have, to farm the Findhorn Valley, or to pasture their sheep there. Banquo turns a blind eye to those who use the king's lands, for he hunts there himself. But he cannot ignore Macbeth's demand for more warriors equipped with new armor and horses. To satisfy his king, Banquo must press his tenants for their rents and tax the villagers. If he were not such a good and generous man, the people of Dunbeag would grumble even more.

I, too, feel a loyalty to Banquo because of his kindness to me. Like a favored hound fed on marrow-filled bones, I want to please him.

"Do you have a kiss for your foster father, my daughter?" he asks, and I oblige him, finding a bare spot high on his bearded cheek. He smells of smoke and sweat and, sometimes, stale food. Whenever he brings a gift for Breda, he brings one for me as well. My favorite is a shiny brass buckle decorated with knots and the figure of a bird. I wear it on my belt every day.

Fleance is as rude to me as his father is kind. He sees that I sometimes limp and calls me a "hirple-foot," an insult I endure in pained silence. I wonder if Fleance is cruel because his father is rough with him and his mother cold and distant. Even so, that does not excuse his meanness.

Twice a week the village priest climbs the hill to Dunbeag to teach Fleance and me something called Latin. It twists my tongue into knots. Fleance, who has had lessons for years, calls me a lame-brain. He has taken to staring at my chest as if trying to see my breasts growing beneath my dress. The priest notices my shame and steps between us, his white hair like a cloud encircling his head. With infinite patience he teaches me to recognize the strange marks and the sounds they represent. Using a quill pen I learn to form letters, then words, but none of them make sense. One day at the tiny church at Dunbeag, while Breda and the other worshippers stare blankly at the cross, I realize that I understand the prayers the priest intones. It is as amazing as hearing words in the sighs of the wind and the melodies of birds.

This priest is a moral man and a lover of learning, with a pretty wife in the village and two children. He loves to tell about the past, when the powerful Picts ruled, battling the Scots, the Romans, and the other barbarians, until Ninian and Columba arrived and vanquished all enemies with their single god. Then they planted stone crosses for the people to worship. After that, the great Kenneth MacAlpin united the Scots and the Picts, and our land became known as the kingdom of Alba.

"Knowest thou," the priest adds in his learned manner, "that thy name, Albia, is akin to *alba,* the Latin word for 'white,' and thus signifies goodness and virtue?" Then he murmurs, more to himself than to me, "Though our country's whiteness is marred by the evil and strife afoot in the land." He looks at me sharply. "Never let thy goodness be so stained! Ask thou the Lord God's help." He touches his forehead, then his chest and each of his shoulders, an odd series of gestures he often makes.

"I will. I promise," I whisper, thinking he is warning me about Fleance.

⁂

A cold and sunless summer follows the barren spring. I am sitting outdoors, using small tablets to weave a braid to decorate the hem of a dress. The warp threads attach to my belt, pass through the tablets, and are secured to a timber post. The wind lifts my hair, which has grown long enough to reach my lap as I bend over my work. In the yard beside the fort, Banquo is training his warriors, and I hear shouts and the clash of swords.

Then Fleance and another fellow stumble into my sight, straining against each other in a contest of might. They wear nothing more than linen clouts over their loins. Their arms and torsos gleam with sweat. Thinking that the priest would not approve of my watching, I peek through the curtain of my hair. With a mighty heave Fleance throws off his opponent, who falls on his back with a grunt of pain. Fleance kneels on his chest and pins his arms against the ground.

"That's two out of three for me, and I'm more fit than you for the king's army," he says loudly. Then he lets the fellow get up and hobble away.

Fleance looks over and catches me watching him. I lower my gaze, but it is too late. He saunters over and stands before me.

"Did you see how I wrestled that carl to the ground? He has ten years on me."

I keep my eyes on my weaving. Fleance must not see that

his show of strength did impress me. "I think he let you win," I say with a shrug.

Fleance scowls. "What makes you think you can disdain me so? I am not ill-favored, am I? Look at me." He holds out his sinewed arms, then crosses them over his chest. "I am the son of the king's best general. And who are you? Nobody! You don't even have a father."

Boiling with rage I leap to my feet. "And you don't deserve yours! Why, you are nothing but a rude braggart. And I should clamor for the attention of one so ignorant? Pah!"

Fleance steps closer. Heat flows from his body and he smells of sweat. But I cannot move away. I am tethered to the post by my weaving.

"Rude I may be, for what warrior is not? But I'll not have you call me ignorant. I have studied Latin longer than you."

"I wouldn't give a piece of tin for your wit."

"Try me with a riddle," he demands. "Make it a good one."

I swallow hard. The Latin riddles are still too difficult for me. I will have to make one up.

While I am thinking, Fleance shifts from one foot to the other as if impatient for another wrestling contest. Finally I have a riddle I think is clever enough.

"I'll make you go blind, but without me you cannot see," I begin. "You may feel me on your skin, but you cannot touch me. I make earth appear and water disappear. All things reach for me, but whatever comes too near me will die." I look directly at Fleance, challenging him. "What am I?"

"That is easy," he says without hesitating. "I am the sun."

I feel my confidence wither. I blink and drop my eyes.

"I have more wit than you know. And I will be paid for it." Fleance smirks at me and tugs on my weaving, trying to pull me to him.

Suddenly I am the doe pursued by the hunter, the rabbit before the stone strikes. I turn to run but only succeed in wrapping myself in my weaving. Fleance steps closer, takes me by the waist, and turns me back to face him.

"I won't hurt you, *sister*. If you pay what you owe."

His voice is more mocking than threatening, his hands firm but not forceful. This surprises me, but my humilation is even greater. As he draws me nearer, I reach up and strike his face with the back of my hand.

"Take that for your payment!" I tear myself away and stumble backward, leaving my half-finished weaving dangling from the post.

Fleance cradles his jaw with his hand, looking stunned.

"Remember this, Fleance, son of Banquo: *I am the sun*. Dare to touch me and you will die. I do not jest."

⚜

For days Fleance and I exchange neither words nor looks. He does not attend our Latin lessons, and I am pleased to think that I have dealt with him for good. But one day I am on my way to the village, carrying wool for the weaver, when he steps from behind a boulder into my path. He wears a sword in his belt and carries another one in a leather scabbard. My first impulse is to throw my basket at him and run, but I hold my ground.

"Do you mean to cleave me in pieces right here and thus have your revenge?" I ask.

"Nay, I mean to teach you a different lesson." He pulls the sword from its scabbard and tosses it at my feet. It clangs on the rocky ground.

Puzzled, I look from the sword to Fleance, who leans on one leg, his hands resting on his hips. He does not look like a carl about to cause me trouble. His massy brown hair blows back from his face, making him almost handsome. He nods at the sword on the ground.

"If you can match me in wits, you can match me in arms."

"You expect me to fight you?" I say in disbelief.

"I will teach you."

"Why?" I say, full of suspicion.

"You have a warlike spirit I mean to hone."

"But what girl ever uses a sword?"

"You are no longer a mere girl, as I can see." His gaze travels from my face down to my waist.

I feel myself blush. Stupidly, I can think of no rejoinder.

"Pick it up," he says, drawing his own sword. The sun catches the long blade, making it gleam.

I set my basket aside and pick up the sword at my feet. It is not very heavy.

"'Tis the one I learned with when I was a boy."

I turn it over carefully, then exclaim in surprise, "I don't have a chance here. This blade is blunted!"

Fleance lowers his sword and gives me a hurt look. "Albia, why do you wish me harm?"

"Well, isn't that the point of the battle?"

"Nay, the point is to defend yourself," he says. A furrow creases his brow. "This is a dangerous world for a woman with a strong will but a weak arm. Now watch, and do as I do."

With two hands on the hilt and my feet planted firmly apart, I hold the sword over my head and bring it down as Fleance shows me. I slash from side to side until my shoulders ache. Sweat beads my forehead and prickles between my breasts.

"I love the sound of the blade cutting the air!" I say, panting with exhilaration. "Do you hear it?"

"Aye. See that you don't strike me!" Fleance yells, jumping back with an oath.

I barely heed him, now imagining myself in combat with the beast Nocklavey, thrusting my sword into his fiery eye, fighting until his black blood empties from his veins.

"Stop! That is not how to do it," Fleance cries, interrupting my wild thoughts. Standing behind me, he reaches around and grasps the hilt of my sword, covering my hands. So quickly did he move that I am too startled to protest. His chest presses against my back and his breath tickles my ear.

"You must learn the proper way to thrust at your opponent without exposing your flanks," he says. "You'd better have a shield."

Are his lips brushing my cheek or do I imagine it? I twist one hand free from beneath his and thrust my arm backward so that my elbow strikes him in the abdomen. The heel of my right foot comes down on his toes. I do this all without thinking.

Fleance drops my sword and falls back with a cry. I pick up the sword and whirl around to face him.

"A fine move, sister!" he says, grimacing and holding his stomach.

"Stay there," I warn. "This doesn't have much of a blade, but I can make it hurt anyway. So that's your plan, is it? Seduce me with swordplay?"

Fleance looks stricken. "I thought you were enjoying our sport."

I say nothing. I *have* been enjoying myself. Too much.

"I could not make you admire my strength or my wit, but you turned and hit me," he complains. "Now I teach you how to use a sword, and you want to kill me. What is a fellow to do?"

"Oh, you'll think of another trick, no doubt," I say, trying with my trembling hands to put the sword back in its scabbard. "But I'll be ready for it."

"I am not the enemy, Albia," he says in a tone of reproach.

"And that makes you a friend?" I want to sound outraged but hear my voice quaver instead.

I slide the sheathed weapon onto my belt and refasten the bronze buckle Banquo gave me. The sword drags my belt down over my hips. I pick up my basket and brush the dirt off its contents. It takes all my self-control to walk away without looking back.

On the village streets, people give me strange looks, the thane's foster daughter, armed with a sword and carrying a basket of wool. I ignore them, my thoughts fixed on Fleance. Twice

I have struck him, yet he did not seem angry, only disappointed. I leave the wool at the weaver's and hurry to the mill to buy flour. Remembering Fleance's arms around me and his breath on my face makes me blush. I hurry back to Dunbeag, up the hill. The unfamiliar sword beats against my leg. Breda will wonder what has taken me so long. I wonder if I have misjudged Fleance. He could easily have overcome me with force, but he did not. Does he want me just to notice him? Wrestling half-naked in front of me and teaching me to fight with a sword are strange ways of getting my attention, but what if the poor fool does not know any other way? I spend hours and days in such speculation. Meanwhile Fleance leaves with his father for Dun Forres, the king's dwelling.

Despite my aching arms and shoulders, I want to practice, but my little room is too narrow a place to swing my sword. So I go outside and choose a stone, not too heavy, and lift it over my head and swing it from side to side to increase my strength. I go to the far slope of Dunbeag and throw a shaft as I have seen men do in contests, fetching it and hurling it until it breaks against a rock. I whet the blade of Fleance's old sword against a hard stone, then swing and stab at a dummy made of straw until it is nothing but a pile of chaff. My blood pounds in every limb of my body, filling me with satisfaction.

While Fleance and Banquo are away, Breda teaches me to play simple tunes on the lute. I dress my hair in braids and ornaments of bone and wonder if it makes me look more like a lady. I practice my Latin with little interest, weave an entire length of cloth without a single mistake, and think about the unpredictable Fleance. What does he want from me? Something more than what he can take by mere strength.

After a few weeks, I realize that I miss him.

So, apparently, does Breda. Although she does not seem to like her husband or her son, she is morose in their absence.

"What can I do to please you?" I ask dutifully.

Breda shakes her head and gives me a look that says *You are not my daughter.*

"I know I cannot take her place," I say in a voice barely above a whisper. "I don't even wish to try."

Breda sighs. "She was nothing like you, but had the whitest hair and bluest eyes."

"Fleance has such eyes, too." I bite my tongue, seeing Breda's sharp look.

"The boy takes after his father," she says firmly.

The silence that follows is weighted with her disappointment in Fleance.

"A man's every deed is an act of war," she says suddenly, stabbing a needle into the cloth she is sewing. "And we women are mere spoils."

I do not know what to make of these statements. Is Breda simply lamenting her lot as Banquo's wife? Or is she warning me against her son?

"I will be no man's spoil," I say, "even if it means I will have no man, ever."

I vow to myself that I will learn to fight like a man, so that I will not need one to defend me.

Chapter 10

Dunduff

Albia

A thick and pestilent air has fallen over Dunbeag. Breda, afraid of becoming ill, is busy preparing for a visit to Fiona Macduff, wife of the powerful thane of Fife. It will be a two-day journey by horseback to Dunduff.

"I shall keep everything in order while you are away," I promise her.

"Nay, you will come with me, for Fiona will expect to meet my fosterling," says Breda, making me understand that she herself is not keen to have my company.

Two soldiers accompany us because of the threat of brigands, but we meet with no danger on the road. Macduff's stronghold is built on the open heath, for there are no hills around. But it is palisaded around with pointed timbers, and high watchtowers afford views in every direction. No one, friend or enemy, can surprise the Macduffs.

Fiona is as robust and warm-hearted as Breda is thin and cold. Her children flock around her like ducklings. I count four little ones, then five, and realize that two of the children are exactly alike. The long-limbed girls hold hands as they gaze at me shyly, and I am reminded of a swan and its reflection in the water. The oldest child, a boy, tries his best to stand apart from the others, like a bird eager to be fledged from the nest and find his own food.

I sit among the children and ask their names, patting their heads in turn. They climb into my lap, play with my hair, and tug on my hands, while I close my eyes and imagine myself among the sheep on the summer shieling. The children tickle me and I laugh. I have not been this happy since I played with Colum. I long for him so intently that tears fill my eyes. It is autumn now, so he has gone home from the shieling. I imagine him in the fields with Murdo, swinging his scythe as the barley falls.

Fiona's eldest son, who is called Wee Duff, soon warms to me like the others. He brings me his toys—animals carved from bone, a leather ball, and a wooden sword—and bounces up and down as I admire each one.

One of the twins taps my shoulder.

"Are you the queen of Faeryland?" she asks, pointing to my red-gold hair, loose about my shoulders.

I look into her wide and serious eyes, green pools in her face, and the voices around me seem to fade.

"I wish I were," I whisper. Something tugs at my awareness from within, perhaps nothing more than the brief longing to be a child again, with the Other-world as close as the next copse of trees.

"I believe she is," says the girl eagerly to her twin sister.

"We saw the queen—" says the second twin.

The other girl finishes her sentence. "In the forest at night."

"And she had hair like yours—"

"But you are much prettier in the day."

I take the hands of the twins and say, "It was a lovely dream, wasn't it?"

They shake their heads stubbornly.

"It was real," they insist. "You must come with us next time."

Seeing their earnest faces, I remember how I, too, imagined playing with faeries and visiting them in my sleep. Those memories have faded like the dye of a cloth washed a hundred times.

I hear myself say, "I will meet you there one day, I promise."

The girls exchange looks of delight, like a face and a mirror, and dance away.

In the company of Fiona Macduff, Breda warms up. She smiles at the children and I can believe that she loved her daughter and perhaps Fleance, too, when he was small.

"Maybe you will beget another bairn," says Fiona hopefully.

Breda shakes her head. "My courses do not come as they used to. It is something to do with the moon. Nothing in nature is as it should be."

I listen while pretending to play with Wee Duff's toy boat.

"Aye, everything is disordered since Macbeth became king,"

says Fiona. "Some say it was he, and not the princes Malcolm and Donalbain, who killed Duncan while he slept."

Breda sits forward, her brow contracted. "Since his death, not even the sheep are breeding rightly. And my husband's best mare bore a creature with two heads! It lived only a week."

Fiona rests a hand on her arm. "We should not be overly fearful. Similar times have come and gone with no lasting ill. My own Macduff was born—and almost died—in a cursed year like this one."

"What happened?" Breda asks.

"By some mishap that befell his mother, he was torn before his time from her womb," Fiona explains.

Breda looks amazed. "Yet see how he thrives today! He is all goodness and strength." She looks around her, finding reassurance. "Indeed, all is well here. Look how your children love you. Wee Duff will grow up to be just like his father."

"I pray he will!" Fiona says, pride in her voice. "He is a good son, and my lord a generous father." Her voice descends to a whisper. "Unlike our king, who is worse than the cruelest father. My Macduff has gone to beg him to rescind his unjust laws against the people."

I glance at Breda. Will she reveal that Banquo sometimes ignores the king's laws and poaches his game?

"Discontent grows, like a weed spreading along bare ground," she says. "Many thanes want war. And we—women and children—will be the victims." Bitterness fills her words.

"Nay, we must trust our men to keep us safe. Before he left,

Macduff promised to do nothing that would endanger us here, and I believe him." Fiona stands up and shakes out her skirt. "Let us no longer speak of men's affairs. Come and see my garden. You too, Albia. Children, let her be!"

I smile with relief as Wee Duff puts down his wooden sword and the twins untangle their fingers from my hair. Following Breda and Fiona into the garden, I draw in my breath with delight. Defying the blight that afflicts all of Scotland, colorful flowers bloom, green ivy twines up trellises, and trees bear globes of ripening fruit.

Fiona touches the fruit with loving fingers and reaches down to pluck a stray weed.

"My children like you, Albia. Tell me about your kin," she says.

I don't want to think about my mother and Helwain stooped before the fire in the smoky roundhouse. I inhale the scents of lavender, rosemary, and lemon balm, wanting only to lose myself in this garden. But Fiona is waiting for an answer, and I must not be rude.

"My mother is a sister of the queen's lady, Rhuven."

She nods. "And your father?"

A memory comes over me. *I don't have a father,* I once told Colum. *No one needs a father.*

I look at Fiona and shake my head.

"He is dead?" Fiona says softly. "I am sorry."

I don't correct her. I cannot explain it.

You are nobody. Fleance's voice now. *You don't even have a father.*

"Banquo is as good as a father to me." I glance at Breda to see if this offends her. Her eyes are moist.

Now I feel the lack of a father like a hole inside me. Until Banquo treated me like a daughter, I didn't know what it was like to have a father. Until I met Fiona and her brood, I didn't think that one needed a father to be happy. I recall Murdo's kindness to me when I was a child, the touch of his hands as he fitted the ashwood to my leg. How lucky Colum is, to have a father to care for him!

All the way back to Dunbeag, the thoughts will not leave me. I must have had a father. Who was he? Why does Mother never speak of him? Did he die or did he leave us? And why? I will ask Rhuven the next time she visits. Or I will go home and demand the truth from Mother.

One way or another, I will find my father out.

Chapter 11

Dun Forres

Grelach

I was born for this. Descended from a king, I am at last a queen! The crown of beaten gold and the fur-trimmed robes become me. My proud lord looks lofty; none dare meet his eyes. I stood behind him as he was crowned, not beside him, so that no one could call me ambitious. Now I am at fortune's blessed height with Macbeth. Our secret is as safe as a jewel locked in a hidden kist. The deed binds us to each other more firmly than any marriage vow.

I admit that in the aftermath of that terrible night a year ago, I feared my husband. I thought he would murder me, the only witness to his crime. So I flattered him, praising his manly courage. I promised that the worst torment man could devise would never work our secret from me. Why would I put our greatness at risk? But I did not lie down at night unless Rhuven was awake beside me, keeping watch.

Rhuven, my most trusted servant! She soothes me when I am afraid to close my eyes because of the nightmares. She quiets me when I awaken screaming from the horrid visions, my heart fluttering in my throat like a bird against the bars of its cage. Of course Rhuven fears the consequences if Macbeth discovers that she knows our secret. I promise her that I will protect her as long as I am queen, and I make her swear to guard me as well.

"If my husband kills me, Rhuven, you must trumpet his crimes to the world."

"Indeed, and who would believe me?" she replies with a doubtful look. "My tongue—or my throat—would be cut. No, I can best serve you with my silence."

"Still, keep a dagger about you, as I keep this one." And I show her my weapon, small enough to fit in my sleeve.

She recoils and will not touch it. Thus I know that neither Macbeth nor I have anything to fear from harmless Rhuven. But have I made her afraid of me? I put the knife away, smile, and speak lightly.

"I only mean that we must protect ourselves, for no one else will."

These days I am always thinking ahead. If my lord were to be found slain, who would be surprised? Every king has enemies. And in the event of his death, who would become king but my own son? With my father's men behind him, Luoch would rise to the throne. I would be twice crowned—the widow of a king and the mother of a king!

Macbeth abhors the thought of my son on the throne. He knows he could secure his own legacy by declaring the boy his heir. But he will not. The blood-pride that fills him to the fingertips and stains every lock of his hair yearns to pour itself into a mold of his own making. Surely I will yet give him a son! Perhaps a new potion will help quicken my womb? Oh, a queen with many sons is the most powerful of women! Sons are her protectors, her hedge against all worldly misfortune.

But on this tip-top peak where we stand, nothing touches us; everything serves us. My lord rules Scotland with a strong arm, and what grew weak under Duncan's lax reign has been shored up: the armies enlarged and newly outfitted, the fleets repaired, castles restored. The people must be brought to heel and made to work for the good of the country. But instead they grumble out of ignorance and laziness, and foolishly fear that one unseasonable year means starvation and ruin forever. Shall we let England overrun us or the Norsemen sweep down from the seas? Not while Macbeth is king and I am queen!

But my lord is not well lately. He meets with his thanes and generals far into the night, then paces the chamber like a fox in his lair, fretting and scheming until dawn. He charges one thane with insubordination and another with plotting against him. He refuses the posset I bring to calm him, sniffing the cup and eyeing me with suspicion.

Tonight Macduff, the thane of Fife, has riled him with some demands. My lord has also learned that Duncan's sons, who fled to England and to Ireland, are spreading rumors about my lord.

"Don't worry about Macduff," I reassure him. "And the princes? Their self-exile condemns them. Let them return to Scotland, then dare to speak against you."

"That is exactly what I fear—that Malcolm *will* return, with England's army behind him. The boy would sell Scotland to King Edward just to call himself a king and rule as England's lackey."

"Malcolm has a big head but no brain," I say with scorn, "and should he come back with an army, your thanes will fight for you."

"Will they?" he muses darkly. "We were not loyal to Duncan. Why shouldn't my men betray me?"

"Duncan was weak. He was not worthy to be king. You are both strong and worthy. And you were acclaimed by all to succeed Duncan." I remind him, as always, of the truth of our greatness. "All that the soothsayer foretold has come to pass."

Instead of being comforted, he grinds his teeth and clutches his head.

"What is it, my lord?" I demand, startled by his reaction. "Who among your thanes would conspire against you?"

"Banquo," my lord whispers.

"Banquo? Is your brain fevered? He is your most trusted general, the companion of your youth—as dear to you as Rhuven is to me!"

"Nay, Grelach, he must betray me. You don't know—"

"I know you torment yourself without reason. Our fortunes have been fulfilled. Content yourself!"

"I have not told you all that the Wyrd sisters foretold."

"What have you withheld from me? Tell me now," I demand coldly.

"That night on the moor, when they promised me the throne, they also prophesied—" He hesitates, and though he looks in my direction, his gaze goes through me. "They prophesied that Banquo would be greater than me."

"No one is greater than the king of Scotland," I say. "What could they have meant?"

Macbeth shakes his head. "At the time, I hardly gave a thought to what they said to Banquo. I only cared about my own future."

"Did they say more? Did they explain?"

"They said that he would beget kings, though he would be none."

The thought of Fleance as a king makes me laugh. "Fleance is nobody. The offspring of a minor thane. A boastful, strutting cock, nothing but noise. No one minds him."

Macbeth only grows more riled.

"Nay, they hailed Banquo as father to a line of kings. Upon my head they put a fruitless crown and in my hand a barren scepter. If the fatal hags do not lie, it will be wrenched away, no son of mine succeeding!"

I feel a surge of excitement at this revelation. Perhaps it does not matter that my lord and I will remain sonless. Luoch, *my* son, will succeed my husband!

"The hags were mistaken. Banquo is no threat to us," I say, trying to soothe him.

"My time has come, and it will pass." Macbeth's tone is dire. "And then Banquo's time will come—unless I stop it!" He leaps to his feet.

I see murder in his eyes. No doubt or hesitation, as on the night he slew Duncan and the grooms.

"No, you must not! Don't kill again," I plead, breathless.

"At least not until you are certain he is disloyal. What if you are found out?"

My lord laughs sharply. "When it is done, not a drop of their blood will touch my hand."

I am too afaid to ask who will do the deed for him. I do not want to know.

That night I dream that I am standing at the edge of a loch. My hands are covered with blood. I dip them into the water, but they will not come clean, though I rub them together, then wipe them with great swaths of linen. The stain is set in my skin. I immerse them again, and the entire loch turns red. I cry out in my sleep and wake up trembling. My lord, not Rhuven, is beside me in the bed.

"Quiet!" he growls in a threatening voice. His hand covers my mouth.

Chapter 12

Dunbeag and Wychelm Wood

Albia

When we return to Dunbeag, Breda treats me no differently than before. Perhaps it does not matter to her whether I have a father or not. Nothing more is said about him. She is being kind, in her own way. Then Banquo and Fleance return from Dun Forres, Fleance swaggering and swearing like a soldier. No wonder Breda envies Fiona her sweet-faced bairns.

The second winter of King Macbeth's reign roars in like a hoary beast, colder and more cruel than the last one. Neither rebels nor loyal warriors leave their hearths to fight. The only battle is the one for survival. I worry about Mother and Helwain but have no way of knowing how they are faring. Rhuven does not even visit. The roads are deserted, even by the bandits. But at the king's behest, Banquo and Fleance leave Dunbeag, wrapped up like bears against the cold, and do not return for weeks. Banquo is grim-faced and silent about their business, but he has brought rewards from the king: marten-lined cloaks for themselves and yards of madder-colored silk for Breda. Rhuven has sent me a new gown, and Banquo gives me a pair of shoes, soft and sturdy, made from a cow's hide. I kiss his hairy cheek and thank him, but this time the word "Father" sticks on my tongue and will not come out.

"I have something for you, too," Fleance announces. "I will give it to you later."

I wonder what new trick he has devised to trap me. This time I will be ready for him.

"I hope it is a shield," I say, eyeing him with suspicion. "Meet me on the path to the village. I will bring the sword and you can give me another lesson."

I arrive there ahead of Fleance and wait, jumpy as a rabbit. Finally he comes, wearing a fine yellow tunic and carrying his sword and two shields.

"You brought me what I asked for. Well done!" I say as someone might praise a hound, but I smile to show my goodwill.

"And I brought something you left *undone*, some time ago," he says, holding one hand behind his back.

"What did I leave undone? Is this a riddle?"

In reply, he holds out a folded piece of cloth. Frowning but curious, I take it in my hands and unfold it, revealing a bright girdle made of silk. It is as smooth and blue as the surface of a loch and trimmed with a woven braid in a pattern I recognize.

"Why, it is the braid I broke last year—when you—" I stammer, remembering how he tried to corner me while I was weaving and I struck him. "Why did you even save it?"

He shrugs. "It was too fine a piece of work to leave in the dirt."

"But how did it come to be finished?"

"I took it to the weaver woman in the village."

I examine the braid and cannot tell where it was broken, so well did she complete the design.

"It is so lovely, I cannot accept it," I say with a shake of my head. "I have nothing to give in return."

"Only grant me leave to put it on you," he says, his blue eyes on mine.

I hesitate. Still, I long to wear something so beautiful. Where is the harm?

I hold up my arms and Fleance passes the blue silk around my waist once, twice, and a third time. He has to lean close to me, but his hands do not stray. He ties the girdle and lets the ends fall. I feel the cloth snug against me yet not binding, a light thing of beauty.

"Thank you," I murmur.

"I want to kiss you." His words come out in a single rapid breath.

I freeze. I feel hot tears begin to form and I close my eyes to keep them from falling. I have been so lonely since coming to Dunbeag.

"Now . . . may I?" he asks.

Where is the harm? I nod, and as his lips meet my forehead I feel a pleasant tingling of my skin beneath the girdle.

Oh please, now on the lips!

But instead Fleance draws back. Disappointed, I open my eyes.

"Where . . . where did you learn that?" I whisper.

"To kiss? Why, that was hardly anything."

"Nay, I mean, to *ask*."

He cocks his head to the side. "The other ways did not work with you."

I smile and finger the ends of the sash. "But why?"

"Why what?"

Why are you, with your rough manners, now being kind to me? I thought you considered me too plain for your attention. Why does your father treat me like his daughter? Why am I so confused?

"Why did you give me this gift?" I ask.

He smiles. "I don't know. It wanted doing."

I peer into his face but cannot read his feelings. I yearn to shake him until his words and deeds fall into some pattern I might understand.

"Fleance, what do you want of me?" I say with all the earnest longing in me.

He steps back, dodging the question. "I want to teach you to fight!"

"And I want to learn," I say, letting the question drop, for I don't think I am ready for an honest answer.

Picking up the shield, I clumsily fasten its leather bands to my left forearm. I let Fleance show me how to protect myself while striking a blow, and how to fend off blows.

"Use the edge. If your enemy's sword gets stuck in the front of your shield, it will be useless."

We practice until I am nearly breathless.

"Now you are ready," he says.

I raise the sword and it promptly slips from my sweaty hand. I groan with dismay.

Suppressing a laugh, Fleance takes a thin piece of deerskin and wraps it around my hand. I try not to think about his hands touching my fingers and wrist.

"This will improve your grip," he says. Then he picks up a sword, and I see that it is made of wood.

"Why, that is a mere toy!"

"Don't frown so," he says. "It wouldn't be a fair match otherwise."

Determined, I face Fleance in the small clearing. With a shield in one hand and a sword in the other, I feel balanced and secure. I match his every move. My knees are bent and I lean a bit forward, waiting for the opportunity to thrust. Has Fleance noticed that my sword is now sharp?

"Just so you know," I say, with a hint of teasing in my tone, "if I hurt you, I don't mean to."

Fleance laughs in a loud burst. "I think I can defend myself. I've had harder opponents."

At that moment his attention falters, and I bring my blade briskly down upon his wooden war-toy. With a crack it shivers into pieces and he is left holding the hilt. He lets out all his breath at once and stares at me, stunned.

Now it is my turn to laugh.

"By Saint Brigid!" he cries. He looks me up and down, his eyes stopping at my waist. "Could the old woman have woven some magic into that girdle?"

"If so, I must never take it off."

"Let me see that sword."

Beaming with triumph, I hand it to him and slip the heavy shield from my forearm.

"It is the same one, surely, but you had it sharpened," he observes. "Did you put a charm upon it, too?"

"I am no sorceress! But I have been building my strength. See?" I hold out my arms, letting the loose sleeves slip back, and tense them so that my sinews show, small but hard.

Fleance grasps my wrists, then slides his hands along my forearms, cupping my elbows. He presses upward, bunching the cloth of my sleeves until he is holding me by the shoulders. There he stops and regards me, his eyebrows raised, mutely asking, *May I?*

I feel the tingling start up again beneath the girdle, deeper this time. I clap my hands against Fleance's back. It is damp with sweat, and the muscles ripple beneath the skin. I pull him to me.

Where is the harm?

I press my lips as hard as I can against his. My teeth bump into his. He kisses me back and we almost fight to hold each other the tighter, until he lifts me off my feet. Soon I feel my strength begin to falter and release my arms, letting him hold me in the air, with nothing to ground me.

Rhuven comes for me the very next day, like one of the priest's angels who save those who are about to lose their souls. My pulse is still racing from kissing Fleance. How could Rhuven have known what happened between us?

Of course she does not know. The reason she has come, she says, is that the pestilence infecting Scotland has reached the Wychelm Wood. My mother is very ill. In fact, she is dying.

We leave Dunbeag at once. Even on Rhuven's palfrey, we cannot travel fast enough to satisfy me. I yearn to see my mother. But my thoughts are also full of guilty desire for Fleance. When I fall asleep sitting up, I feel his hands on me and with a start realize that it is Rhuven holding me up as we ride.

We stop for the night and I have a dream about Banquo. His face is pale beneath his beard, like a ghost's. His look reproaches me as he whispers through bloodless lips, "Avenge me, daughter of evil!" The dream frightens me. It makes no sense. I ask Rhuven if Banquo is my father.

"What gives you that idea?" she asks, looking at me as if I am crazy.

"Never mind." I decide to wait and ask Mother who my father is. But she is dying. What if we are too late?

When we come to the edge of the wood, I leave Rhuven and run ahead. The spreading branches of the wychelms reach out to welcome me home, but they are leafless. The burn rushes along as always, but there are no flowers blooming on its banks, and the birds sing plaintive notes as if protesting the loss. The roundhouse looks darker and more ancient than before, as if it conceals an entrance to the Under-world. Hel-wain stands in the low doorway, her eyes sunken and her hands twitching. She says nothing, yet her eyes speak of the fear that her sister will die.

Inside Mother lies, too weak to rise from her bed, yet glowing with gladness to see me. If she can smile so warmly, perhaps she is not dying after all! I kneel down and take her hand, and then I see that her skin is as thin and white as the bark of a birch tree.

"Mother, I am sorry that I left you last time, without even a kiss!" The words tumble out of me. "But why did you send me away? You must have been sick even then. I should not have left you. Will you forgive me?"

"There is nothing to forgive, daughter," she says, shaking her head. "Tell me, are you happy at Dunbeag?"

Like a child I am eager to tell her everything.

"It is never dull there. I have learned to read and write. I can even fight with a sword. Don't look surprised, it is more for the sport. The lady Breda dislikes me, but the lord Banquo is most kind and fatherly to me, and Fleance—" Here I blush. "He is . . . as rough as one would expect of a brother."

Mother smiles. "They are good people and will see that you are married well." She closes her eyes.

"Married? Mother, I have no wish to marry. I only want you to be well!" The tears fill my eyes, leaving her face a blur. "Helwain, can you cure her?"

Helwain pays no attention to me. She is plying Rhuven for news of the king.

"My lady suffers terrible dreams and wakes nightly, her clothes as wet as if she had fallen in the well," says Rhuven, her face creased with distress. "She cries over and over, 'What's done is done and cannot be undone.' Your potion of poppy did nothing to calm her."

"I will make a stronger elixir with nightshade and belladonna," says Helwain. "Better yet, something that would hold a child within her loins. What of the rue that was meant to strengthen the king's seed?"

"He tasted its bitterness in his wine and demanded to know who poisoned him," says Rhuven. "I think he suspected me and my lady. I was as afraid of him as on that terrible night!"

I listen in disbelief. How can they fret over King Macbeth and his queen at a time like this?

"Then what poison shall I concoct for His Majesty?" Helwain's voice drips with malice. "The deadly nightshade, ground with the bones of night-flying bats. That is the way to end a tyrant's life. It does its deadly work inside, where the evil dwells."

"Nay, you shall do no such thing, nor shall you even think it," says Rhuven fearfully.

Finally I can bear it no longer. I stand up to Helwain, inches from her hairy chin. My hands shake and the words seethe from me. "Enough! How are the troubles of the king and queen any business of yours? My mother is dying. Why don't you heal her!"

"I have tried and it is beyond my powers," says Helwain in anguish.

"O peace. Between you two, peace," pleads my mother.

Helwain sinks down on the hearthstones and begins rattling

bones in her hands. The sound irks me as always, but at least she is no longer ranting.

I take a deep breath. If I do not ask Mother about my father now, I will never again have the opportunity. I kneel down beside her again and smoothe her thin hair. I am loath to displease her while she lies at the brink of her death. But I must learn a simple truth.

"Mother, tell me please, who was my father?"

The soft hiss of the peat fire answers me. The rattling of bones stops.

"Please. I am old enough to know whose name I bear."

From the corner of my eye, I see Rhuven stiffen. In the silence and the swirl of smoke, I hear the intake of my mother's breath. She exhales without speaking.

"It is time for her to know the truth," says Helwain.

After a long pause, my mother speaks. Her voice is barely above a whisper, and I must strain to hear.

"Macbeth, Scotland's king, is your father."

I sigh and turn to Helwain. "Does her mind often wander so?"

The old woman shakes her head.

"I am dying, Albia, I cannot lie." My mother's voice is stronger. She lays a hand on my arm.

I suppress my tears and decide to humor her. "How did you come to bear Macbeth's child? It would have been long before he became king. Tell me, it must be quite a story."

My mother shakes her head. Then she confesses, with the little breath remaining in her, that she is not my mother at all.

"You were born of Grelach, Macbeth's lady. Though I have loved you all these years as truly as any mother."

I stare at her, openmouthed. Then I turn to Rhuven. "Your *mistress?*"

Rhuven nods. Her face is twisted with sorrow.

"No. That can't be! You're both lying."

I see my mother—no, not my mother, simply *Geillis*—wince with pain.

"Then explain why I grew up here," I demand. "Did the faeries steal me from this Grelach and leave me . . . in this pitiful house?" My voice is full of scorn.

Rhuven says, "In a manner of speaking, yes—"

"Don't lie to her!" thunders Helwain. "She is no child. She must know the truth, black as it is!"

"What truth? That I am kin to that painted warrior you conned on the moor? The tyrant who seizes land and lets his subjects starve? That is madness! The king is not my father."

"Your hair is exactly the color of his," says Rhuven, reaching out to me. "And you have his temper."

I push her arm away. "How should that make me his daughter?"

"Albia, you are Scotland's daughter, and here is proof," says Helwain darkly. She holds out a gold armlet set with a large gem the color of thickened blood. I gaze upon it in fascination but recoil from touching it.

"What is this bauble?" I demand.

"It belonged to your mother," Rhuven says. "My lord gave it to her when they were wed. Now it is yours."

"That proves nothing. For all I know, you stole it last week."

Rhuven is on the verge of tears. "Do you think we would make all this up? We would never torment you so."

"Then let me take this gem to Dun Forres and see if I am welcomed as the long-lost daughter of the king and queen." I try to sound defiant as I thrust out my hand for the armlet, but my voice wavers.

"Foolish girl," says Helwain, snatching it away. "Do you want to be killed?"

Her words, like a wintry blast, pierce to my very bones. Clearly there is more to this matter than learning who gave me birth.

"Tell me everything," I say in a small, tight voice. "Tell me who I am and how I came here."

Throughout the remaining hours of that long night, Geillis, Rhuven, and Helwain unfold the long and complicated tale. From hand to hand they pass the thread of my life, until I am dizzied by the whirling, falling spindle and vexed by the tangled strands they weave. I hear how the lady Grelach bore me and tried to hide my lame foot from her husband; how Macbeth, believing me cursed, seized me from her arms and put me out as food for the wolves; how Rhuven saved me and brought me to Geillis, who raised me as the child of her own, never-filled womb.

"Do they even know I am alive?" I ask, my voice rising as if it would leave my throat altogether.

"No, and they must never find out," says Rhuven.

"You are not to seek out Macbeth and his lady," Helwain orders.

"Why not?" I ask, lifting my chin. The time when I let Helwain tell me what to do is long past.

Rhuven shakes her head at Helwain. There is something else she does not want spoken. But Helwain says that I must know, despite the risk.

So I hear the dark and terrible secret that Rhuven has shared with no one but her sisters: that Macbeth and his wife, whetting their ambition until it was sharper than a steel blade, slew King Duncan as he slept under their very roof, innocent and unsuspecting.

Thus I learn that I am the daughter of a murderer and his wife, Macbeth and Grelach—my father and mother? No, monsters who did not scruple to kill their very own flesh and blood, and hardened by that first crime, boldly took the life of a king and his harmless servants. How can I live with this terrible truth? It shakes me to the marrow of my bones. I no longer know myself. Why did I not leave the past buried?

I hurl bitter words at the sisters, charging them with malice against Macbeth for slaying Gillam and making them homeless. I accuse them of raising me in hopes of restoring me to the queen for reward. But my ranting subsides when I see the grief in Geillis's eyes, Rhuven's fear, and Helwain's pain. They have done me no wrong. They are also victims. Now I understand that it is because of Macbeth and his wife that all of Scotland suffers.

"I hate them! Not you," I cry. "And I am their fruit. I fell from that rotten tree." My voice rises to a wail. "Oh, I hate myself, too!"

"Nay, Albia, their crimes cannot stain you," says Geillis with earnest feeling in her failing voice. "You have none of their wickedness in you."

I think of my quick temper with Colum, my hatred of Helwain, the times I struck Fleance, and my sudden passion for him.

"Aye, I do have a violent nature," I whisper.

The peat fire has died down to embers. A few birds begin to twitter. Soon it will be the morning of another sunless day. Geillis's breath grows ragged.

"Come here, Albia," says Helwain.

I get up and obey her. She puts my hand through the armlet with the red stones. The chill of the metal goes through me like a knife blade.

"I don't want it, if it was hers."

"You cannot refuse it. Wear it," she orders. "Your mother is descended of a just king. Macbeth has corrupted her. But you can remedy their evil." Her eyes are shining with conviction. "Albia, you have been chosen!"

A harsh laugh escapes me. "What shall I do? Ride up to Dun Forres and kill Macbeth for you?"

"This is no matter for jesting," Helwain says sharply.

Rhuven adds her own rebuke. "Albia, never speak of what you have learned. It is dangerous—for all of us."

"I didn't ask for this," I say, shaking my head.

"Leave her be, sisters," Geillis pleads. "It is too much for her. Dearest Albia, give me your hand."

I kneel down and put my fingers in her dry palm. The red gem in the armlet gleams like an eye between us.

"Forgive me, daughter. Forgive us. All that we did, was done to save your life."

⚜

I fall asleep from exhaustion and wake up to the sound of Rhuven and Helwain weeping. Geillis no longer breathes. I am holding her lifeless hand and lying beside her like a newborn. She is my mother in the truest sense. As are Rhuven and Helwain, for all three of them gave me life again after Macbeth and Grelach took it away.

Helwain and Rhuven wash Geillis's body with fragrant herbs and wrap it in a cloth. They place her on the sledge and hitch it to the horse. I follow them, my limbs heavy as iron, to a grassy verge near the ancient oak tree, Pitdarroch. Murdo is there, digging a hole. It is late spring and Colum must be on the shieling already. I want him to be here! We place my mother gently in the earth, then use the sledge and Murdo's cart to gather rocks. Wordlessly we pile them on the grave, making a cairn. Each stone seems to weigh as much as the world. Helwain and Rhuven are weeping still. I wonder dully where my tears have gone. Have I, the daughter of evil, no tender feeling left for this good woman who mothered me?

When Rhuven and Helwain leave, I do not go with them. I stay at the cairn, fighting off sleep. The nightingale sings and the owl sends out its quavering cry. Beneath my sleeve, the gold and ruby armlet holds me in its cold grip. My mind turns over and over the history of Macbeth and Grelach and dwells on the awful image of a red-haired man, his dagger poised over the king's breast. Though I try to banish the image, my mind's eye gazes fixedly at the hand and the dagger. Slowly a memory surfaces of a long-forgotten dream that came to me on Wanluck Mhor when the thorn drew blood from my palm. Did I not see a bloody dagger in a man's hand then? Could it have been the very hand and the very dagger that would slay Duncan?

A cry escapes me at the sudden awareness that I do have the Sight, as Helwain suspected. I can deny it no longer. On the moor, I glimpsed the Asyet-world where Macbeth would murder the king and his servants. What other bloody deeds have I foreseen? Just now I cannot bear remembering. I realize I have not slept in two days or more. But I am afraid to sleep, afraid of what I might unwittingly dream.

"O Mother, what shall I do with this unwelcome knowledge?" I call out in the darkness.

The moon has risen, wrapped in clouds. A sudden silvery gleam, like light glancing off the water, makes me blink. It illumines the mist before me and I rise to follow it, stumbling on the rough ground. The feathers of an owl's wing whisper through the air, a flash of white.

Come back! Don't leave me!

The moon shrugs aside its clouds and shines upon the tangled branches of the ancient oak. The owl settles among its leaves and becomes invisible. I kneel down at the base of the tree, where the thick trunk casts a deep black shadow as if the earth gaped open there. And like a cloak snatched from my body, I feel Geillis leave me and know that she has entered the Other-world.

Finally my tears come, and afterward a sleep so profound that nothing can be dreamt there.

When I open my eyes, Colum's face is before me with its nimbus of curly hair. His hands cradle my head in his lap.

"I'm sorry for you," he says. His thumbs brush the corners of my eyes, where the tears have started up again. I close my eyes and open them and he is still there. This is no dream.

"How did you know . . . I wanted you to come?" I say, still half-asleep. His arms around me are a comfort. "You know about my mother. But how?"

"I didn't know. Caora only said that you needed me," he admits. "So we came at once. And when I saw the cairn, I knew why."

Caora's face appears beside Colum's. Her gold eyes sparkle, and her long, fine hair blows across her cheeks. She puts her hands on Colum's shoulders, and he stops moving his thumbs against my temples.

So Colum is in love with Caora! I sit up and slide away from him.

"How did you know about Geillis?" I ask Caora.

"It doesn't matter," she says. "Let me get you some water."

Caora leaves and I gaze at Colum, his familiar face a welcome sight.

"Why didn't you visit me at Dunbeag? I hoped you would." I take his hand to soften the reproach.

"I thought about it. Then I decided that in a new place you would forget me and make new friends."

I feel myself redden, thinking of Fleance. "Why would I forget you?"

Colum searches my face and sighs. "Have you found a fellow, then?"

I ignore the question. "I missed going to the shieling this year."

Colum frowns. "Be glad you were not there. The thane's warband torched my bothy and stole half the flock. Caora and I were lucky to escape unharmed."

Anger stirs in me. "It is King Macbeth's fault!" How strange to speak his name now, knowing that he is my father. "He claims the land that should be free to everyone."

"He is the king, so all of Scotland belongs to him," Colum says with a shrug. "We will find a more remote pasture next year."

"The king is a tyrant!" I cry. "You have no idea how terrible he is. He doesn't deserve to live."

Colum looks astonished. "Albia, you must never say such things. It is as much a crime to denounce the king as it is to blaspheme against God. The priest says so."

"The priest does not know what I know. I will tell you something, Colum, but you must keep it a secret."

As soon as I speak, I remember Rhuven's warning. The knowledge I have is dangerous. But Colum is my dearest friend. What harm could come of telling him?

"I can keep the greatest secret for your sake," he says solemnly.

"I trust you, Colum, so listen. Macbeth is the worst sinner among men." My voice comes out as a hoarse whisper. "He did much more than speak against the king. He murdered him with a dagger, then slew his two groomsmen and made it look like their deed. All so that he could become king."

Colum draws back, shaking his head in disbelief.

"I have the Sight, Colum. Long ago I saw the murder in a waking dream."

"Albia, you're full of grief now, and what you say—is madness!"

"No, I am as clear-headed as you. Duncan's murder happened just as I dreamt it. Rhuven was there and the queen confessed to her. Colum, as I am your friend, you must believe me. What I say is the truth."

"The king—a murderer?" Colum says. "Our fair land is ruled by one so . . . so foul?"

"More foul than you know. He deserves to have his flesh flayed from his bones for what he did to—" I bite my tongue. I am not ready to reveal my still darker secret, that I am the daughter of this king killer.

Just then Caora returns with a flask of water. I avoid her eyes, trying to concentrate on the pure, cold water slipping down my throat.

"So Blagdarc, the god of night, now reigns through the evil Macbeth," she says to me in a low voice.

Startled, I steal a sideways glance at Caora. How could she have overheard the secret I told Colum?

"All of nature will be out of order until his reign is ended."

Her golden eyes meet mine and she seems to see within me. "Nor will you find peace until then."

I feel the armlet, cold and tight. It reminds me that I am the daughter of the tyrant king and his queen. One victim of their depthless evil, but still alive to thwart them.

I thrust the water-flask at Caora and jump to my feet so fast the world seems to spin around my head.

"I am going back to Dunbeag now, where I will tell Banquo about Macbeth's crime. He is already unhappy with the king's rule. Certainly he will take action."

The sudden idea gives me confidence, shores up my broken self with a sense of purpose. Later I will consider the consequences, but now I will act.

Chapter 13

Dunbeag

Albia

Colum and Caora travel with me until Dunbeag comes into view. We say our farewells, and I almost cry as Colum embraces me and walks away with the fleecy-haired Caora at his side. I want him walking beside me. I want Geillis back.

The streets and alehouses of the village are filled with rowdy soldiers and the stables with restive horses. From every tower of Banquo's house colorful standards fly. I quicken my steps in anticipation of a festival or a display of war-games.

Breda meets me at the door and pulls me roughly inside.

"At last you've come back! Can't you see I need your help?" She spares not a word of sympathy or a glance of pity. "You must help the cook dress the fowl. Go now."

"What is the occasion?" I ask.

"Why, the king himself is here. Banquo is with him now."

I freeze and grasp the frame of the doorway.

"Did the queen come, too?" My voice is a hoarse whisper.

"Nay, she is said to be unwell. 'Tis our misfortune."

I want to flee, but Breda has her hands on me. She steers me into the kitchen, and the cook sends me outside. In the yard, a fire burns under an iron spit. Fleance is cutting apart a boar's carcass while shrieking crows fall upon the guts. A servant plucks feathers from dead fowl and tosses them into a pile. Nearby is a creel full of headless fish, their scales slippery and glistening with blood. I carry the plucked birds into the kitchen, and the cook sets me to work on the pastries. My hands shake. I break eggs and spill flour like a clumsy child.

My own father is in this house. Its walls are all that separate us.

My awareness that he is near fills me with dread and desire alike. I put down the pastry roller and walk out of the kitchen. The house is not very large, and when I see the guards in the central hallway, I know that *he* is in the nearest chamber, the one directly beneath my room. I climb the stairs on the tips of my toes and lie down with my ear pressed to the floor. I hear a demanding voice, not Banquo's. It must be the king's.

"My warrriors must have the best horses and helmets of bronze. Without pride, they fight like old women. Woe to your blacksmith, the damned Viking, if he forges me a weak blade! I will use it on his neck."

I hear the thump of a fist against the table.

"Nay, he is a man I trust," comes Banquo's voice, deep and firm.

"You are a luckier man than I am. I cannot trust my own wife."

"My lord, the queen is a most virtuous lady," says Banquo.

I press closer, straining to hear the king. His voice has sunk low.

". . . Eadulf tastes every dish and every cup before I do. My wife and her greedy father . . . dispatch me with some poison . . . place that damned Luoch on my throne."

"My lord, surely you are mistaken," says Banquo.

"Nay, once I prove their treachery, their eyes will not close again in sleep. And you, Banquo!" Macbeth's voice is sharp. "You are either with me or you are against me. Which shall it be?"

"My liege, you have had too much to drink."

The king utters a harsh laugh.

"If I had a son all would be well. But my lady's womb is cursed. The fateful sisters did it. But you have a son. Tell me, do you not dream of him ruling Scotland?" The king's voice insinuates, even threatens.

But Banquo does not take the bait. "My lord, I pray you, question not my loyalty," he says. "I have no ambitions for myself or my son, except to continue to serve you with good faith."

I hear the sound of one man clapping another on the back.

"Banquo, you have satisfied me, withstood the test. I trust you as always."

"Whatever you ask of me, that I can do, I shall perform," Banquo replies.

To my ears, it is an awkward-sounding assurance.

"My Viking blacksmith will—"

The king interrupts him. "Then I ask that your fosterling bear my cup at the feast. I hear she is a comely lass." He laughs.

"I will see if she can be found, my lord."

My heart pounds, sending the blood pulsing into my ears.

My fingers curl, trying to clutch the boards nailed to the floor.

⚜

When Banquo comes into my room, I am sitting stiffly on my bed. I stand up and bow, hiding my face so he cannot see my terror.

"My dear, you will attend the king at his table tonight."

"Must I?" I say, not raising my head. "My hands will shake, and I may drop his cup and displease him."

"I know you are grieving for your mother, but the king must be satisifed."

"I am afraid of him . . . Father," I say, swallowing hard. I want to tell Banquo about the king's great crime, but where and how do I begin?

Banquo hardly looks at me. He seems preoccupied. "There is nothing to fear. Do this for my sake, daughter. And wear something that becomes you."

I have no choice, so I merely nod, and Banquo leaves, satisfied.

My mouth dry with dread, I fasten the ties of a long-sleeved blue woolen gown, an old one of Breda's. I weave my hair in braids. It takes several tries with my fumbling fingers. Then I wrap Fleance's girdle around my waist. It seems to hold me like a steadying hand. Finally I slip on the red-jeweled armlet and secure it above my elbow, hoping it will give me courage.

In the dining hall, men crowd the benches around long trestle tables. A fire blazes in the hearth where a scop plucks his lute, preparing to sing. The hall resounds with shouting, laughter, and the scraping of spoons on plates. When I enter carrying a flagon of wine, no one, not even the king who requested my service, notices me.

From behind the king's chair I study his every feature and movement. His back beneath the tunic of tooled leather is broad and straight. When he turns his face to the side, I see that his nose is long and straight, flaring at the ends. He does not look like a murderer. His skin is fair but deeply lined, his lips thin and stained with dark wine. When he lifts his cup for a toast, I see that his thick forearms are covered with red hairs. A crown of beaten gold sits firmly upon his head, and his hair shines in the firelight, with hardly a streak of gray. I am glad my hair is confined in braids. I hope that no one will notice that it is exactly the same color as the king's.

I dread the moment he notices me, yet I am perversely impatient for it. I move to the front of the table, set down the wine, and pick up a platter of pastries shiny with grease and sugar. The table is narrow, and I am not three feet from the king's face.

"Will you have a pastry, my lord?"

The words I say are empty. The ones I do not speak contain everything. *I know who you are. I know the crimes you have done. But you have no idea who I am.* This thought gives me power. I look directly into the eyes of my father. They remind me of black pools in a dangerous bog.

The king's eyebrows lift in surprise, as if he has read my thoughts.

"You must be the . . . *daughter* . . . of my host," he says, with a sly emphasis that makes my heart pound. Does he know who I am after all? He winks at Banquo and laughs sharply.

Banquo tenses. His hands curl into fists. Fleance touches his father's arm and Banquo glares at Fleance—because he dare not look so at the king.

All at once I understand. The king believes I am not Banquo's daughter, but his mistress! I flush with undeserved shame.

"The lord Banquo is a *most honorable father*," I say, so that the king cannot mistake my meaning.

"And you are a bold child." He takes the tray from me and shoves it aside. "I want none of your pastries."

His look and his words seem to warn me, and I feel my chest constrict with fear. How foolish of me to provoke a man so powerful and merciless. I step back from the table.

"I did not dismiss you. Come, pour me more wine," he orders, summoning me with his cup. Obediently I pick up the flask, but as I tip it the red liquid splashes on his hand.

"I am sorry, Your Majesty," I say, feeling heat rise to my face. "Let me fetch a cloth."

"No, stay." The king raises his hand to his mouth and licks the wine from it, never taking his eyes from me. "I was mistaken. You are no child, but a young woman. A most fetching one. So drink with me." And the king thrusts his cup into my hand.

I do not drink strong wine, so I simply hold the cup. The

king stands up and leans over the table between us. His hand closes over mine on the goblet. The mere thought that it is *my father's hand* that touches me stuns me into submission. He lifts the cup to my lips, and I have no choice but to open my mouth and swallow. The wine, bitter and fiery, makes me cough and sputter.

"Now take a bite of this," he commands, holding out a morsel of pastry. I reach out my trembling hand but he shakes his head and motions for me to open my mouth. Anger and shame battle within me, but I obey, feeling his fingers against my teeth as he places the floury bite on my tongue and withdraws his hand. His gaze is intent and watchful. What is his purpose with me? I close my eyes to avoid looking at him and chew, hating the taste.

After I swallow, I open my eyes to see a sly smile flickering on one side of his face.

"Now you are dismissed," he says. He takes the remainder of the pastry and puts it in his own mouth.

I realize then that the king, suspecting poison, has made me taste his food for him. I have passed the test. But had I fallen dead before him, he would have felt no speck of remorse. Suddenly I cannot bear to be under the same roof as this tyrant. I must get out of Dunbeag!

As I rush by Fleance's table, his eyes meet mine. He has seen what passed between me and the king, and his look is one of rage and jealousy. If only he knew how much I hated the king's attention. Banquo leans his head on his hands as if he has drunk too much.

I am outdoors, running down the path leading to the village. A wild energy flows through me from being in my father's presence and holding back my hatred. *Father?* That word should never belong to Macbeth! When I come to the spot where Fleance and I last met, I stop and wait, praying that he will come. Though my limbs are shaking I feel as strong as a boar. I wish I had my sword, that I could swing it hard, hear it clang, and feel it shiver in my grip.

Hours pass and darkness comes. The moon glows faintly behind thick clouds. By now the feast is surely ended, the scop has sung of warlike deeds, and the soldiers are all drunk or asleep. The fire has drained from me, leaving me exhausted. But I will not return to Dunbeag to sleep in the same house with a murderer. I make a bed for myself among the bracken and lie down. Tomorrow after the king and his retinue depart, I will tell Banquo what I know.

I hear footsteps along the path. It must be Fleance. He alone would know to look for me here. I jump to my feet.

"Fleance?" I call softly. "Here I am."

A tall hooded figure approaches me. At the sound of my voice, he quickens his steps. I feel a twinge of alarm. The gait is not Fleance's. The man throws back the hood of his cloak and I recognize, by the faint moonlight upon his red-gold hair, the king—without his crown. I gasp and stumble backward.

"So it is not my general, but his son who is your lover," he says.

"I have no lover," I reply. The backs of my legs meet the hard surface of a large rock and I lean against it for support.

"Then you will not object to the king's wooing you," he says, touching his chest and nodding his head. It is a gesture meant to look noble, but it fills me with horror.

"I do object, for you have a wife," I say quickly.

"My wife is barren, and I must have a son." His voice is low and urgent.

There is no time to think. Words cascade from my lips before I can stop them.

"Why must you have a son? Why not a daughter? Is a girl-child not good enough for a man?"

I see confusion in his face. And anger. With a few swift steps, he is upon me. I reach out to hold him off but he grabs both my hands in just one of his. His body pins me against the rock.

"What nonsense you speak. Be silent!" His voice is rough. I smell wine and meat on his breath. He reaches up with his free hand and loosens my hair from its ties. He tilts my head back so that the dimmed moonlight falls on my face. There is a tenderness in his touch that confuses me.

"Your eyes are gray-blue, like hers," he murmurs. "So beautiful, so beautiful."

It takes me a moment to realize that he is not seeing me, but someone else. Does the queen, my mother, have gray-blue eyes? He once loved her, I am certain.

The king's breath is hot upon my face.

I turn my head to the side. "Do not kiss me!"

I hear him sigh. His hands move to my waist, searching for the ties to my girdle. Thankfully, I knotted it firmly.

"Do not touch me, I pray you," I plead, pushing away his hands.

"I am the king. I take what I want." His voice is anguished.

"You will not have me. I will kill you first!"

"Do you threaten your sovereign lord? That is treason, my lovely one."

"Treason is no more unnatural than your desires."

In reply he takes my wrists and presses my clenched fists to his face so that he is kissing my knuckles. I squeeze my eyes shut, unable to look at his face so close to mine. As I struggle to free my hands, I feel the cool night air against my arms. Suddenly I hear the king gasp and feel his grip give way. What is it? I open my eyes and look down to see that the sleeves of my dress have fallen back to reveal the gold armlet above my elbow, its red gem gleaming in the faint moonlight.

"Where did you get that?" he whispers in astonishment.

For a moment I feel triumph, seeing his black eyes widen with something like fear. Then terror grips me, for I have no idea how to answer him. If I reveal that I am his daughter, he might kill me at once. But how else can I explain why I am wearing Grelach's gem?

"By all the saints, tell me," he demands.

But I cannot speak. Whatever I say might implicate Rhuven as the thief. I cannot even think while his hands are upon me, knowing the violence they are capable of.

"Unhand me first, for you are hurting me," I say to gain time.

He drops my hands. I rub my wrists and cast around in my mind for words to explain how I came by the armband. I wish I had prepared for this moment. But I never expected to see the king at Dunbeag, let alone encounter him like this. How can I ever say, *Grelach is my mother and you are my father*? Speaking those blunt words would mean claiming the degenerate king as my kin. Yet only the truth will do.

I cross my arm over my chest, bringing the gold and ruby armlet in front of me like a small but potent shield. The king's face is in the shadows, but I know his eyes are fixed upon the gem. I take a deep breath.

"I swear by Guidlicht and Neoni and by the four worlds—"

The king starts at the mention of the old gods. I raise my arm so that the gold gleams as if containing its own light.

"This belonged . . . to my mother."

The king's hands fly up and his fingers tear at his red locks, pulling them down the sides of his face, which bears an anguished and terrible look.

"My . . . *daughter*?" The word escapes him in a guttural cry that seems to tear the fabric of night.

While the shock holds him in its thrall, I seize the opportunity to run. The gods bless me with the swift and silent feet of a rabbit, and they open a burrow in the hillside that hides me as well as if I have become invisible.

Yet I hear him stumble about, looking for me and shouting like a madman, "Where has she gone? Disappeared! Nay, my daughter is dead. I am deceived again. Damn those midnight hags! You, come back to me!"

⚬⚬

I lie all night in the mossy cave, my mind in a turmoil. From my first sight of the king, I felt no speck of the yearning I expected to feel for a father. Not even our shared strands of red-gold hair were enough to stir in me a sense of kinship. I wonder what the king felt when he recognized me. Did he believe that I was his daughter? Or did he run off into the night thinking he had seen a tormenting vision? Surely he could not deny the evidence of his senses, for he had not only seen and heard me, but touched me.

Recalling the king's hands on my body, I shudder and feel sick. But how could he have known—until the moment the armlet was revealed—how perverse his attentions were? It was the jeweled band that stopped him. It was the girdle, Fleance's gift, that protected me. I finger its firm knots gratefully.

Yet as the dawn breaks up the darkness, relief at my escape gives way to a sense of imminent danger. Is it only the fear that the king will seek me out and do me harm? He tried to kill me once before, when I was completely innocent. Now I have openly defied him. I decide to remain hidden until I hear the thundering of hoofbeats that tells me the king's retinue has departed. Then I can safely return to Dunbeag.

Still my unease grows. It is more than fear for myself. *Banquo.* My foster father—my true father. Do I tell him of the king's attempt on my virtue? *Fleance.* I see rage and grief on his face, too. My heart begins thudding as if some threat is near. Into my

136

mind springs Banquo's face, ghostly pale, his bloodless lips intoning *Avenge me, daughter of evil*. How could I have forgotten that vision? The daughter of evil—why that is me, Macbeth's daughter! But what is there to avenge? I start up from my mossy bed. While I have been lying here, has evil befallen Banquo? If it has, I am responsible, for I should have warned him. I should not have riled the king. Has my foster father paid for my carelessness with his life?

As fast as I can, I run up the hill to Dunbeag and dash through the doorway.

A furious Breda grabs my arm. "Where have you been all the night? With some vile soldier? O shame me not so," she hisses.

I shake her off and stumble from room to room on weak legs shouting for Banquo. Without even knocking I burst into his chamber. Fleance is lying on the bed with an arm over his face. Banquo sits in a chair, his eyes bloodshot and his face puffy with drink. My body slumps with relief to see them.

"Forgive this intrusion, my lord," I say, panting. "I must talk to you at once."

Fleance springs up from the bed. His eyes are wide with unasked questions.

"The king departed in a great hurry," Banquo says in a grave voice. "We did not please him."

"It was my fault. I . . . I did not show him enough respect," I stammer. "I am sorry to bring you trouble."

"I saw how he looked at you. How dare he!" Fleance clenches his fists. "Did he—?"

Despite myself, I begin to sob.

Banquo drops his head to his chest. "I am to blame. I should not have let you serve him at supper. All the king's desires are foul! What kind of a father am I?"

"He did not harm me," I finally manage to say. "But you are in terrible danger. You must listen to me."

Banquo looks up, raising one bushy eyebrow.

I close my eyes for a moment, struggling to put my thoughts in order.

"The night when you visited Wanluck Mhor with Macbeth, before he was king, and you met the three women who spoke strangely—"

Both of Banquo's eyebrows shoot upward.

"One of the women was my . . . mother, Geillis. I was there also. I heard the women foretell that Macbeth would become king. And so he did, but by a means most foul. Listen." I pause to regain my breath. "It was Macbeth who slew Duncan. Do not ask how I know this, but believe me when I swear that it is true. The king is a murderer, and the queen his accomplice."

"Stop!" Banquo interrupts me. He is shaking visibly. "How *do* you know such things?"

I cannot admit to Banquo that I dreamt about the dagger in Macbeth's hand. He would hardly be convinced by such evidence.

"Ask Rhuven, if you do not believe me. The queen confessed to her," I whisper, conscious that I am again spilling the secret. But Rhuven is already in danger, if Macbeth should question her and discover that she disobeyed and deceived him.

"Father, there have been such rumors about the king," says Fleance. "What if they are true?"

"Silence! He cannot be so wicked. I will not believe it," growls Banquo.

"My lord, believe it or not, you must understand the danger you are in. Do you remember how the old woman hailed you as lesser than Macbeth, but greater, and said that you would beget kings, though not become one?"

"Double-talk and nonsense," Banquo murmurs, clawing his beard with agitation. "I forgot it."

"Be sure the king remembers. He has no sons, but you have Fleance."

"What do you mean, Albia? Did they predict that I would be king?" asks Fleance in amazement.

"Are you in league with those fate-speaking sisters?" Banquo asks me, sounding suspicious.

"Nay, but I know the king's mind in this, truly I do," I say, growing impatient. "Macbeth killed Duncan to make their words come true. He will as readily kill you to prevent their prophecies. He must be destroyed. Only then will Scotland find peace."

"Albia, my child," says Banquo with a weary shake of his head. "Your thoughts are but fantasies, your fears imagined. It is yesterday's excitement—and the grief over your dear mother—that has made you so distraught. Go and rest."

His words leave me swaying on my feet with the sad memory of Geillis, and I begin to doubt myself. I have scarcely slept in three days. I have lost my mother, learned the unbelievable story of my past, and come face-to-face with that intemperate beast, my father. I have been spilling secrets like blood, bringing danger to myself and everyone I love. I should stop, turn back, and be silent.

But there is no going back. There is no way to undo the past, to unknow the truth, or to unsee what I dreamt. I close my eyes and there, still, is Banquo's hoary, ghostlike visage, admonishing me.

"My lord, you are in danger. I can see it. I pray you, believe me and be wary—" I stop to wipe my eyes. Begging and tears will only hinder my purpose.

Banquo shakes his head from side to side like a tired bear unwilling to be stirred.

My head and shoulders sagging with defeat, I turn away from him and Fleance.

But no sooner have I left the room than Fleance is beside me. He pulls me into an empty chamber.

"They said that my father would beget kings, did they? Am I not then the rival to Macbeth?" he asks, his eyes bright with excitement.

"Fleance, you believe me!" My hopes stir again. "Then you see the danger to both of you?"

"I would be foolish not to consider . . . what may come to pass," he replies evasively.

"Fleance, I don't care if I speak treason. But for the good of Scotland, you must persuade your father to take action before it is too late."

"Don't worry. My father has little love remaining for the

king. It has dried up like a well in a drought. Last night he said to me that the king no longer trusted him."

"That is true," I say, remembering the conversation I overheard. "Neither should you trust him, for he is full of deceit."

"Tell me, Albia," says Fleance, touching my wrists gently. "Did the king . . . force you? Because if he did, I will kill him myself."

"No, Fleance, he did not hurt me. He tried, but your girdle protected me." I manage a weak smile.

Fleance sighs, and I can see by his longing look that he wants to kiss me.

Now would be the time to confess to him that I am Macbeth's daughter. But what if he should react with horror and disgust? Nothing would be gained—and much could be lost—by telling this truth.

"Nay," I say, shrinking away as Fleance puts his arms around me. Even his familiar hands remind me of the king's unwelcome touch. "Let me be, please."

He draws back, offended. "I think you did enjoy the king's attentions," he says coolly. "What woman would not be flattered?"

His words set me aflame like a spark on dry grass.

"If you only knew how much I despise the king—and why—you would unsay those cruel words and regret them a thousand times over!"

"My father is right," Fleance says, angry now. "You are plainly overwrought, a creature without reason. Go away."

"I leave of my own will. And lest there be any doubt, I despise you, too!"

I whirl around and run to my little room, where all my grief spills out in uncontrollable sobs. I do not care how loudly I wail. I want my cries to reach Geillis in the Under-world and awaken her pity. I want to scream in the ears of Macbeth and his wife until they cringe at their crimes. I want my weeping to stir the Other-world to revenge and the Asyet-world to fill the emptiness of my loss.

But not even Dunbeag's inhabitants hear me, or if they do, they make no attempt to console me.

Chapter 14

Dun Forres

Grelach

I confess that when my lord is away at Dunbeag or Inverness or besieging his enemies, I hope that he will not return. With time I might forget the deeds of that awful night and be able to sleep again. The desperate efforts to force a child into my womb would end. I used to look forward to the night, relishing my husband's strength and the intensity of his desiring. Then I realized it was not me he desired, but a son of his own. As I, perhaps, never desired him, but only his ability to make me a queen. Once ambition bound us together. Now what need have we of each other? With a barren womb, I am of no use to him. I fear for my life at his hands and imagine his death at mine. Would I use a dagger? Poison? I do not think I am capable of either. Thus I am left hoping for a mortal wound on the battlefield or an act of betrayal by one of his thanes. Such an end would leave me guiltless. It would set me free.

Then Luoch would rise, and I would see my son rule Scotland as his great-grandfather did. But what if the thanes acclaim someone else as king? Would they choose Banquo? Nay, he is far from the greatest among them. I will not believe the Wyrd sisters. They did not bring us to this height; it was my lord's ambition and courage that made him king! I will not fear Banquo or his offspring. Ranold my father builds his strength in the west, drawing the support of the thanes from north to south along the Great Glen, all on behalf of Luoch. When darkest night comes for Macbeth, my star will still be in the sky.

A storm has broken upon Dun Forres with bellowing thunder, cracking lightning, and a cold wind that rattles the very stones in the foundation. A flood pours from the sky, uprooting grass and drowning small creatures. The midday sky is black. Torches flicker in their sconces. Rhuven keeps them lit, day and night. Poor Rhuven. Her sister has died—though thankfully not the one who provides my medicine—and she returned from burying her with a deep sadness. But she has a new sleeping potion for me. I will need it tonight. The wind howls like a banshee tearing through the castle. A timber from the roof flies off into the storm, and the banshee dips into Dun Forres and puts out the torches, leaving Rhuven and me in the dark.

❧

My lord has returned from Dunbeag in a great frenzy. Surely a rebellion is brewing somewhere. Has Banquo persuaded the other thanes to turn their warbands against our throne? Does he nurse royal ambitions of his own? I wish I had not begged my lord to spare his life.

But when Macbeth comes into my chamber, I see that he is

shaken by something deeper than war. Doubt and suspicion are written on his face, as if he has discovered my disloyal thoughts and knows that I wish him dead.

"What is the matter, my lord?" I ask. "I did not expect you back from Dunbeag so soon."

"How long have you kept it from me?" he demands, his black eyes prying into my very soul.

"I do not know what you mean."

"Are you alone?"

"Aye," I lie, knowing that Rhuven is in the next chamber, listening, and that she will raise the alarm if he tries to harm me.

"She lives. I have seen her with these very eyes." He stabs the air in front of his face with both forefingers.

"Who lives?" I ask, growing impatient.

"Don't pretend ignorance! How did she come by the gold and ruby armlet?"

"My lord, you are speaking madness. Explain yourself." I watch his hands lest they reach for his dagger.

Instead Macbeth grabs my wrist. "The gem I gave you. I put it on this arm when we were married."

I do remember that jewel. It softened me toward my new and strange husband.

"I have not seen it for many years. I thought you took it away from me until I bore you a son."

"I did not. You lie. You deceived me. Like the fateful sisters, you have played foul with me. She lives! Our daughter lives!"

My knees give way and I sink to the floor, slipping from his grasp. The image of a pink-cheeked baby suckling my breast flickers through my mind. Desire tears at me from inside and old grief rises to choke me.

"How can . . . she be . . . alive?"

"I saw her on the heath last night at Dunbeag." My husband's voice is barely above a whisper as he falls to his knees beside me. "She had your jewel. Her eyes are like yours."

"What about her foot?" I ask, testing him.

"She walks like any woman," he says, his black eyes glistening like one who has a fever and sees what is not there.

"How dare you lift my hopes like this?" I cry, striking him with all my strength. "It cannot be her. My daughter was crippled. She has been dead almost sixteen years, and it was you who killed her!"

"Nay, she is Banquo's daughter now. Beautiful. I know her. It was the jewel. She got it from you."

The jumble of words makes no sense. Has my husband been bewitched by some woman—or phantom of a woman? Jealousy pricks me. And fear of what he might let slip in his growing madness.

"Rhuven!" I cry. "Come quickly."

In a moment she is at my side. Macbeth jumps to his feet and grabs her by the shoulders, lifting her right off the ground.

"What do you know of my daughter?" he growls. "Tell me how it is that she lives."

The color drains from Rhuven's face. Only her eyes are bright with terror. She kicks her feet to find the floor again. I pull at my husband's arms until he releases her.

She looks from Macbeth to me, then boldly fixes her eyes

on his. "You are mistaken. Eadulf left her to the wolves. I . . . I saw her body and . . . put it in the ground." A dry sob comes from her throat. It sounds forced. Has she, too, buried her grief so deep it cannot be found?

I stare at my husband with new hatred, that he should burst into my chamber and remind me of my old sorrow. But already he has forgotten us both in his ranting.

"It was Banquo's doing. He shelters the witch. He uses her against me. Now I know he is a traitor!"

Even as I watch, Macbeth's murderous thoughts become manifest. His eyes narrow into slits and his right hand plays over the hilt of his dagger. My pulse quickens in warning. Then he claps his hands together and calls loudly for Eadulf, the rogue who does the deeds he is too cowardly to claim.

⚜

I rub my fingers against my thumbs until the skin is raw and grind my palms together until the bones of my hands hurt. Rhuven gives me poppy crushed in wine to calm me, but it does not help me sleep, so she gives me even stronger mandragora. Still I cannot sleep. I rub my hands without ceasing, but I can no longer feel the pain.

Eadulf left a week ago. My lord and I have barely spoken. I doubt that Banquo is disloyal. But his death warrant is already signed, and that of his son. Will they see the murderers coming and put up a fight, or will they be slain with their eyes closed in sleep? Why must Eadulf kill the boy? He is no threat. I think of how his mother will grieve.

And what will happen to Banquo's daughter, the girl Macbeth thinks is ours because she happens to have a jeweled armlet? Nothing will protect her from a mad king bent on murder. I cannot sleep. I dare not even close my eyes. Rhuven is also afraid. She asks my leave to go away again, but I will not permit it. I must have her by me. I cannot know when Macbeth will succumb to another fit.

Nor can I stop tormenting myself, asking Rhuven, "If I had saved my daughter, might everything be different now?"

And Rhuven replies, "It is no use saying, 'What if this or that.' It changes nothing."

"Is it because I let her die that the saints have cursed me, and the gods given me no sons?"

"The saints don't have such power, and the gods are not so cruel. Remember, you are the queen, and let that be your comfort," she replies.

I laugh bitterly. "To be queen is no comfort! My eyes do not sleep, my hands are raw with rubbing, my husband is crazed, and our love has turned to hate and fear of each other."

Then I begin to sob, choking and shaking for more than an hour, though not a tear falls that might relieve me.

"Grelach, my lady, you must try to stop," Rhuven says worriedly, plying me with wine. It smells of mandragora, sweet and strong. "Tonight is the banquet and you must be fit to greet the king's guests."

Rhuven helps me dress in a long tunic of red silk and links of gold about my waist. I think of a prisoner's chains. She braids my hair, wraps the braids around my head, and sets my crown within. It is not heavy, but it weighs down my head like a rock tied to my hair. Now I am ready to play the king's loving wife.

A fire in the hearth fights the chilly air in the dining hall. Torches blaze, sending up curls of black smoke. The most powerful thanes—Ross and Lennox, Angus and Siward of Northumberland—are all gathered here. I take my lesser seat beside the king's chair and permit them to kiss my hand in greeting. My lord mingles with his thanes, calling out a hearty welcome. I watch their faces and think that I see flickers of discontent when he passes by.

Then I notice that Banquo is not among the party. As the king's general, he should be here. From time to time I glance hopefully at the door, but he does not come. My lord is unusually animated. Is it merely the wine—or another crime—that makes him so excited? My hands begin to throb. I will not think about it.

Luoch sits at a table staring into the fire. He should be among the thanes, listening to their conversations as I instructed him. I glare at him until he looks up. With a motion of my head, I summon him to me. Almost eighteen, he is a tall and awkward carl. He should be more of a man.

"Why do you sit at the table like a child waiting to be fed?"

"I'm hungry," he says.

I resist the impulse to reach up and strike him. What makes me think that he could ever rise to the throne? He has no more ambition than a slug.

"See those men? Put yourself in their midst. Listen to what they say. Speak to them. Win their respect."

Luoch runs his hand through his wild black hair and pouts, as he always used to when he planned to defy me.

"I don't have anything to say. I have been in no battles. They ignore me as if I am not here."

"That is because you make yourself invisible. At least use your ears and listen," I order him. "Go, and don't be such a lackwit!"

"Aye, Mother," he says with a sigh. Obediently he shambles off and greets the thane of Lennox and offers to fill his cup. Then he glances up at me and I nod.

He knows he must please me, and he will yet do so.

Macbeth calls for his men to be seated. I take my place at the table. There is a movement in the doorway. At last, I think, Banquo has arrived, and Fleance with him.

But the man in the doorway is Eadulf. He wears a hood but I recognize the blotch on his cheek. My lord gets up, almost knocking over his chair. He strides over to Eadulf and they whisper in the doorway. My lord's back is to me, but I see him clap Eadulf's shoulders in approval. The next moment he shoves Eadulf, sending him sprawling, and brings his arms back as if to strike him again. Instead he grabs his own head and growls. Eadulf scrambles away. Does this mean Banquo and Fleance are yet alive?

I hurry to my husband's side. The mandragora makes my head spin and it is a struggle to stay upright. Now the thanes have taken notice and they stand up to see better. I have no time to ask Macbeth what Eadulf has done—or not done.

"My lord, you must come to the table now and welcome

the men to eat," I say in a low voice, gripping his arm and leading him toward his seat.

After a few steps he halts. "Good appetite and health to all!" he announces in a forced and hearty tone. "All that our feast lacks is the presence of Banquo. I hope that no mischance keeps him away."

Does he speak in a double sense? I cannot tell.

"Sit, my liege. I may not eat until you do," says Ross, gesturing toward my lord's chair.

But still my lord stands there. He looks at his chair.

"The table is full," he says as a fearful look contorts his face.

The thanes begin to murmur and look doubtful.

"Which of you has done this?" asks Macbeth, shifting his glance from face to face, his body still rigid. "You may not say that I did it."

My pulse quickens in alarm. I dash to my lord's chair and grip its back, urging him to come and sit.

"Don't shake your gory locks at me!" he shouts, pointing to the chair.

The chair is empty. Can he not see that? Who does he see there? Is it Duncan's ghost?

"Dear friends, sit down," I call, my voice rising over theirs. "My lord is not well. These fits sometimes come upon him. He will recover in a moment. Do not regard him, or he will become more disturbed."

I rush back to Macbeth's side and drag him with difficulty into a nook.

"What folly is this? Come to your senses. Be still, and say

nothing more," I beg, terrified that he is on the brink of confessing our crime to all the thanes.

He stares beyond me. "If you can nod, then speak, too!" he demands. He grips my arm, saying, "Look, he goes now."

"What you see is no more real than a painting. An image of your fears."

I glance behind me at the table. The thanes are seated. They are quiet. No one is eating.

"In the olden times, when the brains were out, a man would die," Macbeth whispers, amazed. "But now they rise again, which is a greater wonder."

Then as suddenly as it came, the fit is over. He walks to the table like himself, a king. I follow and take my seat, my legs and hands still trembling. Macbeth raises a cup, and drinks—to Banquo's health! A chill constricts my chest. It is just like my lord to toast Banquo while plotting his death, as he professed his loyalty for Duncan after he had killed him. It is my lord's way: to hide his guilt by feigning love.

The men lift their cups and drink. "Where is Banquo?" they murmur.

My lord jumps from his chair and sends it crashing to the floor.

"Away and quit my sight!" he shouts. His face is as white as a linen sheet.

My hands fly up, knocking over my cup, and the wine pours into my lap. My lord is raving again.

"How can you behold such sights without blanching?" he demands of his thanes.

Only Ross dares respond. "What sights, my lord?"

"I pray you, don't speak!" I cry out before my lord can reply. "My husband grows worse and worse. Good night, all. Go at once."

The men get up and quietly leave. Luoch is the last to go. He glances over his shoulder at Macbeth, his nostrils flared with disgust. I wave him away.

My lord and I are alone in the hall. The untouched food grows cold on the platters. The torchlights flicker and shadows on the wall dance as if to mock us. I can barely speak for the anger in me.

"Did you invite all your thanes here in order to witness your madness? You have no doubt roused their worst suspicions, and they will plot to overthrow you."

"The small serpent has fled," he says, not attending to my words at all.

"What do you mean? Don't speak in riddles," I demand, my patience gone.

"Fleance escaped, but his father lies dead in a ditch."

I sink down onto a bench, dropping my head into my hands.

"And you think that after tonight's display, none here will suspect that you had a hand in the deed?" I ask, dismayed. "How will you justify it?"

"He was caught poaching game on my land. The wardens shot him."

"Even so! To kill a thane without a trial? This is a sure way to turn the others against you."

My lord is not listening. He holds out his hands and examines them. They are powerful and long-fingered, the bloodstains hidden beneath the skin.

"There is still more to be done," he says.

"Fleance? The youth is no threat to us. You are king, as promised. Let the rest be." I am begging him now. "You tempt fate, and I fear it will destroy you."

But I might as well be talking to a stone, for still my lord does not heed me.

"I will go to the Wyrd sisters again. They will tell me what is to come."

I grab his chin, forcing him to look at me. "Hear me, and do not go!"

He slaps my hand away, angry now.

"I will do what I must for my own good. Do not try to stop me." His voice is threatening and his black eyes without feeling.

I let him go. It would be dangerous to rile him further.

I know that my lord is now beyond my reach. While I stand at the shore of a sea of blood, he has waded up to his neck in the gore. And he will go deeper yet. There will be more killing. But I cannot follow, not even to bring him back. I am about to lose him.

Suddenly I do not want to be alone, for without him, I will be nothing.

Chapter 15

Dunbeag

Albia

When I wake up in my tiny room, Breda is holding a cup of warm broth to my lips. The air smells of mustard and wormwood poultices. I feel dull and sleepy and all my limbs ache as if I have been fighting with swords and running with stones around my ankles. Breda tells me that I have been out of my senses for many days.

The last thing I remember is trying to warn Banquo about Macbeth. The fact that Breda calmly tends to me now persuades me that he is unharmed. Perhaps my fears were groundless after all, and grief for Geillis disturbed my mind, then made me ill. I wonder if any warning dreams came to me while I was sick, but I can remember only a few strange images. Trees in a forest stirring from their places and moving as if they had feet. A procession of kings passing me, one holding a looking glass. Mere figments of a feverish mind. And Fleance's face, which brings a feeling of sorrow.

Banquo and Fleance have gone out hunting, Breda says.

She brings me oatcakes soaked in milk, urging me to eat. Her eyes, which once made me think of ice, now recall the cool waters of a loch. When she wipes my forehead, it is like an apology for calling me a whore. I submit to her care, too weak to help myself. It occurs to me that I have mistaken our relationship, trying to please Breda as a companion, when she only wanted a daughter to care for.

But I am not her daughter. I was not Geillis's daughter. Generous, loving Geillis! No, my mother is the queen. I feel no speck of pride in this, for the woman came by that title by foul deeds. Still less can she be called a mother, for she did not even protect me from my cruel father. I deny her. Should we ever meet, I will be as indifferent to her as she was to me. She left me to die!

Yet I did not die, for Rhuven saved me. And I did not succumb to this fever, for Breda nursed me. Macbeth my blood father is a murderer, full of foul lust, but my foster father, Banquo, is upright and kindhearted. He has accepted me as his daughter. Colum is my dear friend. And I think I love Fleance.

I start to cry, not out of grief, but with gratitude for my good fortune.

⸻

Breda's screams make me bolt from my bed. My first thought is that bandits have invaded Dunbeag to rob and rape us.

I reach under my mattress for my sword—Fleance's old

sword. It feels heavier in my hand than before I fell sick. I stumble down the stairs on weakened legs.

Fleance stands in the hallway, covered with blood. Breda's frantic hands flutter over his chest and his arms. She gasps helplessly. Dropping the sword, I run for a bucket of water and a sponge and by the time I get back, Fleance has slid to the ground. Breathless, I crouch beside him. Breda clutches her hair and rocks back and forth on her knees. Before Fleance utters a word, I know the truth: that Banquo has been killed.

"Father . . . tried to fight them. He told me to run . . . save myself."

Fleance's face contorts in agony and tears spill from his eyes.

"Who did it?" I ask, trying to hold in my anger. "Was it the king?"

"Two men. I think . . . one was Eadulf. Macbeth's man. He had a stain like wine on his cheek. He is the one who . . . stabbed my father."

"I was afraid this would happen!" I wail. "I tried to warn him!"

"It was my fault. We should not have been . . . hunting in the king's woods. I should have protected him. Not run like . . . a coward." Fleance's face crumples in shame.

I cannot trust myself to speak. Instead I start to wash the blood away. I open his tunic and feel my face redden as I check for wounds. Fortunately he has only a few cuts.

"You should try and comfort her," I say, glancing over at the keening Breda.

"I don't know how," he says, looking miserable.

"Like this." I wrap my arms around him, drawing his head to my shoulder. My cheek rests against his matted, dirty hair. The words leap out of my mouth like a sob. "Fleance, I loved your father!"

He clutches my arm and for a long moment we hold each other. Then he pulls away from me. His eyes are damp, his chin thrust out in determination.

"I won't be a coward anymore. Ross, Lennox, and Angus are turning against Macbeth. I will join them."

"Where are they now?"

Fleance lifts his shoulders. "I don't know, but I will travel the rivers and glens southward until I find them."

"I am coming with you," I say, having decided just that moment. "I want to help defeat Macbeth."

"Albia, you are brave," says Fleance with a sigh. "But I cannot let you come to harm for my sake."

But I am determined, and I do not like to be denied.

"I can defend myself. Isn't that why you taught me to fight? I only need a better sword and shield."

"No." Fleance holds up his hands, palms toward me. "He was my father. This revenge is mine." More firmly than those hands, his words push me away.

Then he crawls over to his mother and lays his head in her lap like a child. She leans over him and they weep together.

The sight of them fills me with longing. But I suppress it, for the matter at hand is revenge. What Fleance does not know is that it was my father who killed his, even if Macbeth did not wield the knife. The revenge belongs to me as well. I dreamt it, and it will come.

No, I will *make* it happen, for I am Macbeth's daughter.

❦

In the morning, Fleance is gone. No one saw him leave. I am angry that he went away before I could persuade him to take me along, but I am still too weak from my fever to follow him. But I decide to waste not a day before building up my strength again. I go to retrieve my sword, but it is not in the hall where I dropped it yesterday. Instead, leaning against the wall is a round shield with a brass boss in the center. Next to it lies an unfamiliar scabbard tooled with twining ivy and birds. I am surprised to see it attached to my own belt, the one with the brass buckle Banquo gave me. I reach for the sword, and it slides from the scabbard with a sharp and satisfying *zzzzt*. It is lighter than I expect and balances perfectly in my palm. The shining blade is exactly the right length for me.

I am excited—and confused. Fleance said he did not want me to go with him, but he left me this sword. Should I seek him anyway, and the thanes who oppose Macbeth? Seeing me with a sword, they would laugh me out of Scotland. I may be stronger than most women, but it is still a disadvantage to be one. Maybe I should go to Dun Forres instead, and by some deception get the king alone, then kill him. But how? I've only ever killed a fish or a fowl, and that in order to eat. How could I possibly kill a man? But I must act somehow. What shall I do?

The answer comes to me, more silent than a whisper.

Rely upon the Sight. It is your gift. Use it now.

I try focusing my mind, then emptying it, but the images that come and go are of my own making. I wander around Dunbeag at night, but no white deer or black dog appears to show the path to my revenge. In my dreams, no ghost speaks to me, like Banquo's gory head. I have only that same impossible dream of the trees moving out of the forest, as if animated by a wood-sprite. And I see the parade of kings, the last one holding a looking glass. How can trees walk? Why would a king look in a glass and see nothing? It makes no sense.

I decide to visit Helwain. She knows I have the Sight and will give me herbs to sharpen it. We will go to Stravenock Henge and invoke the gods with spells and potions until a vision comes, and she will help me understand its meaning. I will stand under the ancient oak tree, where the four worlds meet, and sleep on Geillis's grave until I receive a sign. And then I will follow it until I destroy Macbeth.

⛄

Breda's misery is boundless. The ice in her melts and flows out in tears that redden her pale cheeks. I never thought she cared much for Banquo. Or for Fleance, gone now to stir rebellion, perhaps to die as well. It would be thankless of me to leave her now. I suggest that she come with me to Helwain's, and she agrees, following my lead like a lost child. We pack food and clothing. Everything that I value fits in one small bundle: the few gifts from Banquo, the girdle from Fleance, the armlet that was the queen's. None of Dunbeag's guard offers to escort us. Some even murmur that Fleance killed his father and ran away. Breda, now without a husband or son, has no protectors. I promise that I will stay with her, and her eyes grow round at the sight of the sword and shield Fleance left me.

"So that is why you met him in secret, and returned so disheveled," she says, finally understanding.

"Aye. It was not what you suspected." I blush, thinking of how Fleance and I kissed and clung to each other.

"You have changed my son," she says. "He will not be the kind of man who sees a woman as his possession."

"Nor was Banquo such a man," I say. "He did love you."

Breda looks away, but she nods just barely.

We leave Dunbeag on a sunless day like all the others. A cold wind whips our cloaks and makes the bushes and bracken rustle. I ride a gray palfrey named Gath, and Breda rides a brown one. The dry turf crackles under their hooves. We travel in silence until we see, in a valley between two looming hills, a small party on horseback coming in our direction.

My first thought is that the king has sent warriors to destroy what is left of Banquo's family. A glance around the wide heath reveals no place to hide.

"Shall we turn back and try to outrun them?" I ask.

"Nay, we will go on and meet them," Breda decides. She has nothing left to lose.

"Let us hope they take us for travelers and pass by," I say. "Still, cover your face."

I take the lead and Breda lags behind me. My apprehension grows as the riders draw closer. Then I see the lead rider carrying the standard of the thane of Fife. They are Macduff's men! We sigh with relief and hurry to meet them.

Rather than Macduff, it is his lady, Fiona, on her way to Dunbeag to console Breda. The two women slide from their mounts and embrace in the middle of the road. In her friend's arms, Breda succumbs to more tears.

"This latest crime is yet more proof of the king's boundless evil," says the indignant Fiona. "The tyrant must be stopped!"

"Fleance has gone to revenge his father's death," sobs Breda, "but how can a single boy bring down Scotland's king?"

"He is not alone!" says Fiona. "My lord leads the thanes who mass against Macbeth."

Breda stares at her with red-rimmed eyes.

"Who are the other thanes?" I ask.

Fiona glances up at me in surprise. "Ross and Caithness in the north, and Lennox and Angus in the midlands. They are my lord's cousins, and blood ties them together. The western thanes follow the queen's father, who has turned against Macbeth. My Macduff has gone to England to ask King Edward to lend his army."

I feel my heart skip with excitement and fear at the thought of Scotland at war. Does Macbeth know how far the rebellion has progressed? Does he have enough loyal warriors to thwart it?

"Tell me, Breda. Will Banquo's men join forces against Macbeth?" asks Fiona.

"Dunbeag is an uncertain place since my lord's death. I

don't know which way his warband tends," says Breda wor-riedly. "They have no love for me because I am not of Scotland born."

Now I understand Breda's willingness to leave Dunbeag with me.

"You must come to Dunduff. My lord left it strongly forti-fied, and you will be safe," says Fiona.

"I will," agrees Breda instantly. She mounts her palfrey again, and Fiona's party turns around. Breda spurs her horse to join them.

It is Fiona who turns around and beckons to me.

I hesitate. I feel responsible for Breda. Banquo and Fleance would want me to take care of her. But I realize that I cannot keep her safe. Macduff's stronghold would be a better place for her than on the road with me.

"I cannot come with you. I must go to Wychelm Wood."

Fiona's eyes widen. "Alone?" she asks with some alarm.

"Don't be foolish, Albia," says Breda, but without feeling.

"I am prepared," I reply, indicating my sword and shield tied to the palfrey's trappings. I realize that I am grateful to Fiona for coming along to relieve me of Breda. I prefer to travel alone.

Breda and I say our awkward farewells. I know she would rather be with Fiona. Yet as she rides away, I am struck with the certainty that I will never see her again. It is not the Sight coming to me, only the fear that either she will die of grief or something will happen to me in this wasteland where the sun never shines, and no one will know or care.

Not even Fleance.

I cup my hands and call after Breda's retreating figure.

"When you see Fleance . . ." I take a breath.

Fleance. Fleance. Fleance. The name rebounds from the hills around me.

"Tell him . . ."

Tell him what?

No one turns around to look at me. Do they not hear me?

I shout louder, "Tell Fleance I seek him!" My voice breaks and the wind throws my words back to me.

"Tell Fleance . . . I love him."

I say this to myself, to hear if it sounds like the truth.

Chapter 16

Wychelm Wood and Stravenock Henge

Albia

I am startled to see how Helwain has changed since Geillis's death. Her back is more stooped. Her hands are gnarled and black from the walnut juice she rubs into them to soothe the stiffness. Dark crescents extend beneath her eyes and shadows haunt the hollows of her cheeks. The pain and loneliness I see there almost stir my pity.

She does not seem surprised to see me. She glances at my sword without any comment. *She knew I would come.* For a moment I wonder if she has been staring into her scrying stone, and if the lump of rock actually works.

"It is Macbeth's daughter," she says in a hard, flat voice.

"What do you mean by calling me that?"

"Like him, you've come to me for advice." She lets out a harsh laugh. "But I am done with telling fates."

All the anger in me gathers into a storm. Words burst out of me like hail and lightning.

"You are done? It was you who began it all. You told Macbeth he would have sons, and so he cast me out for dead. You told him he would be king, and he slew Duncan. You said Banquo would be greater than Macbeth, so Macbeth slew Banquo, who was like a father to me!" I am shouting now. "All this evil is on your hands, Helwain. It is far from done."

The peat fire shudders, as if the winds of my wrath would blow it out, and Tammas the cat claws his way up a post, yowling.

But Helwain stands like a stone, unperturbed.

"You are mistaken. I don't determine anything. I may say the sun will not shine tomorrow, but that doesn't make it dark. Macbeth did those things of his own will. It was not fate," she says scornfully. Holding up a bent finger, she advances toward me. "He chose evil, and his crimes have brought darkness on the land."

"But . . . but you foresaw it all. You predicted what came to pass," I protest.

"I have said before, I see what people plainly desire and I speak it back to them," she says. "I do not have the Sight. You do."

"Then look at me and tell me, what do I want?" I mean to sound forceful, but my question comes out as a plaintive cry.

Helwain turns to the fire and picks up a pipe from the hearth before replying.

"You desire your mother."

"I do not! My mother is a heartless—" I break off, seeing the satisfied look in Helwain's eyes. "Of course I wish Geillis were still here," I murmur.

Helwain puts the pipe to her lips and puffs until bitter-smelling smoke drifts out the end.

"You also desire revenge," she says, letting out a long breath. "But more than that, you desire justice and order. Revenge is merely your means to that end."

"Then tell me—since you know so much—how can I get this revenge? How can I make the world right again?"

"You already know," says Helwain. Her head is wreathed in smoke.

"Macbeth must die," I say. "But how?"

Helwain slowly shakes her head. "*You* have the Sight. Use it."

Another storm bursts from me.

"I don't see anything that makes sense! I cannot make a vision come, and if I could, no sprite of my mind could kill a flea, let alone a king." I dash the pipe from her mouth and wave away the smoke so that I can see her face. "You have potions and charms. Give me something to sharpen my Sight. Help me understand what I see. Now!"

I clench my fists behind my back to keep from hitting Helwain. Geillis is no longer here to stop me.

Helwain picks up a bag and puts some small clay pots into it.

"Here is amaranth for conjuring. Let it burn and breathe in the smoke. This contains elfwort to strengthen the Sight, guard against evil, and attract love. Steep it in water and drink."

I give her a doubtful look. "If this will bring on the Sight, why did you not give it to me long ago?"

"Nothing has power if you don't believe in it," she says.

Then she tells me what I think I already know. That I will see nothing clearly while my mind is disturbed and crowded with angry, vengeful thoughts. That I must know what I want before I can see a way to make it happen. Also, that she does not have the answers. I must go away, alone, to seek them.

I also know before she tells me that I will go to Pitdarroch, where the four worlds meet and Geillis lies beneath the stones.

"Take my hawthorn staff, and be off," she says, dismissing me.

I take the staff and leave without another word.

⤙

At the throw of a stone from Pitdarroch stands the cairn where Geillis lies buried. As Gath carries me by, I whisper her name and close my eyes, seeing her face before she fell ill, her green eyes and round, smooth cheeks. There are no tears left in me, none that will bring her back. Then I wonder about Grelach. Did she weep when she lost me? If I dream tonight, will the Sight bring her face to me? I dismiss the wish. I will not dishonor the memory of Geillis, my true mother.

At the base of the ancient oak tree where the roots form small hollows, I make a nest of ferns and sit with Helwain's staff across my lap. Gath munches dry grass nearby. I listen for wolves but all is silent save for the wind that blows through the gray-green moss hanging from the oak branches like the hair of an ancient crone. I kindle a small fire and burn the amaranth, and I mix the elfwort with water from my flask and sip it, feeling a little foolish. Nothing happens. My mind is still crowded with unwelcome images of Geillis's pale, cold body, Macbeth looking at me with lust, and Fleance covered in blood. Vengeful thoughts stir in me, but they slip away again like water soaking into the ground. The fearsome images also vanish and nothing takes their place. I am left cleansed and blank, no longer afraid. The world around me is soundless, and all within me silent and calm.

Pitdarroch is suddenly charged with spirits. I feel them as a tingling deep in my belly, a coldness on my skin, and invisible fingers lifting my hair. But I see nothing, though I strain my eyes. I think I hear them, though it may be only the sighing of the wind. I inhale, and they smell like humid earth and fresh-cut bracken. A hunger for sleep overcomes me, and I feel myself floating out of the Now-world.

I dream of being in the middle of a battle. My sword clashes against another. A man with a helmet over his face cries *Beware Macduff.* Fragments flit past my inner eye: a baby covered in blood, a child crowned like a king, with a tree in his hand. And again, the trees advancing upon a hill, a parade of kings, with the last one holding up a glass. Still the glass remains dark, but this time the mystery does not trouble me.

Though the dream is violent and still incomprehensible, I awake in the morning feeling calm and somehow wiser. I did not see myself striking down Macbeth, but I feel assured that

I will have revenge. Macbeth himself will bring it about. The time will come, and soon.

❧

My calm is undisturbed even when Helwain and Rhuven appear at Pitdarroch with fear in their eyes to announce Macbeth's approach.

Rhuven looks haggard and her movements are frantic. She has left the queen without permission. The king's madness deepens, she says, for now he sees the ghosts of those he killed.

"And your life is in danger, Albia, for he suspects you are his daughter."

"I am not afraid," I say, surprised to find it true. "Does the queen know that I live?"

"Nay, she believes the king has lost all his reason."

"Has she no hope at all?" I ask.

Rhuven looks at me strangely. Did I really sound so forlorn?

"No more questions," says Helwain. "You must leave, or hide, for the king comes here tonight."

"I will not leave. He comes to know his future, and I will show it to him," I say, not at all sure what I mean.

"Have you seen it, then?" Helwain asks, her eyes wide and greedy. "Tell me, that I may know what to say to him. He found me last night, and I told him to meet me tonight at Stravenock Henge. There we will have the advantage of the gods."

"I will speak to him, Helwain. Not you." I have no idea yet what I will say. "Does he come alone?"

"He has two men with him. With so many enemies, do you think he would travel unguarded?"

"It is too dangerous, Albia," says Rhuven. "He may recognize you. If he discovers that we deceive him, our lives will be forfeit."

"Don't worry," I say. "He will deceive himself."

And so we prepare for Macbeth's arrival, darkening ourselves with peat dust and staining our clothes, using water brown with tannin. It is my idea to weave moss into our hair, so that we look like beings from the Other-world. Helwain kindles a fire and sets her kettle on its flames. As midnight draws on, a storm arises with gusts of wind and rumbling thunder, but no rain to wet the dry earth. Then as the firelight leaps off the face of the great high stones and Helwain chants to the spirits roaming on the winds, Macbeth comes.

I hear him shout, "How now, you secret, black, and midnight hags!" Then I see his hooded figure along the perimeter of stones. My heart starts to pound in my chest as if it would break out from my ribs. Two men flank the king, their weapons ready.

"I conjure you, by all the evil you profess, answer me what I ask you," he demands.

Rhuven's eyes are wide with fear. Helwain chants in a low, continuous monotone, a litany of gods. She throws a chalky substance on the flames, and blue and green smoke rises up.

The king tosses back his hood, and though he stands outside the circle of firelight, I see his gold crown and red hair as if they are lit by the darkness within him.

Step by slow step he approaches the fire. And as if we are locked in a fateful dance, step by step Rhuven, Helwain, and I retreat, keeping the fire and its bitter-smelling smoke between us.

"Stay!" he commands. "Show me what will come." He stares into the smoke, then starts back. "It is an armored head!"

Naturally, kings fear rebellion. I will tell him the truth, for I know who leads the rebellion against him.

"Beware Macduff," I say, taking care to alter my voice. "Beware the thane of Fife."

"You have hit my fear aright, fatal sister. I thank you for the caution," the king replies, sounding unimpressed.

Of course he already knows that Macduff is against him. I see that it will not do to try to make him fearful. No, I must make him reckless instead, so that pride will be his weakness.

A clap of thunder sounds.

I remember overhearing Fiona say that Macduff was born unnaturally, torn from the womb before his time. This bit of truth will be my bait.

Macbeth stares into the fire again. "What do I see now?" He frowns and stiffens. "A bloody babe? Not . . . not my daughter! Begone." His hands claw at his eyes.

Rhuven gasps, and Helwain whispers at my ear, "What power you have! How do you do it?"

In fact, I have conjured nothing. All I have done is to think about Macduff as a tiny infant taken from his mother's belly. What the king sees springs from his own tortured mind.

"Be bloody, bold, and resolute!" I shout. "Scorn the power of men, for none of woman born shall harm Macbeth."

The king's body relaxes. He flexes his arms so that the sinews stand out and nods to his men.

"All men are born of women. So live, Macduff. I have nothing to fear from you," he says with a laugh.

Now I think of that child—whoever it may be in Macbeth's mind—with a crown on its head, and a branch of a tree in its hand, like a staff. As in my dream, I imagine the impossible— trees pulling up their own roots and moving across the land, Nature herself revolting against the evil tyrant.

And I declare to the king, "You shall not be vanquished until the trees of the great wood come against the high hill."

The king claps his hands against his thighs and roars like a storm wind.

"That will never be! How shall great Birnam Wood rise from its earthbound roots and climb to Dunsinane?"

His black eyes gleam through the smoke. "Tell me now," he demands, "shall Banquo's issue ever reign in this kingdom?"

I remember the procession of kings from my dream. The last one carries a mirror. Closing my eyes, I imagine him with Banquo's face.

Then I say to Macbeth, "I see a line of kings—"

Macbeth interrupts me. "I see them, too." Then he speaks to them, looking right through me. "You are too much like the spirit of Banquo. The second like the first, the third . . . like the former." His voice rises. "Why do you show me this? Another! A seventh . . . and an eighth, who bears a glass in which I see . . . many more." Spittle forms around his lips as he shouts, "What, will Banquo's line stretch out to the crack of doom?"

It seems that I have dreamt the king's greatest fear: that no son of his will rule Scotland.

"He grows disturbed; let us go now," whispers Rhuven, pulling my arm.

Helwain throws an armful of dried moss onto the flames, sending up billows of smoke. While Macbeth slashes the air with his hands, we retreat to a hollow at the base of one of the standing stones.

"Where have you gone?" the king cries, stumbling from stone to stone like a child looking for his mother. Then he shouts, defiant, "Hear me, you foul, fateful sisters! No one born of woman shall harm me. Damned be those who trust you!" His curses grow fainter, but these final words come borne on the wind, as clear as if spoken at the porches of my ears.

"Yet I'll make assurance double sure. Traitor, you shall not live."

And the king disappears into the black night of his own creation.

Chapter 17

Stravenock Henge to Dunduff

Albia

Traitor, you shall not live.

Macbeth's threat lingers long after the sound of his voice has died away.

"You have pricked the king into a mad rage," Helwain says, her eyes glittering. "Now reason and law are usurped in him, and he is most dangerous."

"I only spoke of what I saw in the dreams that made little sense to me. But the king recognized his own fears in them," I say, trying myself to understand what happened.

"Because of what you told him, he thinks himself invincible," says Rhuven. She is clearly displeased with me.

"Rather, I think he is more afraid—that in the end, Banquo's heirs will hold the throne for which he schemed so foully," I say.

"Aye, and only by killing his enemies can he control his fear— and hold his throne," Helwain adds.

The thought strikes me like a fist to my gut, depriving me of air: *Who is a greater enemy to Macbeth than Banquo's heir, Fleance?*

"I must find Fleance!" I cry out. "I must warn Macduff! He and his allies are in danger."

"What can you do? You could be harmed or even killed," says Rhuven in alarm.

"Let her go," says Helwain, to my surprise. "She has made up her mind. And she is well equipped to defend herself."

I fasten the sword-belt around my waist and my shield to Gath's saddle and ride back through the woods to pick up the road where I left Breda. According to Fiona, Macduff has gone to England. Still, I can warn his cousin thanes that Macbeth intends to murder their leader upon his return. But what if I encounter the king on *his* way to Macduff's fort and he should recognize me, either as the fateful sister at Stravenock Henge or as the girl claiming to be his daughter? I shudder to think of the consequences. And what if Macbeth or his henchmen should find Fleance searching for the rebel thanes, alone? His life, too, is in peril.

I must find Fleance. I must warn Macduff.

The urgent words, repeated to the rhythm of Gath's galloping hooves, blur like the ground passing beneath us. I ride him so hard that flecks of white foam fly back from his mouth.

The road skirts a wide bog strewn with tufted cottongrass and crowberry, passes through some stunted pines, then emerges onto pasture land. Sheep dot the hillside and a shepherd's bothy stands in a grove of myrtle.

The peaceful scene slows me down, then draws me from the path. I dismount to drink the cold, clear water trickling down a rocky cleft in the hillside. My sword gets in the way, so I take it off and tie it to Gath's harness. When we are both refreshed, I lead Gath up the hill to where a shepherd sits in the lee of a rock, overlooking the low hills that lie like a rumpled mantle all the way to the horizon.

Cupping my hands, I call into the wind, "Hail, shepherd, do you know my friend Colum?"

The fellow stands up and flings off his hat, and I see that it *is* Colum. Unable to believe my good fortune, I run to him and we embrace, laughing. He gathers his sheep and leads me to the bothy. The shadows are long, heralding night. But there is enought light left for me to make out Caora with her bright silken hair.

"Welcome, Albia," she calls, looking pleased to see me. "You can stay here tonight. It will be too dark to travel." She feeds Gath a handful of oats, tugs on his mane, and makes noises into his ear.

Seeing my sword and shield, Colum is full of questions. I feel overwhelmed, for so much has happened since I last saw him, just after Geillis died. I have met my father and pricked him to a murderous rage. I have lost Banquo and left Dunbeag behind. I am now homeless. I am searching for Fleance, whom I love and whose life is in danger. So what am I doing stopped at a shepherd's bothy?

I explain to Colum that the king's men have slain Banquo and that I am looking for his allies in order to warn them of the danger they face. I do not mention Fleance. Nor do I reveal anything that has occurred between Macbeth and me. I feel guilty keeping all this from Colum.

Frowning, he picks up my sword and slides it halfway out of its scabbard. Gingerly he touches the shining blade.

"The only weapon I have is a slingshot," he muses.

Caora goes into the hut and comes back with a long, graceful bow made of yew wood and strung with deer sinew.

"You could borrow this, Colum," she says softly. "You have some skill in hunting with it. Nothing is as swift as one of my arrows."

"I am a shepherd. Deeds of arms are not for me," Colum says, frowning.

I feel heat rising to my face. "You would not judge me if you knew my just cause!"

"Albia, that sword is made to slay men. I cannot believe . . . that *you* would use it so!"

"I do not plan to kill anyone, Colum, but to keep others from harm."

"And how do you plan not to get hurt yourself?" asks Colum.

"I . . . I'll use my shield."

Colum regards me doubtfully. Suddenly the fine sword lying on the hearth looks like something that could not possibly belong to me. How could I hope to survive a fight against trained warriors more than double my size and strength?

Colum turns his attention to gutting the rabbits for our supper. He hands them to Caora, who spits them to roast on the fire, then goes to fetch water. I can see they have done this many times while I was away at Dunbeag. I envy them the simple daily rituals of life on the shieling.

Caora reaches up to turn the meat, exposing the red and

white scars on her arm, marks of the fire-breathing Nocklavey. I see a small child stumbling into the fire and screaming as flames lick up her sleeve. A pot of water is dashed upon her, putting out the blaze. Of course. The beast is only afraid of water.

"Your story of Nocklavey used to frighten me," I say. "But I don't believe it anymore."

Caora frowns, her brows hiding her golden eyes. "Believe it or not, it is true."

"Scotland is troubled by a far worse monster now. The king himself is the beast who brings everything to ruin. I have felt his evil touch."

"As I knew Nocklavey's touch," she says evenly.

"My wound is not visible. But it is old, and deep." I don't know why I am needling Caora. Yes, I do. I want to know how much she knows about me, and *how* she knows.

Caora gazes directly at me. "I have the Sight as well as you."

"Then tell me what you have seen, that you know so much about me."

Caora shakes her head. "I may not."

"You must! Do you know how much is at stake?" I am all but shouting. "While you and Colum keep your cozy hut on the shieling, Scotland is being destroyed!"

"Aye. So hear me," says Caora, her voice urgent. "You must not go on your way alone, if you want to live."

"Tell me more!" I reach out to seize Caora's arm, but she is quicker, leaping to her feet and running away into the night.

When Colum comes back to find Caora gone, I admit with some shame that she and I argued. He cups his hands and calls for her, but she does not come back. I cannot sleep, knowing that Colum is sore with me.

In the morning I am up before dawn and on my way, alone.

~

Late in the afternoon, when the shadows have grown to impossible lengths, I finally see Dunduff in the distance. I can even make out a figure in the watchtower. It is a relief to find the fort still standing, its palisades sharp and erect. I half expected a smoking ruin. Welcoming pennants flutter from the towers. But there no longer seems a need for haste, so I slow Gath to a walk, then stop altogether by a mossy bank to rest. My limbs ache from so much riding.

Soon the wind changes, and faint shouts echo behind me. I turn to see a figure galloping toward me, and my first impulse is to leap on Gath and ride for the safety of Dunduff. But I am slow and sore, and the other horse comes on with surprising speed. I only have time to buckle my sword-belt and strap on my shield with fumbling fingers before a heavy black war-beast, snorting and pawing the path, is upon me. Its shape fills my sight, and in my terror I wonder if it is Nocklavey. It halts suddenly, rocks fly up from its hooves, and two leather-clad riders slide to the ground. They pull off their caps and I groan with relief to see Colum and Caora.

"How dare you give me such a fright!"

Colum looks shaky on his feet. I would wager he has never ridden such a beast. Caora is self-controlled but tense.

"Why did you leave alone, after I warned you?" she asks.

"What is there to fear? Look, it is peaceful here." I gesture in the direction of Dunduff. "But tell me, where did you come by the horse?"

"I stole it from a thane in the glen beyond our bothy. I meant to be back by morning, but the stables were well guarded and it was no easy task to take him."

Caora wears her bow and quiver strapped across her back. I suspect she had to use them when she stole the horse.

"We left the sheep in the care of a friend and came as quickly as we could," Colum says.

"I'm glad you are here," I say truthfully. "Though I am not as helpless as you think. Let's go now."

Caora boosts Colum onto the black horse, then lightly leaps across the beast's back as if there are wings on her feet. I step on a rock to hoist myself onto Gath's back and hurry after them.

We are almost within the shadows of Dunduff's towers when Caora halts the black beast and puts up a hand to warn me. Following her gaze, I see that the person in the watchtower is not moving. In fact, he leans over the battlements at an odd angle. I feel my gut twist. Caora nods to Colum seated behind her. He takes her bow and fits it with an arrow, holding it ready. I feel helpless and exposed as we approach the gate. Why don't we run away? None of us wants to turn our backs to Dunduff now.

"Look up!" I cry, seeing a movement in the opposite tower.

An arrow whizzes by inches from my face and lodges in Gath's neck. The horse lets out a high whinny and paws the air, almost throwing me from his back. Colum looses his arrow, but it falls short of the tower. While Caora holds the warhorse steady, he aims another arrow. It splits the air and finds its mark. With a cry, the figure falls from sight behind the wall of Dunduff.

Colum, the peace-loving shepherd, has shot a man. He did not even hesitate.

No more arrows come from the tower. Everything is still again, except for the banners flapping in the wind. Gath shakes his head from side to side, trying to dislodge the arrow. Blood trickles from his wound. We dismount and, using the horses to shield us, make our way with slow steps to the gate. To my surprise it swings open at our touch. Broken staves are strewn about the yard, where chickens peck the dirt. Caora picks up a stick to use as a weapon and Colum does the same. I count six bodies lying on the ground, twisted in violent death. The one Colum shot is tangled in the rungs of a ladder that broke his fall from the tower. Anguish shows on Colum's face, but none of us speaks.

The heavy door of the dwelling has been hewed with axes. The hinges are broken. Caora hesitates. Her face is paler than usual. So I go in first, my sword drawn, my arm tense with dread. All the furniture is smashed, the cupboards looted. The back door is open, and I pass through it to Fiona's garden. The once-green bushes are withered, the flowers and fruit trees all brown and sere.

Under a leafless arbor they lie, covered in blood. Fiona with a bloody baby in her arms. The twins clutching each other, their limbs whiter than a swan's down. A boy stabbed in the act of fleeing. And by the pool, her arms flung over her head, her fingers trailing in the water—Breda.

I draw in my breath to scream, but no sound comes out. I am dizzy, the world spins around me, and I close my eyes to keep from falling. My sword drops to the ground. Caora and Colum hold me up, one on each side.

"I am too late!" I finally manage to utter. "The monster has come and gone. O damnable father, tyrant king, hellish beast!" My voice rises to a scream. I turn and push my head into Colum's shoulder.

Caora trembles beside me. "The women and the children, all of them?" she murmurs in a daze. "Not one of them spared?"

I open my eyes again. I must count the children, though I cannot bear to look at their still bodies. There are only four of them. Wee Duff is not here.

"Duff! Where are you?" I shout. "Wee Duff, answer me!"

I tear through the house, yanking open doors and flinging aside bedding. No one is there. I run outside into the yard. *The archer who fell into the ladder.* I run to the base of the tower and look up to see Wee Duff with the broken shaft of Colum's arrow in his shoulder. Colum and Caora are right behind me. Colum climbs up the ladder and brings the boy down, laying him on the ground.

"He's only a boy," he says, his voice hoarse with emotion. "O holy God, I have killed a child."

Caora leans down and puts her ear to Wee Duff's mouth.

"No, he is breathing," she announces.

A groan comes from the boy's lips and his eyes flutter open. They are bright with fear.

"Wee Duff, do you know me? It is Albia, and these are my friends. Don't be afraid."

The boy's eyes fill with tears. "I thought you were . . . them," he whispers. "I didn't want to die."

"You won't die," Caora assures him. "The wound is not deep."

The boy's brief smile turns into a grimace of pain.

"Oh, Duff, you are a brave boy," I say, rubbing his hand. "Can you tell me what happened?"

"My uncle Ross and his band had just left when they came. . . . The king's men." The boy struggles to speak. "They asked for Da, but Mama told them he was away. We were not scared at first. But then they called Da a traitor and . . . showed their daggers . . . and killed my brother first!"

Wee Duff begins to cry. I kiss his hands, leaving my own tears on them.

"Next they came for me and got me . . . here." He points to his stomach. His eyelids flutter as if he wants to sleep.

Caora tears open the boy's stained tunic. Besides the arrow in his shoulder, he has a wound in his belly, and fresh blood seeps from its ragged edges.

"He has lost everything," Colum whispers. "Not his life, too!"

Emotions churn inside me like the contents of a boiling cauldron. Grief for Fiona and her children, for Breda. Rage at Macbeth, rage at myself.

"Their deaths are my fault. If only I had not stopped—"

"If you had not stayed the night with us, still you would have been too late, and still the boy would have mistaken you.

But you would have been alone, and the arrow would have stuck in *your* throat," says Caora fiercely.

"Nay, I let Breda come here, thinking she would be safe. Now she is dead like her husband. Oh Fleance, now you have no father or mother!"

"Albia, take heart that he was not here," Caora whispers.

But nothing can console me as I think of the slain children.

"The blame is all on me. I told the king to fear Macduff. I dreamt of a bloody babe, but I did not know what it meant— that he would kill the children!"

Caora bites her lip and looks at Wee Duff, lying with his eyes closed.

"His thread of life is frayed," she says softly. "But it still holds."

A new determination fills me. I will not let the boy die.

"Caora, you must take charge of Wee Duff. Take him to the Wychelm Wood, where Helwain will heal him. Tell her it is my wish. Colum will go, too, and show you the way."

She nods and says, "I will take Gath, and leave you the war-horse."

I thank Caora. It will be an advantage to have a fast, fierce, and strong steed. Taking the beast by his harness and pulling his huge head down, I speak into his cavernous ear.

"Your name is now Nocklavey. And I will ride you to my revenge."

Chapter 18

The Spey Valley

Albia

We wash and bind up Wee Duff's wounds and lay him where he cannot see us burying the bodies of Fiona and her children. It takes us several hours. As soon as we are done, Caora springs onto Gath and Colum lifts the boy to ride in front of her.

I stroke Gath's long nose and peer at the wound in his neck. It will rankle until it heals. I touch Wee Duff's leg. "May all the gods be with you. One day your father will know how brave you are." My voice starts to break.

Suddenly I realize I have no idea how to find Macduff's allies.

"Wait. Duff, where did your uncle Ross go, when he left here?"

The boy frowns, thinking. "He said he was going to meet my uncle Angus. His lands are to the south, beyond the River Spey and across the Grampian Mountains."

"Then we'll be traveling in opposite directions." Because

Gath cannot carry three riders, Colum will have to walk, and that will slow them. So I urge them to leave. "If you hurry, you can reach the shelter of the glen before dark."

Caora turns Gath toward the gate. But Colum crosses his arms over his chest and makes no move to leave.

"I am staying with you, Albia. I am in this now."

I look at him in surprise. His jaw is lifted with determination.

"But why? What are these people to you?" I gesture toward the fresh graves.

"They were all innocent. The boy . . . I almost killed him." Colum's voice stumbles, then steadies. "I owe it to him to punish those who did this to his family."

"So you would join a rebellion against the king? You, a peaceful shepherd?"

"Aye. For now I know the king to be a tyrant and a hellish beast. But tell me, what did you mean, calling him a . . . damnable father?"

I can no longer hide the truth from Colum. Caora, too, must learn it all—whatever she does not already know. I take a deep breath. There is no easy way to break this to him.

"Unbelievable as it may seem, Colum, I am the daughter of Macbeth and his queen."

Colum stares at me and says flatly, "That is indeed beyond belief."

"But it is true. And now you must decide if you want to remain my friend." I swallow hard, half-afraid to look at him.

Colum strides away from me, turns around, and comes

back to face me. "You are making this up so that I will leave you here."

Caora's voice rises over his. "Believe what she says, Colum. It is no lie."

"And how do you know?" I challenge her.

Caora doesn't answer. "I must be going now," she says. "The boy needs help. May the gods protect you both." She passes through the open gate of Dunduff, riding my gray palfrey into the gray dusk. I watch her until she disappears.

Colum is staring at me with a strange look on his face.

"How can you possibly be the king's daughter?" he says in a hoarse whisper.

"It is a long tale," I say, letting out a weary breath.

"I have all night." He sits down on the ground, indicating that he means to wait.

I sit down next to him, and though I have no wish to remain any longer at Dunduff, among the dead, I begin the story of my birth and banishment. We do not rise until I have finished the story just as the sisters told it to me. I even admit that I have the Sight and that long ago I dreamt about the murder of Duncan. I describe my dream of Banquo and how he was killed and how Fleance fled, leaving me a sword and shield.

I do not tell Colum that I might be in love with Fleance.

My history must sound as fantastic as a tale of bogles and goblins told on the shieling. But Colum does not question it. He does not recoil when I tell him that the king shamefully touched me, his own daughter. Nor does he

shrink away when I describe how I used my Sight to foretell the king's doom, which spurred him to slay Macduff's
family.

"So you see," I conclude, dropping my heavy head into my
hands, "I am his daughter, and like him tainted with innocent
blood."

"You are not the guilty one." says Colum.

"But think of the deaths that I did not prevent, even though I
foresaw them. I cannot shake off that burden. Hear me, though,
for I have made a vow, and you are my witness." I pause until our
eyes are locked together. "When I meet Macbeth, I swear I will
not hesitate to lift my sword against him, even if it means my
own death."

Colum stiffens. "Is it justice you seek, or revenge?"

"They are the same," I say defiantly.

"Nay, revenge springs from malice, but justice I think . . ."
He pauses, searching for words. "Justice comes from wanting
what is good. Not for yourself alone, but for others."

"A fine thought for a mere shepherd!" I snap. "There is no
justice, if the king himself, who should be its source, is cor-
rupt. There is *only* revenge."

"I don't wish to argue, Albia," Colum says with a sigh.
"Rather, let's decide what to do now."

I gaze over the ruins of Dunduff, the dead guards, the graves.
Only a few days ago a joyful household thrived here.

"We find Macbeth and kill him."

Colum looks sideways at me, his brows knit together.

"Perhaps I *will* argue with you. Shouldn't we find Ross and the other allies of Macduff first? You and I alone . . . are not very strong."

I know he is right. But every bone and sinew of my body longs to find the king now and strike at him, revenging all the wrong done since the days of my infancy. I press the heels of my hands into my eyes, trying to hold back the hot tears. I press so hard that wild patterns dance there like hellish sprites against a black curtain.

I hear Colum moving around. I blink until my blurry sight clears and see him struggling into a tunic made of iron mail. He has taken a helmet from one of the guards, as well as a bow and arrows. I begin searching and find a small steel and leather helmet and a jerkin fitted with overlapping brass plates that is lighter than Colum's tunic. We gather dried fruit and meat from a storehouse and fill waterskins from the well. Before going, I pull a banner down from the tower. We now have something to show our allegiance to Macduff. All the horses have been stolen, so Colum and I both ride Nocklavey, who is strong enough to carry double our weight. Because I am shorter, Colum lets me ride in the front.

It is easy to tell which way the king's men took after finishing their rampage. The road leading south is trodden and strewn with debris. Ross's men also went that way, according to Wee Duff. So we take the same road. The weak sun hides behind thick clouds, yet the heat rising from Nocklavey's back is enough to warm us.

I know each landmark in the Wychelm Wood as well as I know my own body, and Colum can traverse the shieling by smell alone. But for both of us Dunduff is the gateway to an unknown country. We have no idea how far it is to the River Spey, how wide the Grampian Mountains may be, or how we will recognize Angus's lands.

"If we ride south, as Wee Duff said, I can't believe that we would miss the river," he says. "But I don't like taking the road. We are as likely to run into Macbeth's men as Ross's."

The thought of meeting the murderers gives me chills. But what else can we do but follow the way and hope it leads to the river?

"We'll trust our luck, Colum, and keep the standard of Macduff hidden until we find our allies," I say, trying to sound confident.

His long legs grip Nocklavey's side, and his arm encircles me. Ever vigilant, our eyes scan the wide landscape. Instead of a grassy sea strewn with mid-summer flowers, a reddish brown terrain swept by harsh winds surrounds us. I wonder if the land will ever thrive again.

Meanwhile it seems that Nocklavey leads us, not that we guide him. Colum holds the reins slack. I hold on to Nocklavey's coarse mane and find that his strength reassures me. Finally I have the courage to ask Colum a question that has been bothering me since we left Dunduff.

"Colum, now that you know who I am, does it disturb you?"

I feel his arm stiffen around me. After a long pause, he says, "You are the same Albia you have always been."

But I am not the same. The knowledge of my past has changed me. Colum must sense that.

"Did you ever suspect there was something unusual about me?" I turn around in the saddle, trying to see his eyes, but we are too close. He looks over my head.

"I thought you were not much like your mother—like Geillis."

"I wonder what my mother *is* like. Grelach, I mean. Is she as coldhearted as my father?"

"If she is anything like her daughter, she must be strong-willed and hard to please," he says in a teasing tone.

I dig my elbow into him. "Those may be her *best* traits," I say with a wry smile.

"She must have some kindness in her, for your nature can be as soft as a lamb's coat."

I feel Colum's cheek resting upon my head.

"If I am at all good or gentle, that is due to Geillis's care," I say. "My own mother, you remember, left me for dead."

"You don't know everything that happened then. Perhaps she longs for you every day."

"She doesn't even know that I am alive. She never even tried to find me!" I am gripping Nocklavey's mane so tight my hands hurt.

"If she thinks you died, why would she look for you?"

Colum's reasonable tone only irritates me, and I toss my head impatiently.

"I only know that I never want to see her," I say, but my voice lacks the conviction that I intend.

"One more thing about your mother. She . . . must be very beautiful," says Colum in a low voice.

"Perhaps she is," I admit. "But it is my father's red hair and pale skin that I have."

Colum sighs. "I don't care if you were born from sheep-stealing wolves. I will always be your friend."

⟡

At the end of the second day of our journey, the River Spey reveals itself in the distance, a glistening gray ribbon winding through a wide, flat vale. By dusk we reach her banks, where grasses, crowberry bushes, and birch saplings flourish, a small paradise fed by the rushing river. Colum and I dismount, doff our weapons, and drink deeply.

But Nocklavey, though his mouth is flecked with foam and his sides glisten with sweat, shies back from the riverbank and will not drink.

"You gave him a fitting name," remarks Colum. "The monster Nocklavey could not abide fresh water."

Colum jumps into the river and while he splashes like a delighted child, I linger on the bank, cooling my feet and dipping my hands in the water. The swaying underwater grasses put me in mind of the thin arms of the Greentooth hag that stole away Colum's little cousin. Should I warn Colum to stay close to the shore?

Colum rears up out of the water, his long hair sleeked back from his face.

"Come in, Albia! If you cannot swim, I will teach you how."

There seems to be nothing to fear from this river. I take another step into the stream, feeling the slippery stones beneath my feet. The river tugs at my legs, inviting me into its cool depths.

Nocklavey lets out a high whinny of warning. I freeze in my footsteps, suddenly afraid of the swirling water. I hear his heavy hoof paw the ground and turn to see a man running toward us in a crouching position, a dagger in his hand. Does he mean to steal Nocklavey or to attack me? My shield and sword are lying on the ground near Nocklavey. It is easy to see that the man will get to them first.

"Colum, help!" I scream.

Nocklavey lightly leaps in front of the man, giving me time to dash from the water and grab my sword. The man tries to hold Nocklavey's harness, but with a swing of his great head the beast knocks him to the ground. He scrambles to his knees and lays his hand on his dagger, but I am already upon him.

"Don't move. Who are you?" I raise my sword over him.

The man lets out a garbled, throaty noise. I see that his clothes are torn and filthy with mud or maybe blood, and his feet are bare. But his arms are thick and strong. He could easily leap up and overpower me.

"Who are you? Speak!" I demand, louder.

"Is he alone?" asks Colum. Dripping with river water, he fumbles in search of his bow and arrows.

The man stares up at me. His mouth is a hollow O in his face, which is pale except for a mark like a splash of wine upon his cheek.

Rhuven has described this man to me. Fleance, too, knows his evil face.

"Eadulf," I whisper, my skin prickling with horror. "Murderer!" My sword-arm trembles with the desire to strike. "Do you know who I am?"

In a single motion he lunges to his feet, clutching the knife. I leap back, barely avoiding his blade, and bring mine down, cleaving the bones of his hand. The dagger falls from his harmless fingers.

"You'll never strike at me again, villain. Now speak, or I *will* kill you." I am so angry, all my limbs are trembling.

Eadulf's reply is a guttural howl from deep in his throat. His mouth opens wide in agony and a trail of bloody spittle drips from his lips as he stares at his broken hand.

"Albia, he cannot speak. He has no tongue!" cries Colum, seizing my sword-arm.

"By the pitiless gods," I whisper, staring at his mouth. "Who did this to you?"

With his good hand, Eadulf points to his head and makes a circling motion.

At once I understand. "Colum, it was the king! Macbeth punished him because he failed to kill Fleance as well as Banquo. Silenced him, so that he could never speak of his crime. Am I right?"

Eadulf nods. Then with further gestures he manages to convey that he meant only to steal the horse.

"Were you at Dunduff?" Colum demands. "Do you know what happened there?"

He shakes his head vigorously and indicates that he is alone, that the king drove him away.

"Colum, I don't trust him. He slew Banquo and tried to kill Fleance. If I were to kill him it would be a just revenge."

"Your quarrel is with the king, Albia; this man is only his instrument. A broken, discarded one at that." Colum begins to clean and bind up Eadulf's hand, using a strip of cloth from his own tunic.

"He doesn't deserve our mercy," I say, still holding my sword. I am wary, knowing that Eadulf's good hand could easily smash the side of Colum's head.

"Remember, he spared your life once before," Colum says softly.

"But he took Rhuven's virtue."

"A price she willingly paid," he reminds me, having listened well to my story.

Eadulf has been following our conversation, his eyes growing ever wider. Now he grunts with the desire to speak. He points to me, his hand circles his head again, and he makes the motion of cradling a baby, then points to me again. He is asking me a question.

"Yes," I reply, "I am the king's daughter. But no more like him, I pray, than the daylight is to the darkness."

At that Eadulf, careless of his broken hand, throws himself at my feet and wraps his arms around my legs, and by the noises coming from his throat, I think he must be sobbing.

Chapter 19

The Grampian Mountains

Albia

Eadulf will not be left behind. With fervent signs he indicates that he fears Macbeth and that he wishes to join us in seeking the rebels.

"What shall we do?" I whisper to Colum. "Unless we tie him up, he will follow us."

"If we leave him tied up here, he will die. We must bring him with us."

"Colum, you are too innocent. Even with an injured hand, he is still strong enough to harm us."

"Albia, I am certain he will not hurt you. Did you not see the look that came over him when he realized who you were? You are his savior."

Still I am reluctant. "Even if he does not plan to murder me, he might steal Nocklavey while we sleep. He has spent so long serving Macbeth, he must be a master of deception."

"Can't a man change? Look at him, as much a victim of the king as you once were."

Seeing Eadulf in pain and looking desperate, I wonder for a moment if he had been unwilling to murder Banquo. Did he let Fleance escape? And all those years ago, was he perhaps relieved not to carry out Macbeth's command to leave me for the wolves?

Colum's pleas finally persuade me to give the rogue a chance, and the three of us set out together. Eadulf travels on foot. He holds up his hands and will not come near Nocklavey, as if to assure us of his good intentions. For his part the beast eyes Eadulf as if warning him and stamps his mighty hoof, showing his strength.

Following the winding River Spey, we journey for several days, crossing the broad strath, the valley where the distant moutains can be seen disappearing into the clouds. We travel through groves of trees that close around us protectively, then open again into dales where the river spreads out like a lake. A few dwellings nestle at a point where a tributary stream flows into the Spey. As we approach, an acrid smell greets us. The huts seem deserted; one smolders from a recent fire. Nocklavey comes to a halt and throws his head to the side as if bidding us turn around.

"Macbeth's men are not far ahead," I say to Colum. "We are no match for them. Which way should we go now?"

Eadulf makes a noise to get our attention. Taking a stick, he draws on the pebbly shore and points to the mountains in the distance.

"The Spey flows on, then doubles back?" I ask.

Eadulf nods. He makes another mark on his map, then taps the ground firmly.

"Do you mean we should leave following the river and cross those mountains?"

Eadulf crosses his arms over his chest with a satisfied look.

"We might head them off and reach Angus's lands first," I say to Colum.

Together we gaze at the mountains, their steep sides streaked with snow. Their peaks are hidden. How high do they rise? I have no idea what to expect there.

"Those must be the Grampian Mountains that Wee Duff spoke of," Colum says, sounding awed.

Then I look at Eadulf and see not the man who killed Banquo, but one who wants, almost as badly as I do, to vanquish Macbeth. I will have to trust him.

"We will go the way you advise," I decide.

We turn our backs to the river and face the mountains. Soon we enter the fringes of a pine wood whose fallen needles soften our steps and deaden every sound. Unlike the arching wychelms, these trees grow straight and tall, their branches so far above our heads they would be impossible to climb. While the bracken and bushes are brown, the distant tops of the pines are still green, as if death has not yet reached that high.

There is no path through these untraveled woods. Fallen trees lie across one another, their trunks so thick that not even Nocklavey can leap over them. We backtrack around them and climb and climb, skirting ravines that open in the earth unforeseen. We cross icy streams and pass under cataracts that plunge from overhanging cliffs. We sleep in the caves that gape beneath huge boulders, making our beds from fern fronds and pine needles. Not a single berry on a withered bush remains for us to eat, but Colum has the luck to shoot a gray fox. It makes a small feast, and the fulness in our bellies distracts us briefly. But the uncertainty, like hunger, soon returns. How long will it take us to cross these mountains? What will we find beyond them? What if Eadulf leads us astray, by accident or intent?

The higher we climb, the colder the air becomes until our breath hangs in the air before us. Nocklavey's flesh, dark with sweat, steams. Then the pine forest suddenly ends and we find ourselves facing an implacable ridge of rock. Only the nimblest of mountain sheep could find a footing there. We dismount and Colum leads Nocklavey while Eadulf and I go on foot, seeking out a path. Our ascent is slow and perilous, but at last we reach the crest, only to see a higher one beyond, scattered with scree and snow. A cry of dismay escapes me but Eadulf, undeterred, plunges onward. Colum and I have no choice but to follow, stumbling on the loose rock and slipping in the snow. For two days we scramble up and down the steep faces. My feet, bruised by the rocks, ache with cold, and my hands are raw from gripping the rough stones. My recent fever has sapped my usual strength, and the muscles in my legs tremble from exertion.

The third night draws on since we left the Spey, and the fading light turns the snow-spotted mountainsides blue and gray. I ride Nocklavey to spare my sore hands and feet, while Colum and Eadulf scout ahead for the easiest passage. All at once an icy wind blows up as if from the rocks themselves, and huge flakes of snow swirl around me. Nocklavey and I are enveloped by a whiteness as all-encompassing as night. He stops, turns, takes a few steps, turns again, as if seeking a way out of this strange darkness. I no longer know which direction we are facing. The world has become invisible. We might be on a precipice, about to fall to our doom. But I cling to Nocklavey's mane, for I am less afraid to be on his back than on foot.

"Colum. Where are you?" I shout into the snowstorm that roars in my ears like a god who is angry that we trespass on his frozen lands.

No reply comes back to me. What if I cannot find Colum and Eadulf? How will any of us survive without shelter? I tell myself that Eadulf is not the sort to perish from a single night of cold. And Colum can make a fire anywhere, dry or wet. But what about me? I am already shivering like one with a deathly fever.

A low whinny reverberates in Nocklavey's broad chest. He throws his mighty head from side to side and steps backward as if avoiding some danger. The skin on my neck and arms begins to tingle.

"What is it?" I whisper, peering into the thick gray-white fog. I make out a dim shape near the ground, like a rock. But then it moves. A gust of wind scatters the snow and mist like a hand parting a curtain, and I see, not twenty feet away, a large gray boar with a long snout. I close my eyes and quickly shake my head to clear my mind of the dreamlike figment. But when I open my eyes, the animal is still there, snow on its back, its dark tusks curving upward in menace. It stamps the ground on short legs and lowers its head. My hand scrambles behind me for my sword, just as the beast begins to charge. I see its red eyes glowing like fiery embers the instant it leaps at Nocklavey. The furious horse rears up. Unprepared, I tumble from his back and my sword flies from my hand into the snow.

What happens next is as unreal as a dream yet vivid as life. The boar's tusk nicks Nocklavey, who roars in anger. His hoofs like anvils strike the stones, missing the boar that dances nimbly away despite its bulk, then comes at him again with greater fierceness, aiming for his flank. I clamber in the wet snow for the hilt of my sword, and finding it at last, leap up only half-armed, without my shield.

Then the boar turns from Nocklavey to me, perceiving an easier prey. Its tusks are red with Nocklavey's blood, and yellow fangs protrude from its snarling mouth. It fixes me with a malevolent stare and begins to circle me, like a foe waiting for the moment when I will try to flee. But I do not run. I feel as if I have drunk a potion that courses through my veins, making my heart race with the desire to fight. I plant my feet wide on the snowy ground and pray that I will not slip. The sword feels firm and sure in my grasp. I feint to the side and the boar, fooled, rushes toward me, but I reverse my step and the beast passes by me, so close that I smell its foul animal stench. I've missed a chance to strike it. The beast turns and paws the ground, snorts, then charges again. I do not take my eyes off of my target, its thick neck, and I bring down my sword there, but it glances off the boar's tusk with a force that sends a shudder down my arm and so angers the animal that it whirls around at once and lowers its head to lift me on its tusks. This time I bring my blade down on the monster's neck with a singing sound, cleaving skin and sinew and stunning the boar. My arms burning from the blow, I draw back and thrust my sword into its throat, just beneath the ear. A black stream of gore gushes forth, yet the beast, still strong, snaps its mighty jaws at me.

Then Nocklavey is on his hind legs, his mane flying, his flared nostrils steaming. His forelegs beat the air an instant before his huge hoofs deliver the final blow, snapping the boar's spine.

The boar's unearthly scream subsides into a rasping hiss, then silence. Its eyes are black and glassy, not red as they seemed before. Lying in the snow, I hear my own ragged breathing. My left thigh throbs with pain, and I realize that my leather leggings are torn. I am bleeding. The beast took a bite from me before it fell.

With trembling hands I touch the wound, feeling sick to see the torn flesh, but relieved not to see the bone beneath. It's too cold to remove my leggings, so I fold the torn flap over my wound and, using the girdle Fleance gave me, bind up my leg. I see that the cuts on Nocklavey's chest are small, for his hide is thick, but the boar gored his side more deeply, drawing thick blood. It looks like a wound that will fester.

As the fire that flooded my veins ebbs again, I begin to shake and shiver. Were it not for Nocklavey, the boar would have killed me. Standing up with difficulty, I seize his mane and pull myself across his back and lie there with the length of my body against his, my face resting on the back of his neck. Slowly his heat begins to warm me.

I can scarcely believe what I have done. I killed a boar to save myself and Nocklavey. Many times I have wept over a sheep slain to keep its sickness from spreading. But I feel no speck of regret at this deed. I did not think; I simply acted. This is how I want to be when I meet Macbeth: merciless and swift with my sword.

The snow has stopped and the light of dawn tinges the snow-covered rocks a pale rose, like blood diluted in a basin of water. I must have dreamt the silken-feathered swan whose brightness melted the snow into a lake for her to float upon. She swam up to me and touched my throbbing leg with her bill. I open my eyes to find myself still prone on Nocklavey's back. Remembering my battle with the boar, I look around but see no evidence of our encounter. Did Nocklavey carry me away from the scene while I slept? Or did I imagine the beast, raising it from the storm with my fears?

The bright girdle tied around my thigh is my answer. I touch it and feel a sharp pain. My senses do not fool me. The battle was no dream. I unwrap the cloth and see a ragged tear in my leggings. But when I probe within the tear, I do not feel the opening of a wound. The skin is intact, not even scratched. Confused, disbelieving, I tie the girdle around my leg again. Sliding from Nocklavey, I run my fingers over his flank, searching for the deep hole made by the boar's tusk.

I find it. A spot, no bigger than a man's thumb, like a dint in a shield, healed as if it happened weeks ago.

With the daylight, I do not recognize my surroundings as the place where the snowstorm struck. Nocklavey and I must have wandered far. Weak sunlight shines and I squint, unused to it. The sky is blue, and hints of color seem to touch the browned grasses and gray stones. The edges of the new snowbeds are melting and the water gurgles as it flows down the crevices in the rocks. To the sound I add my own voice, calling for Colum as I steer Nocklavey in one direction, then another. Finally I hear an answering cry and Eadulf comes into view with Colum a few steps behind.

"There you are, at last!" I cry, running to embrace Colum. The pain in my left leg causes me to limp. "How did you survive the night?"

My ardent greeting surprises him. "Why, we found shelter under a rock," he replies, patting my back.

"But it was a terrible snowstorm. Didn't you worry about me?"

"It snowed some, but I knew you were riding Nocklavey close by, and that we would meet up again. And so we have," he says cheerfully.

My reply is terse. "It seems we have not been on the same mountain. *I* was lost in a snowstorm and had to kill a boar who was about to devour me."

Colum lifts his eyebrows with surprise. "Did you? Where is it?"

"I don't know," I admit. "Somewhere in the snow." I can tell that Colum does not believe me.

Then the blue girdle tied around my thigh catches his eye. "Were you hurt? Let me see."

"Nay, it is nothing," I say with a wave of my hand. How can I explain the wound that disappeared overnight? Or the sudden appearance of the boar, when we had seen not a single such creature during our several days in the wilderness? Where had it come from, and why did it choose to attack me in the midst of a storm? I have no answers to these questions, but I know what *did* happen: I fought the boar, and with a strange, fierce relish, took its life.

Later when I am alone, I unwrap the girdle from my thigh. There is still no sign of a wound, nor is the girdle even stained with blood. I wrap it around my waist again, and think longingly of Fleance.

⚜

Our way through the mountains is becoming easier. The highest peaks are now behind us. Eadulf has brought us through a pass. Below, a string of lochs shimmers like a chain of blue gems leading out of the rocky wilderness. By holding up two fingers, Eadulf indicates that it will take us two days to descend the wooded mountainsides and reach the valley beyond the lakes.

What we will find there? Macduff's allies gathered on a plain? The king's men still on their killing spree? Perhaps no one at all. What if Eadulf led us on a long detour to prevent me from reaching Macduff's cousins? Or to allow Macbeth's party of murderers to find Fleance before I do? But if he meant us ill, it would have been far simpler just to kill us in the mountains.

"So the boar didn't leave a scratch on you?" Colum asks, interrupting my thoughts. He points to my torn leggings. "You were lucky."

"Yes, I was," I agree. "I wish I had cut off its tusk as a trophy."

But it is not the boar that interests Colum now.

"That blue girdle you had tied around your leg. You wear it all the time." Colum looks at my waist. "Where did you get it?"

"It was a gift."

"From . . . ," he prompts.

"Fleance," I reply, striving to keep my voice even.

For a while Colum doesn't speak. We walk side by side through the woods, Colum leading Nocklavey. The pine trees are so big that it would take six men with their arms outstretched to circle a single one.

"What is Fleance to you?" he finally asks. I see him struggling to hide his jealousy, knowing it is unworthy of him.

"He is Banquo's son, hence my foster brother," I say, feeling warm blood rise to my face.

Colum stops and takes my arm. "Look at me, Albia."

I glance up at him. His brown eyes are serious.

"What am I to you?"

"Colum, you are the dearest friend of my life," I say.

"No more than that?"

"What more could you be?" I ask, becoming exasperated. "I have known you since before I could walk." Then I say in a softer tone, "Do you remember how I followed you around then? I wanted to do everything that you could do."

Colum smiles, but it is a stiff one. He sighs and opens his mouth as if to speak. I turn away, for I am not ready to hear what I fear he will say.

"I see you often play with the ends of it," he says.

I look at him in confusion. Then I realize I am holding the end of the sash.

"You're thinking of him," says Colum softly.

"I . . . I wasn't . . . aware of it," I stammer.

But I do think of Fleance. I wonder if he cares for me at all or if he left in secret to avoid me. I remember what it was like to kiss him and wish I had not refused him the last time he asked.

"Is that the purpose of this journey? To take you to Fleance?" Dismay creeps into Colum's voice.

I feel the forest surround me. The pines stand as straight as arrows in a giant's quiver. Colum and I are mere specks. Our feet make no sound and leave no print in the earth. The wind in the pines seems to whisper, *Why have you come here?*

"Albia?" he prompts me. "Are we looking for the rebels, that we might help revenge the wrongs Macbeth has done you and all of Scotland? Or is it your desire just to find this fellow?" He presses his lips together. Then he blurts out, "You love him, don't you?"

"I don't know if I love Fleance!" I cry out. "Or if he loves me. He might be running away from me, for all I know. But still I need to find him, for he set out alone and Macbeth's men are looking for him even now. They mean to kill him, Colum."

"Because he is Banquo's son," says Colum, grasping the

situation. He looks grim. "I'm afraid we've lost time in these mountains."

Ahead, Eadulf waits for us to catch up. With long strides, Colum hurries toward him and I follow. The pines still whisper to me, *Why are you here? Where do you go? Whom do you seek?*

I wish I knew the answers. I can only hope that whatever I find, I am prepared to meet it.

Chapter 20

Dun Forres

Grelach

Rebellion threatens our throne. Banquo's death has roused his cousins Ross and Angus, and they have pulled Lennox and the others into their plot. Duncan's son Malcolm is in league with England and with his uncle, the powerful Northumberland. Anyone with eyes to see and ears to hear knows that our enemies are springing up like mushrooms on a rotten log. Only my fool of a husband does not see the danger. Rather, he sees what is not there—Banquo seated in an empty chair. And all the thanes beheld his madness! I could not persuade him that he looked at nothing. I remember the days when my lord called me his dearest partner of greatness and sought my advice before acting. Now he heeds none but that trio of unholy hags, from whose dark haunts he has just returned.

"Listen, Grelach," he commands, a strange excitement gripping him. "This time a different sister spoke to me and showed me sights meant to shake my courage," he says, his entire body quivering. "But I did pierce their doubleness and see the truth. Thus I am assured that none of woman born shall ever harm me."

I resist the impulse to laugh at him. "I think you are the one deceived. How can you believe that no one can kill you? Every man is mortal."

" 'No man of woman born shall harm Macbeth,' she swore. Tell me, who is not born of a woman?" His tone is brazen with confidence. "Why, even Christ was born of a woman. Thus not even God can touch me!"

Certainly he is mad. Why, I could kill him myself while he stands before me, raving.

"I tell you, fate favors me still." He strikes his breast with his fist. "I will not alter my course."

"You will have Macduff to contend with. Even the fateful hags say so. He is a leader among the thanes."

"Macduff and his sons are all dead by now, and soon Fleance, that spawn of Banquo, will also greet his mother earth."

"Has Eadulf . . . ?" I begin, dreading to hear that the unfortunate lackey has been sent to kill the boy.

"Eadulf has already been punished," Macbeth interrupts with a wave of his hand. "He will not speak of our deeds ever again."

I hear Rhuven, who has been sitting in the shadows, utter a cry as faint as a mouse's. What is that stupid carl Eadulf to her? She, too, has been acting strange lately, fearful of my lord, looking like a startled rabbit and wanting to flee when I have most need of her here. I make her lie in my bed, for nothing calms me but her presence there. When she was gone a few nights ago,

I cried and wandered in and out of Dun Forres, terrible visions arising in the blackness. The child plucked from my arms, her startled pale look. Duncan's innocent face bathed in blood. My husband's ruthless hands, reaching for me. I tried to push the dreams away and wake myself, but of course I was not even sleeping. I never do.

"The Wyrd sister showed me a parade of kings, all like Banquo," my lord is saying now. "But he is already dead! It was an illusion meant to frighten me." He laughs. "But it did not. For I shall never be vanquished until Birnam Wood comes to high Dunsinane."

Macbeth takes my wrists and draws me to him. I feel the heat of his body and smell its familiar, slightly rank odor. Ambition, that old desire, stirs in me again. Dunsinane Hill lies across the mountains, near Scone, where my lord was crowned. It is the best-defended crag in all of Scotland, with a fort built on foundations a thousand years old and a stone tower that will stand a thousand more. Could the Wyrd sisters be right that we are invincible?

Still I am suspicious. "What did they mean? How can Birnam Wood ever come as far as Dunsinane?" I muse aloud. "Seeds scattered in the glen would take a hundred years or more to grow into a forest. Not the strongest of them would take root on the steep and rocky face of Dunsinane Hill."

My lord smiles. "You see, my sweet chuck, it is impossible that we should fall."

Indeed, how is it possible? We are Scotland's king and queen. It was not fate that made us, but our own will and cunning. And these shall keep us on our thrones.

And yet. . . . My lord has killed one of his best thanes on the merest suspicion of betrayal. Discontent breeds among the rest. Rumor has it that Macduff is their leader.

"Beware Macduff," I whisper. "They warned you of him."

"I am not afraid of Macduff." There is now a settled stubbornness in his features.

"But your thanes betray you and flock to him."

"Do you doubt me, too, wife? Are you with me or against me?"

"Of course I am with you. Am I not standing here?" I can barely hide my impatience. "But I see a rebellion brewing against you."

"No harm will come to me," he scoffs.

"Don't be a fool! Defend yourself. My lord, we must go to Dunsinane," I plead, thinking of its double-thick walls, of safety beyond what Dun Forres or Dun Inverness afford. But this is not the plea to move my lord.

"To strong Dunsinane," I repeat, summoning courage into my voice, "where we will prove the truth of the Wyrd sister's words: that no man can harm you."

Chapter 21

Angus House in the Midlands

Albia

Once we leave the Grampian Mountains behind, the way is easy, taking us beside a river flowing through a pleasant glen. Arriving in a village we are directed to a stone and timber dwelling surrounded by defensive ditches—the thane of Angus's house. At the outermost defenses, Nocklavey snorts and tosses his great head as if demanding to enter.

"How shall we make ourselves known?" Colum asks. "For we are an odd trio to be coming to the thane's gate."

I glance at Eadulf, sturdy as an ox, but with his maimed mouth a dark O in his face. Colum wears his mail tunic over his shepherd's garb. Though he carries a bow and a quiver of arrows, his lean build shows his lack of battle training. I am wearing my war-gear, but my long red hair spreads out over my shoulders and back, revealing my sex.

"We will announce that we have come to join the rebellion against the king," I decide.

"Will you tell them who you are?" asks Colum.

"I will say that I am Banquo's daughter. That is no lie, for he considered me so."

"And we have come from Dunduff and seen the king's wicked work there," Colum adds.

"Yes. Then I will tell them that Macbeth believes his stronghold at Dunsinane to be unassailable. They will welcome the report."

Eadulf is shaking his head and trying vainly to speak. Colum and I glance at each other in confusion, able to determine only that he is afraid of Angus's men.

"We will protect you, Eadulf. You have brought us this far in good faith," Colum assures him.

I see Eadulf hesitate. Finally he thrusts his head toward the fort, consenting to go with us.

Colum dismounts from Nocklavey and leads him, while my legs cling to the charger's side to stop them from shaking. Eadulf follows behind. We approach the gate and, holding up Macduff's standard, announce ourselves. The gate opens to admit us, but once we are inside, nothing goes as planned.

"I know this man. He is the king's spy!" cries a guard, grabbing Eadulf.

"Nay, he is the king's victim, as you can see. Release him," I plead. "I will vouch for him."

"What—a lady, vouching for this murderer?"

The deep voice belongs to a man of almost giantlike proportions. He stands before us, unarmed but surrounded by members of his warband.

I take a deep breath before speaking.

"Oh, great Angus, kinsman to Banquo, the man I called father—"

My voice breaks. I have never spoken aloud with so many men staring at me. Some look surprised, others hostile, their hands touching their weapons. With halting words, I name myself and Colum and describe our journey from Dunduff through the mountains, assisted by Eadulf.

"Thus, having seen with our own eyes that King Macbeth is an evil tyrant," I conclude, "we are here to join you in restoring justice and order to Scotland." By the time I finish, I feel breathless and slightly dizzy.

The thane of Angus slowly claps his hands.

"A pretty speech from a pretty lass. Cousin Ross!"

A man with a brow like the precipice of a cliff detaches himself from the warriors and steps up to Angus.

"Ross, have you ever seen such a pair? A lady in arms escorted by a sort of huntsman?" Angus says in a tone of mock awe.

Fury rises up in me. Without even thinking how far I am from the ground, I slide from Nocklavey's back, stumbling as my feet hit the earth. Looking up into the stern faces of the thanes, I feel suddenly very small.

"How can you doubt me, lord? I have lost a dear foster father and his wife to the tyrant, and I fear for the safety of my brother, Fleance. I saw Macduff's slain family, all but the boy whom we saved. And you dare to laugh at me?"

Ross peers at me from beneath his daunting brow.

"You are traveling with Banquo's murderer. Why did you

not slay the wicked carl, unless you are are in league with him?"

My mouth is dry. I don't know what to say. I am truly in a bind, until Colum steps to my side and speaks for me.

"She almost killed him, but I bade her let him live. We trusted him and were not betrayed. Eadulf is no spy and neither are we. I am a humble shepherd, with no understanding of war and politics."

"And she?" asks Angus, regarding me with some scorn.

"You underestimate this lady at your risk, my lord. Albia has more than mortal knowledge of the king. Don't ask how she comes by it, but listen and heed her wisdom, for her very life is charmed."

I am surprised—and touched—by Colum's eloquence, but his tone of defiance worries me. Angus, however, seems merely amused. He walks around me, looking me up and down.

"What is it that you know, charmed lady?" he asks mockingly.

"I know that Macbeth believes Dunsinane Hill to be invincible—"

Angus interrupts me. "The king is already at Dunsinane with his men. We know the fort cannot be taken. Tell us something that we don't know."

Sweat prickles on my skin as I ponder my choices. Shall I tell them that Macbeth killed Duncan? The thanes already suspect as much. Shall I reveal that I am the king's daughter? That I have the Sight? That the king is doomed? I realize that I have not actually seen the king's end, how it will happen or when.

Or who will deal the fateful blow. Could I be mistaken about my mission? Is Macbeth's end merely my earnest but vain wish?

Angus and Ross frown at me, awaiting my words. They want an excuse to clap me in irons. I must speak with care.

"The king is full of superstitions, as you know. Of late a woman—a soothsayer—told him that he would not be vanquished until great Birnam Wood came to high Dunsinane Hill. This woman . . . is known to me," I add, seeing their doubtful looks.

Angus snorts. "How can such a thing happen?"

"If we cut every tree in Birnam Wood and with a thousand horses haul them to the foot of the hill, then build a great pyre surrounding it, we could smoke him out of his tower," says Ross. I think he is jesting. He looks at me with eyes that are no more than slits. "The woman is a liar."

My chest constricts so that I can barely breathe. I close my eyes and look deep inside for the old dream in which the forest moves. I remember pine branches upright and swaying, not being dragging on the ground or burnt. They are carried aloft, like standards. I hear the sound of marching feet and see warbands swathed in greenery advancing up a hillside.

"You must cut the trees and cover yourselves in the greenery," I say, my breath coming easier now. "Use the branches to hide yourselves, your horses, and your arms. Carry the saplings upright as you advance upon Dunsinane Hill, and you will bring yourselves unseen to the very foot of the hill from which you can surprise the king and take his tower."

"And when he sees the forest move, will he not suspect our ploy?" Angus demands. His feet are wide apart, his arms folded across his chest.

"He will not see it move, because he does not believe it to be possible," I say.

Ross shakes his head. "But his men will show him."

"And he will deny it."

"Deny his own senses?" Angus bursts out. "Rather, he will attack and slay us."

Even as they press me with their doubts, I grow more certain of my plan.

"If his own reason forces him to see the forest move, he will know that his downfall is at hand," I argue. "Then he will see the soothsayer's words fulfilled and be unable to fight against his fate."

"If she is right, we cannot lose," murmurs Ross. "We know how fitful the king's mind is. At the feast we both saw him gaze upon the air and swear it was a man seated at the table. Not even the queen could calm his madness then."

I can see that Angus is still not convinced. He looks at me hard, as if trying to force me to confess myself an agent of the king.

"Who is she, really, and how does she know this about Macbeth?" he asks Ross through clenched teeth.

Under Angus's suspicious gaze I grow more uneasy. I am afraid he will notice how red my hair is and guess that I am Macbeth's daughter. But everyone believes the king to be childless. What if Angus decides I am a sorceress instead?

But in the end I am spared more explanation, and we are allowed to stay at Angus House. We are even permitted to keep our weapons. Eadulf is put under guard, Angus promising that he will not be mistreated. Nocklavey is the object of many greedy-eyed warriors but will let none but Colum and me touch him. We take turns caring for him and that night I sleep in his stall, the only place I feel secure.

No one seems to have any news of Fleance, nor do they appear concerned by his absence. Someone supposes he is with the thane of Sutherland or the thane of Lennox. Perhaps he has met with Macduff returning from England. One thing is clear from the messengers galloping from camp to camp: the rebel thanes are closing in on Dunsinane like a knot in a rope.

Angus's fort bustles with battle preparations. Hammers clang upon anvils as smiths forge sword-blades, mail, and spear-points. Sweating slaves feed the fires and haul burdens on their bent backs. Rows of lathes scrape in rhythm as woodworkers carve shields, axe handles, and cart wheels. Leather crafters make harnesses and belts. I pause before a waist-high heap of leather strips and turn to Colum with a questioning look.

"Don't you see?" he says excitedly, picking up one of the long strips. "These are to bind the greenery to the warrior's bodies. The thanes have taken your advice."

"Yes!" I clench my fists and smile secretly. How I long to see the sight of Birnam Wood marching to Dunsinane! Yet so much is at stake, I should be terrified. For if the strategy fails, the defeat—and all the ensuing deaths—will be laid at my feet.

⚶

That night I dream of Fleance. His hands on mine, teaching me to hold a sword. His thick brown hair blowing across his face, my hands reaching up to push it back, touching his cheek. Fleance wrapping the blue braided sash around me, again and again. His mouth covering mine. A sob escapes me. I see my hand slapping his face, the hurt look in his eyes, my instant remorse. His blood-ied body slumped in the hall at Dunbeag, weeping for his father. I reach out to kiss him, but my hands grasp only dark, empty air. I wake up and find that my eyes are wet.

I pore over the dream as if it is a Latin text, looking for meaning—for a clue to Fleance's whereabouts, a warning image, a message about the future. Nothing comes to me. It was merely an ordinary dream built on memories and wishes, foretelling nothing. I press the sides of my head in frustration. What good is having the Sight if it doesn't show me what I need to see?

In the wake of the dream, restlessness comes over me. Within the walls of Angus's fort, I suddenly feel trapped. Every time I turn around, I see the same fellow nearby, a young man with straight black hair and serious dark eyes.

"See that carl over there? About your age? He watches us wherever we go," I whisper to Colum.

"The men all wonder at you, Albia," he says. "Can you blame them for staring?"

"This one does not smile. He is not admiring me. I think Angus has told him to watch me."

Colum shrugs. "Let him. You have nothing to hide."

"Why do the thanes still not trust me?" I grumble.

"They have to be careful, Albia. What they are doing is treason, and the price of it is death." Colum meets my eyes, and I see that he is aware of his complicity, of the price he, too, will pay if the rebellion fails or if we are taken for spies. I regret drawing him into this danger, which deepens every day.

"Colum, does it seem to you that we are being held here like captives of war?"

"Nay, for if that were the case, Angus would have taken our weapons away." He sighs. "You are too suspicious, Albia."

"Think about it, Colum," I insist. "We have been given no duties, no role in the preparations for battle. I am certain they mean to keep us here when they leave for Dunsinane. I can't let that happen."

"What will you do about it?" he asks, frowning.

It takes me a while, but I come up with a plan. "I will go to Angus now and tell him that I am leaving to find Fleance. If he refuses to let me go, then I know my suspicions are true."

"Why don't we just leave without telling him?" Colum suggests.

"No, that would alarm them. And we cannot leave Eadulf here alone. You must stay with him."

Colum looks hurt. "I have not come all this way to be parted from you at such a dangerous time."

"And I have not come all this way to be kept from my revenge by anyone!" I try to control my mounting frustration. "Whatever Angus says, I am leaving here tonight."

When I find Angus, I notice the black-haired fellow among his men. He seems to be the son of a thane, for his garments are fine and he carries a sword, but no one pays him much mind as they polish their weapons and play at dice. Surely he is a spy.

Angus laughs at my request. "It is the eve of a great battle, and she wants to go find her brother!" He looks from side to side, trying to draw Ross and others into his amusement.

Ross regards me warily. "I understand you are worried for Fleance, but what can you do for him? You are only a lass, and likely to come to harm yourself."

The thane of Ross may mean well, but his words anger me. It is all I can do to remain calm and wait for Angus's judgment.

"A lass or not, consider the harm she can do," says Angus. He jabs a finger at me. "With what you know of our preparations, you could go to the king and betray us."

"Who would believe me, a mere lass?" I ask, glaring at Ross. "But though I am not a man"—I raise my voice and meet Angus's eyes—"you may believe me when I say that I will give up my own life rather than Macbeth should rule Scotland any longer."

At this, several of the men glance up with sudden interest.

"Brave words," says Angus, clapping his thighs. "Go, then. But your companions . . . will stay . . . here." By the way that he draws out the sentence, his meaning is clear. If anything goes wrong, or if anyone gives the king information, I will be blamed and Colum and Eadulf will suffer.

I had not expected this. How can I put them at risk? And just why is Angus allowing me to leave? The thane and I lock eyes. Who will call the other's bluff?

It is my turn to speak. I take a deep breath. "I will do nothing to bring harm upon them. So, I go."

I turn to leave, but Angus calls my name sharply. He makes me wait while he and Ross confer. *So he thought I would back down!* I can barely hide my smile of triumph.

"We would not have you go alone, lady," says Angus finally.

"For your own safety," adds Ross, with a tone of apology.

Angus turns and scans his ranks. His gaze falls upon the young man with the black hair.

"Luoch. You will accompany her."

Luoch? Isn't that my brother's name?

Chapter 22

Dunsinane Hill in Perthshire

Grelach

My lord and I have taken refuge atop Dunsinane Hill, which rises far above the plain, its steep flanks strewn with scree, impossible to scale. The only path to the summit is defended with high stockades set in grooves of stone. The walls of the fort are many feet thick and made from oak logs and planks filled with earth and rocks, and the tower is built of dry stone and oaken beams. No king has ever been defeated at Dunsinane.

Warbands loyal to Macbeth approach Dunsinane from the north and south, camping on the plain below because the fort is too small to shelter them all. Day and night the sounds of their carousing drift up to me. My lord joins them, raising their mettle with his confidence. At night he retires to the fort for safety, bringing his officer Seyton and several thanes, including his new general, the aged Atholl. They fight each other, drink ale, and prick their bodies with needles dipped in woad, marking themselves for war.

It is noisy and crowded on this hill, but I may as well be alone.

From where I look, wooded hills stretch in every direction like a rolling brown sea. But instead of the churning surf and the shrieks of gulls, I hear the ghostlike cooing of the doves fluttering in the eaves. Where have the songbirds gone, with their merry notes? Perhaps they are all nesting in the great, thick Birnam Wood. Oh, breathe easy, Grelach! How should those trees move, unless the ground itself gape open and release their roots?

Is that how the end will come? Will Dunsinane Hill quake and crumble to the plain, burying us under rock and earth? I would prefer to die in my sleep. But such a quiet death comes only to those who deserve it—those who are innocent. *Duncan*. Did the old king die in his sleep or did he wake to feel the blade in his throat? Did he see his lifeblood spilling forth? Oh, the blood! The redness seeps from my own chafed hands, a stain that will only be cleansed when a second flood purges the wicked earth.

But Duncan's death is old guilt, old grief. Something fresher tears at me, strong enough to pitch me from this tower to the ground below. It is the sorrow that never leaves a mother who has lost her children.

For now my son—my only hope and comfort—has left me. He has abandoned his mother, and gone—I know not where. I should have seen the signs. When Macbeth was taken with the fit and thought he saw Banquo's ghost, Luoch could not hide his disgust.

"He is not fit to be king," he said to me the following day. "I spit upon his crown."

"You owe Macbeth the duty of a stepson and a subject," I rebuked him, pressing my hand over his mouth.

Luoch pushed my hand away.

"He has never been a father to me. He has no love for anyone but himself. Mother, he doesn't even love you."

I could not speak. I could barely breathe. How can a son see such things? And how dare he speak of them to his mother! Did Macbeth and I not hide our hate with shows of love?

"I have heard the rumors of his crimes, Mother," Luoch said, not sparing me with any tenderness. "I see his eyes with no spark of feeling in them." He paused and gripped me by the arms. "Tell me. Is it true that he killed Duncan?"

For years I feared this question from my son. I held him at a distance and forced his quiet compliance in everything. When did that wayward infant pulling at my breast, that sullen boy, become this man who will not be silenced?

"You must not ask me that." I shook my head. "I cannot speak of it."

"But I must know. Were you a part of it? And if you cannot speak, I will take your silence for guilt."

For a long moment we stared at each other, barely breathing.

"How could you, even for all the wealth and power in the kingdom?" His voice was thick with emotion. He glanced down at my hands. I had been rubbing them together with such force that the knuckles stood out. "They will never be clean," he said, and walked away from me.

"Come back, son!" I cried, clutching the air behind him. "You are my only hope, my future."

He looked over his shoulder at me.

"Mother, you are past any hope. And you are not *my* future. Therefore I must go."

And he left, and I wanted to weep, but of course my eyes were as dry as these ancient stones.

So I spoke of my grief to Rhuven, lamenting that Luoch's rejection was what I deserved for abandoning my daughter so long ago.

Rhuven said that I should not give up hope, that perhaps someday I might begin anew.

What feeble consolation. How shall I start over, when more than half of my thirty-one years has been misspent with Macbeth? Can the heart bloom again after it has long withered? I have not loved anyone since my daughter was lost to me. Not Luoch, not my husband. And Macbeth does not love me, as even my son knows. Oh, had we loved each other more than our own ambition, would there have come the son that would have satisfied Macbeth? Then there would have been no need for even that first crime.

Alas, it is too, too late for such supposings. Too late for regret or repentance.

I tell Rhuven she must leave me. "I am fated to end my life alone. I no longer care what happens to Macbeth. Let him live a tyrant or be killed by his enemies. Nothing matters to me."

"I will not leave you," she replies, almost in tears. "You are dearer to me than my own sisters. I will do anything for you."

Her devotion moves me. There is yet one thing she can do.

"I gave you a dagger, Rhuven, did I not?"

She nods, looking fearful at what I might ask.

"If we should be defeated here at Dunsinane, do not let Macbeth or his enemies touch me. Rather, you must take my life. Do it quickly and with a sure hand."

Rhuven shakes her head so hard that her braid whips from shoulder to shoulder.

"Never, my lady! It will not happen."

She wraps her arms around me and runs her hands from the top of my head to the base of my spine like she often does to calm me. This time, she is the one shaking, so I hold her and kiss her hair. We sit like this until we are both still.

I will not mention the dagger again. It was too much to ask her. No, I have enough mandragora to bring my ending, the quiet death that I desire. I am only sorry for Rhuven, my faithful gentlewoman, who will be the one to find my lifeless body and consign it to the earth.

Chapter 23

Near Dunsinane Hill

Albia

My mind is in a turmoil as I leave Angus House accompanied by the young man with the same name as my brother. We head southeast, toward Birnam and Dunsinane. Luoch rides a gray charger with a blaze of white across its muzzle. He seems as nervous as I am. But riding the proud and swift Nocklavey gives me courage, and I remind myself of how I killed the vicious boar with my steady sword, now ready at my side.

We barely speak, but from time to time eye each other warily, like foes measuring each other before an encounter. Whenever I take the lead, he goes ahead and cuts me off and alters our course, slowing us down, until finally I lose my temper.

"You are of no help in getting me to Dunsinane. In fact, you seem determined to prevent my progress!"

Luoch looks abashed. "The king's men are converging on Dunsinane from all directions. If we ride in plain sight they will see us."

I am impatient to be at the site of this stronghold, but I see the wisdom of being cautious.

"Then let us hide in the woods here until it is dark, when we can advance unseen," I suggest.

We find a secluded copse of linden trees and dismount, tethering our horses. Luoch lies down with a weary sigh, holding his short dagger folded in his hands. Moments later he is dozing. For a guard, I decide, he lacks vigilance. I consider going on by myself, but remembering that Angus is holding Colum, I sit down under a tree to keep watch instead. Whoever this Luoch is, he does not seem to have the ruthless nature of a warrior. His arms are thrown over his face as he sleeps. I watch his long limbs twitch, as if they are still growing. When he wakes up, I will rebuke him for being so careless.

The woods are silent for a summer day. I hear only the persistent notes of a bird, a rapid twitter that rises, then ends on a long, plaintive note. Is the bird calling for its mate? Or is it lamenting the lack of food for its young and the sun that no longer shines to green its nesting place?

Where are you, where are you . . . FLEE . . . ance?

As I listen the bird seems to sing my sorrows, too. Then from another tree comes a reply on the same mournful note.

Roaming in suffering . . . SCOT . . . land.

The two lone birds sing the sadness of this land, crushed under the heel of the tyrant Macbeth, and to their tune, I fall asleep.

Again I have my recurrent dream about the parade of kings, the last of whom holds a looking glass. Their faces, blank before, now are filled in with Banquo's features. *No, that is Macbeth's vision, not mine.* I try to shake my dreaming mind clear, but the vision grows even sharper. The last king's face is unmistakably Banquo's, his form as lifelike as Banquo himself. But he wears no crown; he is not a king after all. I seem to smell his sweat and ale as I lean over his shoulder to look into the glass. Then the dream-Banquo shifts the mirror so that its light glances from my eyes. He is holding it out toward me and nodding. I take the mirror and gaze upon its glassiness.

Like a pond where the ripples spread out and vanish until the surface is smooth, the mirror gradually reveals a face. It is not my own, but one I know almost as well, with its sardonic smile and determined blue eyes, the face of Fleance that I love and miss.

Then in my dream Fleance holds the girdle with its bright braided pattern. He wraps one end around me. I see and even feel his arms touching mine. Then he wraps the other end around himself and knots the ends together. There is no need to ponder the dream with my waking mind. I already know its meaning: that my fate is bound to Fleance's and has been since the day he gave me back the braid I broke, woven into the wondrous girdle.

The urgency of this knowledge awakens me. I feel in me Fleance's desire to destroy Macbeth and revenge Banquo's death. This we share. But Fleance yearns for more. That I also know, for in his dream-face shone the desire for greatness, that same ambition that drove Macbeth to his cursed crimes. No! My Fleance must not follow the king's way. I will find him now, before this day ends.

I leap to my feet, only to fall down with a startled cry. For a moment I think my weak leg has somehow betrayed me, until I feel the pulling on my ankles, and I realize that my feet are tied to the tree, and Luoch is nowhere in sight.

Damn him! The fellow has tricked me, made me the fool.

He pretended to be asleep, and once I fell asleep, he tied me up. I, not Luoch, am the careless one. And my blue girdle is gone from my waist! A wail of dismay escapes me at the loss of Fleance's gift. I fumble with the knots on the rope around my ankles. I will find Luoch and stun him senseless for stealing it. Then I realize that he is not so clever after all. Why would he tie my legs but not my arms? I wonder, rubbing my sore ankles.

Then I see the band of blue lying on the ground. My girdle. Relief floods me. I pick it up and a tingling sensation courses from my fingertips to my shoulders. And I know that while I dreamt of Fleance's touch, Luoch was removing my girdle and tying my hands with it.

"So much for my fateful dream!" I groan.

And yet I awoke with my hands free. Had Luoch bound me so poorly? Did I work the knots loose while I slept? I finger the girdle, remembering how I had wrapped it around the wound from the boar, which had healed overnight. Before that, it had prevented the king's hands from abusing me after the banquet at Dunbeag.

The truth dawns on me like sunlight. Luoch was unable to tie me up with my girdle. The knots fell away of their own accord. Only Fleance could bind me with it; only I could tie it in a knot that would hold fast, a knot whose purpose was to protect me.

I take the sash and pass it around my waist securely and tie the ends, feeling courage and strength fill me again. I whistle and Nocklavey whinnies and comes to me, his head lowered so that his nose nudges my arm. I leap onto his back.

"Luoch, you will soon know who I am!" I shout into the trees.

I barely touch Nocklavey with my heels, and he leaps in pursuit of the trickster, his mighty hoofs striking the earth like hammers, his nostrils steaming like a furnace.

The black-haired carl cannot hide his surprise when we overtake him in the woods. I cut off his path, giving him nowhere to run, and his gray charger cowers before Nocklavey.

"How dare you betray me?" I shout at him. "I came with you in good faith."

Luoch's eyes widen with amazement. "How did you get free?"

"Magic," I snap. "Why did you tie me up?"

"I wished you no harm. It was Angus who bade me restrain you."

"You are a villain to leave me like that, and a coward, to blame another!" I slide from Nocklavey's back, quickly unfix my shield, and stand with my hand upon my sword hilt. "Get down now and you will learn who it is you deal with."

Without hesitating, Luoch jumps down and draws his sword.

"Nay, girl, you shall know who *I* am!" he shouts back, his blue eyes blazing.

I swallow hard. I have no wish to match swords with this boy, who is taller and stronger than I am.

"I already know you," I say, taking a chance. I try to recall everything Geillis and her sisters told me about my brother. "You are Grelach's son. Your mother is ambitious for you, but the king will not call you his son. Is that why you seek his overthrow?"

I see that I have hit my mark. Luoch's face pales beneath his black hair.

"How do you know this?" His eyes narrow. "Who are you, a witch?"

I pull off my helmet and shake out my red hair.

"Do I look familiar?" I step closer, keeping an eye on his sword hand. "Look in my eyes. Do you know them?"

I see in his eyes a glimmer of recognition, but then he looks away and shakes his head in denial.

"Luoch, I am your sister, Albia, the daughter of your mother and the king."

"I had a sister." His voice comes out as a croak. "But she died. I hardly remember her."

"I was left for dead but Rhuven saved me. Here is proof, a gem that Macbeth gave to the queen—my mother." I raise my sleeve to show him the armlet, though I see that it means nothing to him. "Can you look at me and deny that I am Macbeth's daughter, that I have Grelach's eyes?"

Luoch stares at my face and my hair for a long moment.

"What do you want? Why have you come here?" he asks, sounding more confused than suspicious. "Are you ambitious for the throne, too?"

"Me—ambitious?" The thought makes me laugh. "No, I want only to see the end of Macbeth's reign. And . . . the safety of . . . someone I love." My voice falters despite my efforts to control it.

"Fleance," he says knowingly. "You spoke his name in your sleep. He is not your brother, if I am."

I blush, but cover it up with stern words. "And you are going to help me find him now, or be forced to fight your own sister."

"I will help you," Luoch agrees. "And I'm sorry for tying you up." He looks ashamed. "Angus can be cautious. He didn't even trust me at first, though he has known for years how much I hate Macbeth."

For a moment I almost feel sorry for Luoch. Clearly Angus sent him with me to keep him out of the way, and Luoch left me behind out of his own determination to join the battle.

"We'll show him," I say. "Let us make for Dunsinane double quick, lest we miss the battle. Fleance must be there by now."

But Luoch doesn't move. "Albia? Are you really my sister?" He tilts his head to the side boyishly.

Until now I have not let myself think about having a brother. I feel no kinship toward Luoch. He is someone with a different life from mine. We have nothing in common but the womb that bore us before we were aware of anything. But could we, over time, come to care for each other?

"I swear that I am your sister." I force a smile as I say this.

"Then I am glad to know you, Albia." Luoch's smile is genuine.

The words come out of my mouth before I can think. "Luoch, tell me about my mother. What is she like? Is she beautiful?"

At once his smile fades.

"I cannot bear to think of her, even less to speak of her," he says. "Aye, she *was* beautiful, once. But Macbeth destroyed her beauty and her goodness." His dark eyebrows almost meet as he scowls. "Together they have done unspeakable wrong. Now there is no hope for her."

"You also know . . . about Duncan?" I whisper, stunned.

Luoch glances away. When his gaze returns to me, I see his eyes are moist. But when he speaks, his tone is rough.

"Grelach has nothing to offer you. Forget her, as I have."

Chapter 24

Dunsinane

Grelach

Cries and clashes rise from the plain, resound off the rocks. Breathless messengers run in and out of Dunsinane, bringing reports of battle and bearing Macbeth's orders back to the field.

With oaths and curses, my lord rages against the rebellious thanes. His mighty arms are painted blue-black from the shoulders to the wrist. He strides back and forth in this room that is too small even for what remains of his ambition. And yet it will take more than mortal strength to escape from the noose that now tightens around Dunsinane.

A whey-faced lackey runs in, breathless. "Malcolm's soldiers number in the thousands," he reports. "Siward, Earl of Northumberland, is among his allies."

So Duncan's son has arrived to seek his revenge, joined by his uncle, England's most powerful earl. This is grave news indeed.

My lord merely scoffs and says, "Who is Malcolm but a man born of woman and therefore damned?"

The lackey backs out of the room, fear and confusion on his face.

Two more messengers arrive with the news that the thane of Caithness and Atholl, my lord's newest general, have deserted. I hold my breath as they speak.

"Cowards! Let them fly all, till Birnam Wood come to Dunsinane," Macbeth snarls, wolflike.

The messengers stare at him as at a madman. I push them out of the room, afraid of what they will say next. It cannot be long before Macbeth learns that Luoch is among the rebels, and my father, too. He will accuse me of treason and no doubt slay me on the spot. And though I do not love my life, I—not he—will determine its end.

My son—how proud he makes me by standing against Macbeth! It is a risk to gamble on the king's fall, but it is the the only way for him to rise. And rise he will, my son, descendant of a king, once Macbeth falls. We will be reconciled, and I will forgive him the pain he has caused me, for it is only natural that a son leave his mother in order to become a man.

My thoughts are interrupted by Seyton, my lord's officer.

"I looked toward Birnam, and . . . saw the trees begin to . . . to move," he announces, stammering in surprise.

My heart pulsing in my throat, I run to the window, but the high, sharp palings block my view of the woods.

"That is impossible! You are a liar and a slave," cries my lord, beating Seyton about the head. "Go, bring me my armor. I will meet them on the plain below."

The frightened Seyton leaves. My lord begins talking to himself as if I am not even in the room.

"I have lived long enough. My course of life is dry and withered," he laments, rubbing his head with his great, thick hands. I see silver hairs glinting among the red ones. "I know no honor, love, or loyal friends, but only curses and false speaking."

There was a time when the anguish in his voice would have moved me to comfort him. That time is gone. He deserves every stab of self-torment and more. I will not reassure him. I cannot even bear to touch him anymore.

Seyton returns with my lord's hauberk, helmet, and greaves and dresses him in silence, placing his crown in a groove over his helmet. Then without so much as a word to me, his wife of seventeen years, Macbeth strides off to fight his fiercest foes, the men of Scotland who once served him.

"My lord—" I start to say.

He turns around. His eyes are invisible, shadowed by his helmet.

"Nothing," I whisper, shaking my head. I don't know why I called, what I thought I would say to him.

"I go now, Grelach. I will fight till my flesh is hacked from my bones. Seyton, give me my sword."

Their footsteps retreat, and the jingling of the mailed hauberk grows faint.

The end is almost come.

"Rhuven!" I cry. "To the tower!"

Chapter 25

Between Birnam Wood and Dunsinane

Albia

In the woods of Birnam, chopped saplings and branches leave a trail like the wake of a warship at sea. Luoch and I follow it, knowing it will lead us to the plain before Dunsinane Hill. The battle is already engaged. I hear shouts and curses, animal cries of pain, the clash of steel on steel, the neighing and stamping of horses, all growing louder as we come to the edge of the forest. My mouth is dry and my pulse is beating fast, but I urge Nocklavey forward. If I once stop, I may lose all courage, turn, and run the other way.

"Albia, wait!" Luoch calls to me. "We cannot just blunder out there. We might fall directly into the king's hands."

"Yes, but how else can we find out where our allies are? We can't see the field because of the trees."

Even as the wood thins near its edges, the rise of land prevents us from glimpsing more than the tower atop Dunsinane Hill. I consider venturing out, using branches for cover. Then my eye falls upon a lone elm with high, spreading branches.

I draw Nocklavey close to its trunk. It takes me only a moment to shed my plated tunic and helmet. Standing on Nocklavey's wide back, I can just reach the lowest branch. Using all my strength, I pull myself up while walking my feet along the trunk until I have gained the branch. A squirrel clinging to the bark flicks its bushy tail at me. I right myself and stand up, holding the trunk for balance. My legs are not even shaking. Exhilarated, I reach for the next limb and find a foothold on a knot in the trunk. Soon I have gained two more limbs and the ground is far below me.

"Luoch, follow me!" I shout.

Confident now, I climb upward. A sparrow hops from branch to branch, as if guiding me. Soon I can see over the trees and down the slope to the wide field of battle. Luoch joins me on the branch, breathing hard. Together we study the scene below.

Thousands crowd the plain, so that the ground itself seems to undulate with horses and footsoldiers brandishing weapons and waving banners. Men battle one on one, two on one, three on two, swinging swords and axes and knives. They grunt and scream as their bodies and shields thud dully against one another. Men stumble over their fallen fellows and are soon trampled in the mire. Their swords fly from their hands; disabled shields, shot full of arrows, drop to the ground; bright standards fall in the dirt, and men raise their arms in desperate surrender.

From the south a triple line of horsemen, their lances thrusting out from a wall of shields, advances against a ragged row of men on foot with spears and cudgels. The footmen scatter and fall back upon themselves like a wave, crushing one another. Then archers behind a palisade on Dunsinane Hill unleash a volley of arrows that sing through the air and clatter like hail on the horsemen's shields. The barbs find soft flesh, and wounded soldiers slide from their horses' backs, while the beasts themselves fall with lances stuck in their throats, screaming like demons from the Under-world.

Who can tell one thane from another under their helmets and hauberks? Who fights for Macbeth, and who fights against him? And where is Fleance in all this confusion?

But Luoch has assessed the situation. He points out the Englishmen commanded by Malcolm, the archers and the infantry that belong to Macbeth. Then I recognize Macduff's red and gold standard at the foot of Dunsinane Hill, where soldiers assault the defenses that, once breached, will open the way to the fort above.

"Fleance must be there, and Macbeth as well. We will join the battle at the foot of the hill," I decide, and Luoch nods in agreement.

Descending the tree proves trickier than climbing it. When my left foot touches Nocklavey's back again, I feel an ache there, a reminder of my old weakness. I seem to see my infant self, lying on my back beneath a tree, filled with wordless longing.

"Luoch, do you know, I have never climbed a tree before," I announce with a wide smile, forgetting for the moment the dangers before us.

"Sister, everything about you surprises me," Luoch replies with grudging admiration.

Once armed again, we skirt the field, then fly into the fray so swiftly that none can stop us. A great din assaults my ears; the smells of muck and blood and sweat sting my nose; lances, stones, and arrows fly all around me. But Nocklavey, like the prow of a great ship, divides the sea of foes. I see the startled faces of men who stop their fighting to stare at me, and I realize that my red hair, stirred up by the wind, rises like flames from my head. Doubtless they have never seen a woman in battle before.

"Fleance, I am here!" I shout, but my voice is lost in the mayhem like the mewing of a kitten. I want him to know that I have come. But seeing me might only distract him. Rather, I must focus upon my own revenge.

My eyes search through the thick crowd of identical-seeming warriors for the one who must be the king. It is like looking for a single stone on the wide strand. Suddenly Nocklavey rears up and a high shriek issues from his throat. Has my valiant partner and protector been shot? I lose my grip on his mane and slide back over his haunches to the ground, then leap to my feet. Nocklavey's hooves find the earth again, scattering men before them. They strike the earth again—at the very feet of Scotland's king.

Macbeth stands before me, his legs planted wide apart, his thick arms painted with battle-marks as they were that long-ago night on Wanluck Mhor. I hear him breathing hard and fast. Or is it Nocklavey beside me whose mighty nostrils flare like a bellows? Thick red hair, damp with sweat, curls from beneath the king's helmet. I cannot see his eyes, but I sense their black malevolence. His sword is drawn, and his crown gleams dully, like a tarnished metal toy.

This is my chance. Here is my final test, for which the battle with the boar was but a trial. This time I must gain the advantage, strike the first blow.

I find my balance, lunge forward, and swing my sword. It strikes the king's forearm, glancing off his metal greaves. *What have I dared to do?* I raise my shield, bracing for his counterblow, knowing that I am no match for this warrior-king. His arm is as thick as my thigh. A single stroke of his blade would kill me.

But the king does not even lift his sword.

"So this is how the soothsayer deceives me," he says slowly. " 'No man of woman born shall harm Macbeth.' " A bitter laugh escapes him. "Nay, a *woman* is to be my downfall." He lifts the helmet from his head, drops it on the ground, and replaces his crown.

Now I see his eyes. They are dark, not with the evil I expected, but with something more like sadness.

I had planned to cry out loudly and charge him with all his crimes, but I find I cannot speak. I see that he knows me and why I am here, and that is enough.

"Come, daughter, break my limbs and take the flesh from my bones. I have wronged you, I have wronged your mother, and death is all I deserve." He kneels and presents his neck to me, inviting the blow.

Time seems to stop. The king and I are alone on the battlefield. I raise my sword, using both hands, and feel the jeweled armlet tighten as my muscles tense beneath it. With one blow I can avenge years of wrong, free Scotland from tyranny, and be hailed as a liberator. Like floodwater, the blood rushes in my ears, the blood I share with Scotland's king. The blade in my hands quivers with longing.

But how can I slay my own father? What kind of monster would that make me?

Inch by inch I lower my sword until its tip touches the ground. I realize that I do not want to kill him with my sword. Can it be that I want to touch him with my hand instead? But I do not, yet.

"Renounce the throne, let the thanes choose a new king, and I will show you mercy," I say, struggling to hold my voice steady.

The king's head is level with my shoulder. I can see a struggle playing out on his face. The moment is brief, but it seems long.

"It shall be as you say." He lays his sword on the ground. "I am finished."

"Luoch, be my witness to this!" I cry, but my brother is out of my hearing, fighting somewhere on the field.

And then I see a man in a red and gold tunic, hewing his way toward us with a sword in each hand, his vengeful gaze fixed on the king.

"Turn, hellhound, and fight!"

The king rises slowly to his feet and turns toward the voice.

"Macduff, my soul is too much charged with blood of yours already. I will not fight with you."

"Put on your helmet and fight me, dog."

"I am already vanquished," says the king. "By this woman—"

Macduff does not even glance at me.

"Have you yielded, coward, just to save your life?" He spits out the words. "I'll put you on show in a cage, like a rare beast, and have it written: 'Here you may see the foul tyrant.'" He raises a woad-painted arm, as mighty as Macbeth's. His sword is already bloody.

Goaded by Macduff, Macbeth picks up his sword again. His eyes now blaze like a fire banked for the night and rekindled in the morning.

"Then lay on, Macduff! And damned be him that first cries 'Enough.'"

Macduff drops his second sword and rushes the king, who raises his shield and nimbly sidesteps Macduff's blow, then counters with his own, so that the thane's shield shivers and cracks. Back and forth they strike, blow for blow, the two men equal in strength and evenly armed. But the king lacks his helmet, which he removed when he knelt down. Now his head, with its insubstantial crown, is as vulnerable as an egg.

Soon both men are bleeding from their several wounds, yet their rage only increases. I watch in horror, not knowing whom to hope for, when Macduff's blade glances off the king's bare head, bounces from his shoulder, then finds the soft flesh where the lifeblood throbs in the neck. Macbeth greets the ground, and his crown tumbles from his head.

⤞⤝

A cry goes up and, like a ripple when a stone is thrown into a pond, spreads from man to man.

"The king is dead! Macbeth lives no more! Scotland is saved!"

The news flows across the battlefield, and the combat grinds to a halt. My brother reappears, bleeding from a gash on his leg.

"Luoch shall be king!" someone shouts, and others begin the chant, "Hail, Luoch. Hail, Luoch."

"The tyrant's stepson?" cries an angry voice. "Never."

"But he fought against Macbeth. He is blood-kin to the great King Kenneth."

Curses and shoving commence between Luoch's supporters and his detractors. Macduff's men seize Macbeth's, who flee to avoid being taken prisoner.

"Who is that woman?" I hear someone shout. "Did you see Macbeth kneel to her?"

"Is she a foreign queen?"

"No, she is the witch who unmanned him."

Luoch grabs my hand and pulls me down. Together we crouch beside the king's body. "Cover your hair. Put it under your helmet somehow," he orders me. "Who knows what this rabble will do now!"

I hurry to obey him, but I have too much hair, so I end up stuffing it down the neck of my tunic instead.

Then I see the tears on Luoch's cheeks. They surprise me at first. Macbeth was not Luoch's father. Yet he did raise the boy, who suffered his insults while hoping one day to be recognized as a son. No wonder he grieves. I look at my father's dull and sightless eyes, black as peat, his mouth half-open where his last breath escaped him. I feel no sorrow, only a deep peace, despite the chaos around me. And a sense of release, as if my soul, not my father's, has been freed from the world's cares.

I touch the king's arm. It is still warm.

"I suppose I shall have to tell my mother," sighs Luoch, looking toward the tower atop Dunsinane Hill.

I follow his gaze. My heart seems to turn over in my chest.

"I will come with you, Luoch," I hear myself say.

Chapter 26

Dunsinane

Grelach

A raven perches on my window ledge, its feathers black as my lord's eyes. I wave my arms and the ill-omened bird flies up into the gray sky, cawing and shrieking. A moment later it is back in the same spot, peering at me with glittering eyes. Its fateful presence chills my blood.

"Rhuven, come. I must have light. Bring me a taper."

She stands at my elbow, speaking softly. "There are a dozen burning already, my lady. I have no more."

Seyton bursts into the tower room, his tunic torn and blood-soaked. It was midday when he and my lord left for the field, and now night draws rapidly on.

"How fares the king against his foes?" I ask. Despite everything, I expect to hear that he has vanquished them, for when has ever failed to win a battle?

Seyton crumples, his knees hitting the floor. "My lady, the king has been slain by the traitor Macduff."

This news confuses me. I thought Macduff and his family

were dead. Did the thane somehow escape? Why didn't Luoch and my father slay Macbeth? Then they could claim his crown. It must not fall to Macduff or anyone else!

"Did you hear me, lady?" Seyton says, louder. "We cannot hold Dunsinane or protect you now."

Rhuven leaps up, as if she has been waiting for this moment. "Let us flee now, Grelach, before they reach the tower."

"What about my son?" I demand of Seyton. "Was he victorious?"

"I dread to tell you this, my lady, but Luoch has been taken captive by Malcolm, who acclaims himself the king."

"That cannot be!" I exclaim in a rush of irritation and dismay. Luoch should have roused the others to support him. But no, he let himself be taken by Duncan's worthless son. My last hope, gone. My son, too stupid to be a king.

"Then is Fleance, Banquo's son, also dead?" I ask, trying to recall what the Wyrd sisters showed my lord.

"I do not know. The dead are too numerous to count. Their bodies are ruined, some beyond recognition."

At the thought of all those deaths, a wave of weariness and despair rolls over me, leaving my limbs heavy and weak.

"Why do I yet live?" I murmur.

"My lady?" asks Seyton, anxious.

"Nothing. It is finished, Seyton. You are done. Go. You also, Rhuven. Save yourselves."

Seyton disappears in a flash, but Rhuven does not move.

"I will not go unless you come with me," she says firmly.

"In a moment, Rhuven." I hold up my hand. "First gather my jewels together and fetch my cloak."

While Rhuven is busy, I pour the mandragora into my cup. A week's worth I have hoarded, a deadly dose. I go to the window. The raven has flown away. Dunsinane is deserted, at least until Macduff and Malcolm arrive to claim it. I sip the thick, strong liquid. It will numb all my limbs so that I will not feel the fall. Rhuven will find my body. Will anyone in all of Scotland, besides her, weep for me? No one weeps for Macbeth. Not even his wife.

I lean from the tower window, one hand on the ledge. Down among the stones, in the gray murk of dusk, a white shape catches my eye. Is it a deer? It stands unmoving, giving off a silvery glow. Am I asleep and dreaming already? How quickly this poison works! I breathe its heavy sweetness. The cup is still almost full. I lift it to my lips again.

"Grelach, no!" comes Rhuven's startled cry. She throws her arms around me and the cup flies from my hand, spilling the red liquid into the gathering night. Seconds later the brass cup clatters on the stones below.

"Rhuven, do you see the white deer, too?" I ask in a daze, forgetting the cup. "Or have we frightened it away?"

With her arms still around me, Rhuven glances out the tower window.

"Aye, I see the deer. She beckons us. We must follow now, or lose sight of her. Come."

I let Rhuven lead me from the tower. Down the ladder, step by careful step, from the deserted fort, and down the steep path on the hill's far side, for this is the way the deer went, Rhuven swears. I hear the dull commotion of the battle's aftermath, but soon the sound fades and we come to a barrow half-hidden in the hillside. The mandragora, though I sipped but a little, has made my limbs feel like lead, and I beg Rhuven to let me rest here for a while. She protests, but my body has already succumbed to a heavy, dreamless sleep.

When I open my eyes again, it is still night, but I can see Rhuven's face as plain as in the day, for the moon is shining on the horizon. I stare at it with awe. When have I last seen the moon?

"I had to wake you, my lady," Rhuven says, an urgency in her voice.

I sit up, at once alert. Has the white deer led us not to safety, but into a new danger?

"Now that Macbeth is dead," she says, "I must tell you something—a secret I have kept for years."

"Rhuven, we have no secrets from each other," I say with a sigh. "You have been with me since I was a mere girl."

"I pray you will forgive me for holding it so long. It has been a heavy weight on me."

"What do you know of the burden of secrets?" I say bitterly. I stand up to stretch my limbs.

"Listen to me, Grelach!" she pleads. "Your daughter—"

I cover my ears with my hands. "Do not remind me of old griefs!"

Rhuven takes my hands in her own and whispers, "She lives."

"My daughter has been dead these sixteen years," I say sharply. "Macbeth was mad when he swore he saw her. How could you believe him?"

"Because he *did* see her. She *is* alive, and I have seen her."

I stare at Rhuven, stunned. In all my life I have trusted no one more than her. But now I learn that even she deceived me.

"Then you lied before . . . when you told Macbeth you saw her body." My mind forms the words slowly. "Why should I believe you now?" I pull my hands away from her grasp.

"Because I am the one who saved her life when she was a baby. I took her to my sisters, who raised her in secret. Then Banquo and his wife fostered her, and that is how the king came to see her at Dunbeag. I know it seems impossible, but it is true."

I can only shake my head and wonder, What is true? Is Macbeth truly dead? I have not seen his body, though Seyton did. Does my daughter truly live? Rhuven claims to have seen her. Rhuven has known all along!

"Why did you hide this from me?" I demand. "Why? How different my life would have been, if I had only known!" I clutch my head to stop the whirling of my thoughts.

"Listen, Grelach," cries Rhuven, now in tears. "I hid the truth in order to spare three lives. You would have sought her out, and then Macbeth would have killed you both, and me as well."

I see that Rhuven did what she had to. I must not blame her, yet I am still angry. Not at Rhuven, but at my lord, for taking my daughter away. I have lived with this anger for sixteen years. Then it comes to me: Macbeth is dead, and I am free. Free to seek my child.

"What is her name?" I whisper.

"Albia."

I turn the name over on my tongue. I wonder if she looks like me.

"Does she know about me? Where is she?"

"I don't know where she is now. But aye, she knows the truth. It has made her confused and angry." Rhuven sighs. "Banquo's death has also made her want revenge. She was seeking Macduff—"

"Then she is also against me!" I wail. "Must my children both despise their mother's weakness? Alas, I deserve their hatred. Rhuven, you should have let me die."

Rhuven takes me by the shoulders. "You must not despair, my lady. We will find her and I swear by the face of Banrigh and the soul of Saint Brigid that you shall be reconciled."

I look upward. Above Rhuven's head, the white moon seems to fill the sky. Now even the stars are visible, flickering like countless tapers. My heart expands within the cage of my ribs.

I will find my daughter. I will ask her forgiveness. One day I will hear her call me "Mother." I will wait as long as it takes.

Chapter 27

Dunsinane

Albia

Luoch tries to change my mind.

"I don't think you should come. My mother is not well. Her mind is disturbed."

"I know," I say, meeting Luoch's eyes directly. "For she is as guilty as Macbeth."

Luoch looks away. I can see he is ashamed.

"If we go together, it will be easier for us," I say.

"But it will be hard on her. She thinks you are dead," Luoch reminds me.

"Hard dealing is what she deserves," I reply in a grim tone.

Luoch sighs. "Then let us go, before she hears the news from someone else."

I am eager to get out of this confused mob before Luoch and I are injured. But we don't have the chance. We are standing beside Macbeth's body when six horsemen, their mail-coats jingling, draw up on steeds decked with bright trappings and encircle us. The foot-warriors fall back, all except for Macduff.

Seeing the foremost rider, Luoch whispers, "It is Duncan's son Malcolm!"

But my eyes have passed over Malcolm to rest on the rider beside him, a lieutenant resplendent in a blue-trimmed hauberk and holding a shiny brass helmet under his arm. Its brightness makes me blink and tears fill my eyes. For the rider is Fleance, and he is unharmed.

I put my hand over my mouth to keep from shouting his name. My legs tremble with the desire to run to him. But Fleance doesn't notice me. His eyes are focused on the dead king. Out of respect, someone has placed his dented crown upon his chest.

Macduff steps forward and describes with quick words his triumph over Macbeth, then sweeps up the crown and with a grand gesture offers it to Malcolm. A roar erupts from his men. Luoch and I remain silent. Is this our mistake? Or is it merely that we stand over the king's body, as lambs will often stay beside the body of their tup who has died?

At a nod from Malcolm, two of his men take hold of Luoch and me, disarming us. For a moment I am too stunned to speak, then I begin to struggle. Luoch demands to be released, but Malcolm only laughs.

"You are Macbeth's stepson, the queen's son, and you have some supporters here. But I am Duncan's son, and I will rule Scotland now."

My efforts to free myself have made my hair come untucked, and now it flies about my head. Malcolm turns to me in surprise.

"What have we here? I heard report of a woman on the battlefield but took it for a legend. Who are you?" he demands.

Before I can reply, Luoch speaks out. "She is my sister, and you will not harm her."

Malcolm looks confused. He dismounts and stands before me, peering at my face. "What sister? Is this a family conspiracy then?"

"Unhand me, and let me speak!" I cry. The guard loosens his grip and I shake my shoulders free. "I am the daughter of Macbeth and Grelach, long lost but now returned, not to claim any rights for myself, but only to help unseat the tyrant." I pause to take a breath. "This I have done, yet you treat me like a foe."

"Valiant words," says Malcolm in a wry voice. "Yet for all I know you fought beside him, then when he fell you switched your allegiance."

"I did not," I protest.

Malcolm only shrugs. "It is what they all do," he says. "But I will not be fooled."

"My words and faith are true. This man will vouch for me." I turn to Fleance, my lover, feeling triumph at hand.

But Fleance is staring at me, a look of shock and disbelief on his face. His mouth opens as if to speak, but he can only shake his head.

"Fleance, you know me. Tell them who I am," I plead, growing alarmed.

Then I realize that I never told Fleance who I truly am. Until this moment he did not know that his mortal enemy, Scotland's king, was my father. I kept the truth from him, and now it emerges too late to help me.

Fleance says not a word as Malcolm's soldiers lead me away.

⚘

They take Luoch and me to the fort on Dunsinane Hill. It is a steep climb and I stumble frequently, for my hands are tied together. Macbeth's men have all fled and Dunsinane is deserted. There is no sign of Grelach there.

Luoch's spirits are sunken, for Ross and Angus would not vouch for him. They conferred with Malcolm and agreed that we both should be imprisoned because of the danger we pose as kin to Macbeth and the queen. I reminded them all that my Birnam Wood strategy led to their victory, but they only shook their heads and murmured something about sorcery. In words as dire as I've ever spoken, I warned them that if anything happened to Colum and Eadulf, they would see what sorcery can do. They did not laugh at this. Only I knew that the threat was an empty one.

And now that they have left us here, my spirits fall as low as Luoch's. I am afraid of the harm that must come to Colum because of today's events. At least my loyal friend will never believe anyone who claims that I betrayed him. Not so Fleance. To discover that I am the daughter of the king who killed Banquo and Breda! To see me come to Dunsinane in the company of Eadulf, his father's murderer! How can he ever trust me again? No, I have lost his friendship and all hope of his love.

I wonder dismally how my search for truth, my desire to see justice restored in Scotland could have ended like this: with me imprisoned in a windowless cell in the dead king's stronghold. Why did I think that I could fix the ruin Macbeth and Grelach made? I am a fool indeed. In all of Scotland, there is no one to help me now.

⁂

The sound of voices awakens me. Malcolm and his guards are in the next room where Luoch is being held. It must be morning now, for light streams in at a door or window somewhere. Perhaps they have come to free us.

Then I hear Luoch's voice, a high, keening wail. "Oh you gods, pity her soul!" Then it sharpens with anger. "She would not take her own life. She was killed. Murderer!"

There are sounds of a scuffle. I hold my breath, stunned. The queen is dead? Was she stabbed? My *mother* is dead. Now I will never know her. Regret mingles with horror at the thought of her dying within these very walls. But I feel no sorrow, except for Luoch's sake.

Outside my door, I hear Malcolm dismiss his guards. Then he comes into my cell and locks the door behind him. With my eyes I measure him, Duncan's elder son. He is not tall or muscular, but his head is very large. He tilts his chin upward as if to seem taller. It only makes him look proud.

Malcolm also studies me. Though my hair is tangled and my clothes torn, I will not look away and let him think I have anything to be ashamed of.

"The queen is dead," he says. "We found the poisoned cup."

Through the wall I can hear Luoch weeping.

"I did not know her," I say evenly.

"She and my father were cousins. So you and I are also kin."

"But you are less than kind, after what I did to aid your cause."

Malcolm smiles but without warmth. "I will have some water brought, that you might clean yourself up," he offers.

"That would be a start. Better still, tell me that my companion Colum is safe."

"And the rogue Eadulf, too? That henchman of the tyrant?" Malcolm frowns.

"He has done wrong, I grant you," I say, trying to remain patient. "But he turned against Macbeth, suffering greatly because of it. And I did not choose his companionship."

But Malcolm is no longer listening. His eyes are wandering over me.

"You might be a beauty, with that hair. If you wore a dress." He looks with distaste on my sheepskin leggings. "I'll have one brought to you from the late queen's closet."

The idea of wearing my mother's clothing makes me shudder.

"I do not want a dress," I say firmly. "I want my friend Colum released. He is only a shepherd with no desire to become entangled in your wars."

Malcolm waves his hand. "He may go. He is nothing to me. But Eadulf must stay, for Fleance deserves revenge for his father."

I am relieved at least for Colum's sake. But what comes next in this broken realm? Will Fleance be permitted to kill Eadulf? Will more murders follow?

"Who will be Scotland's king now?" I ask Malcolm.

"I will," he answers without hesitation. "It was I who brought England to the battle. I have the most warriors and the best claim, being Duncan's appointed heir. Not Luoch, that puling son of the tyrant's wife. Not Macduff. Brave though he is, his royal blood is scant."

Malcolm does not even mention Fleance. Perhaps Macbeth's fear—that Banquo's line would rule Scotland—has died with him, and what I thought was the Sight will prove only an illusion.

"It is a pity that the two who could vouch for you are dead," Malcolm is saying, staring at me sharply. "How do I know you are who you claim to be? Many women have red hair like Macbeth's and gray-blue eyes like the queen's."

"Nothing I say will convince you," I reply, giving him no answer.

Malcolm fingers his large head thoughtfully. "Both Seyton and Macduff swear they heard the king lately speak of a daughter who had returned from the dead. They thought he was going mad. But perhaps he spoke a measure of truth." Suddenly he smiles. "Riding into the battle, you shone like a fiery lodestar in the sky."

I am growing impatient with this man's musings. He reminds me of a cat deciding whether or not to pounce on the mouse he has cornered.

"You have no quarrel with me, and I have none with you," I say briskly. "Let me go."

Malcolm shakes his head. "I must know whether Macbeth's daughter can be trusted. You were at Dunduff, where all Macduff's family were slain."

"How dare you suggest that I was of the murderers' party!" I stand only inches from the nose on Malcolm's big face. "I loved Fiona and her children. It was Colum and I who buried them. Tell Macduff that we saved his son, who is now in the care of the wise woman Caora and old Helwain in the Wychelm Wood. Send him there to learn the truth from Wee Duff himself!"

Malcolm takes a step back and regards me with something like respect. "They were not all killed, as it was reported?"

"Nay, the son survived—as I told Angus and Ross. Banquo's son also lives. You, Duncan's son, and I, Macbeth's daughter, live. It is up to us to restore justice and peace to Scotland now."

"I see that you understand the situation." A smile spreads across Malcolm's round face. "Albia, with you as my queen, my claim will be firm. No one will dare to come against the kin of Kenneth and Duncan united."

"Nay, you mistake my meaning. I have no desire to be a queen," I say, holding up my hands.

Malcolm reaches out and grasps them. "Our eldest son will rule after me. And our daughters will marry thanes and princes, bringing us allies, and Scotland shall prosper."

"I am not the spoils of war. You may not claim me," I say, indignant. "I am the daughter of Scotland's king and queen.

As they are now dead, I will marry whom I choose—or not at all."

Malcolm's smile fades. His grip on me tightens. "You are hardly in a position to choose your future. Kiss me now and seal the pact," he demands, leaning forward.

My forearms ache from the tension of trying to pull away from him. "I do not love you, and I will not marry you!"

Malcolm's lips draw back from his teeth in a wolflike snarl.

"Without food or drink, you will change your mind soon enough. Then I will wed you before the thanes and England's earls, and you will put on a show of willingness or live to regret it."

With that, Malcolm releases my hands and I stumble backward. He storms from the cell, letting the bolt fall loudly into place behind him.

Chapter 28

Dunsinane

Albia

The walls of Dunsinane close in upon me, windowless, the locked door unbreakable. It must be night again; it seems an entire day has passed. Sick despair fills me at the prospect of being Malcolm's wife, forced to serve him and bear his children. Did my mother feel this way when she was made to marry Gillam, and then the man who slew him, Macbeth? Will I also end up abetting violence all my life?

I am determined not to replay that same dark role in the drama of Scotland's future. But who in all the land will save me from this prison, Dunsinane, or the bondage of being married to its king? The face of Fleance drifts into my mind, and with it finally come my tears, blurring the sight of my love. No, I must not give in to self-pity. I wipe my eyes with the ends of my blue girdle, still firm about my waist, wishing its magic could help me escape. Perhaps if I sleep, the Sight will come to me, revealing a way out of my prison. Or will it show me what I most fear, a life of miserable captivity to Malcolm?

"Albia, are you all right?"

The man's voice is low-pitched and muffled. I assume it is Luoch, trying not to be heard by the guards.

"No, I'm not." I lean against the wall between us. "I want to be freed."

"Are you hurt?"

Hearing the concern in his voice, I can't hold back my sadness.

"Only my heart is broken. It wasn't supposed to end like this! I wish I could talk to you."

"Keep your voice down," the man whispers. "I am coming in."

Then I realize it is not Luoch after all. A key scrapes against the door lock. Has the odious Malcolm returned so soon? I wish I had something to defend myself with, but the room is bare except for the bedding and mats on the floor. So I hide behind the door with the idea of slipping out in the moment before my visitor sees me, then running.

But my heart leaps up in my chest and my feet refuse to budge, for the man who enters my cell is Fleance. But my joy soon gives way to confusion.

"Why are you here, Fleance? How did you get past the guards?"

"I bribed them with wine." He looks at me uncertainly. "I wanted to see you."

"And I you—" I can say no more; "dear Fleance" catches in my throat. I think of how he looked at me yesterday and condemned me with his silence, and bitterness fills me.

"Why did you not vouch for me to Malcolm? I might be free, if you had spoken."

"I was stunned to see you—and to hear you speak. I thought I knew you, Albia, and then I learned you were someone else." His voice pleads for my understanding.

"I am who I always was," I say, unmoved. "I have not changed since you last saw me."

"But all the while, I did not know—that you are kin to that monster and his wife." The disgust in his voice rouses my anger.

"I am not pleased to be Macbeth's daughter!" The words burst from me. "I did not ask for Grelach to bear me!"

"You hid the truth from me, and from my father," Fleance accuses me. His brow is contracted with grief and hurt.

"I myself did not know who I was until the night Geillis died," I explain in my defense. "And when I tried to warn your father of the danger from Macbeth, he dismissed it. If I had sworn then that the king was my father, you would have hated me and sent me away. I could not have borne that."

"How did I fall in love with the daughter of such a wicked man, and not know it?" Fleance tightens his hands into fists, as if to squeeze all feeling from them.

"You are most unjust to blacken me with his crimes." My chest is heaving as I speak. "I abhorred the evil my father did. Fleance, I begged to come with you and help avenge your father's death. I almost killed Eadulf but instead let him lead us to the bigger prize, Macbeth himself. I wept to see your mother dead, and buried her with my own hands. Dear

Fleance, dear, I have thought of nothing these past weeks but finding you."

Fleance loosens his fists and runs his hands through his hair.

"I am sorry," he says. His shoulders sag. "It is I who should be ashamed. You have shown more courage than the stoutest of men."

"If I was strong, it was due to your gifts, this girdle and the sword you left me at Dunbeag. They kept me safe."

Fleance looks confused. "That old sword? It was a mere toy."

I want to tell him about our journey through the mountains and my fight with the boar, but there is too little time.

"Is Colum still here or did Malcolm free him?"

"The rustic bowman? Malcolm sent him on his way."

Still I am worried, for Colum would not willingly leave while I was still being held captive.

"Where did he go?"

"He was ordered to lead Macduff north to where his son was taken." Fleance smiles to himself. "I have never seen a man so drowned by despair and raised with hope as this great Macduff when he learned his son was alive."

Silently I thank the gods that Colum is safe and feel a twinge of homesickness at the thought of him at Murdo's cottage and in the familiar bowers of the Wychelm Wood.

"Now Macduff is determined to punish every one of the king's men responsible for destroying his family," Fleance says. His brow furrows with grief for Banquo and Breda.

"How I wanted to be the one to deal the king his death blow!"

I put my hands on his shoulders.

"Be glad that neither of us bloodied our hands by killing a king, however wicked he was."

Fleance clasps my hands. "O brave Albia, you held your furious sword still when with one stroke, you could have wrought all our revenge. Was it not hard?"

The awe in his voice embarrasses me. I don't want to revisit those moments of my rage, how it flowed and ebbed, and my father's strange repentance, his submission to me. Not now.

"I regret only one thing, Fleance," I say, touching his cheek. "That I did not let you kiss me when we last parted," I whisper. "You may do it now, if you still wish."

He looks at me. His eyes are full of grief and hunger. "I do, and I will, but I might not be able to stop kissing you once I start."

At once we lean together, and our arms find their natural fit around each other's bodies. Our lips meet like an arrow and its target, holding fast until I almost faint for lack of breath. He whispers what sounds like "I love you" into my mouth, and that gives me air enough to keep on kissing him.

Then I feel his hands at my waist, untying my girdle. I trust his fingers and do not try to stop them. He takes the ends of the girdle and wraps them around himself. We are tied together so nearly that I blush to feel the heat from his body.

"Albia, my fate is bound with yours," he whispers.

The words of my own dream startle me, coming from Fleance's mouth.

"I know," I breathe back. "You and I share a single future."

Then I think of Malcolm's determination to make me his wife. I pull away from Fleance, whose hands caress my neck.

"You must help me get out of here. Malcolm is threatening me."

"He will not hurt you. Don't worry. I will come to you as often as I can."

"You don't understand. Malcolm wants to *marry* me. He will force me if I refuse."

Fleance reels back. "How dare he, the unworthy sot! He cannot have you." His face looks grim as his mind works behind his dark blue eyes. "I see where Malcolm's ambitions tend. With you as his wife, he thinks he can win over the warriors who are loyal to Kenneth's blood, sapping your brother's support. Then, while Macduff is still away—whose voice would carry great weight because he slew Macbeth—Malcolm will have himself crowned. And when the far-flung parts of Scotland, who never loved Duncan, learn that his son has seized power, new wars will break out, tearing the country asunder."

"So to foil Malcolm's plan, I must escape now, Fleance." My mind reels with my own plotting. "The guards are asleep. Bring me my sword, and tell me where they are keeping Nocklavey, and I will ride away tonight. You must break Luoch out of his cell, too."

"I don't want to lose you again, Albia. Stay, and we will find another way," Fleance pleads.

"I will not stay and be forced into marriage with Malcolm. That way you *will* lose me—forever."

"I will not let you marry Malcolm. Stay, and marry me instead," Fleance says, his voice firm and sure.

At any other time, I would melt into wax at these words. Now I only wonder how Fleance can be so thickheaded.

"And then watch Malcolm kill you? No, you must come away with me and Luoch." Once I say this, it seems the perfect and inevitable solution. "That way we can be together."

But there is a long silence before Fleance replies, in a careful tone, "As my father's son, I have a duty to see justice and order brought to Scotland and a new king seated."

I stare at Fleance, stung that he does not even consider leaving with me. I think of him in his bright livery at Malcolm's side.

"Would you then let Malcolm declare himself king?" I ask.

Looking pensive, Fleance shakes his head.

"Why not, when you could become his general? Whom would you choose to rule Scotland?" My tone is icy.

"I might support Luoch," he says slowly.

Fleance is withholding something from me. I try to see his eyes, but he will not meet my gaze. I ought to know him well enough by now to guess what he is hiding. Surely it is related to the question of who will rule Scotland. Then I remember the day I reminded Banquo of the Wyrd sisters' long-ago predictions. Fleance's eyes had shone at the idea that his father would beget a line of kings; that he, Fleance, might be a rival to Macbeth. Yes, he often wants more than he can have. Can he possibly still hope to be king?

"I see now, Fleance. You want to marry me. Malcolm also wants to marry me." I lay out the pieces one by one. "My mother's grandfather was the great King Kenneth. My father was a king. That makes me quite a prize. Whoever weds me puts his hands on a great deal of power."

I fasten my gaze on Fleance. He does not blink, but seems to breathe faster as I speak.

"And if you have little claim to rule through your own blood, Fleance, you would be wise to marry a king's daughter, so that your own offspring have a stronger claim, especially if her brother is the king and you have helped him to the throne." I raise my eyebrows. "Have I not hit it?"

"I will not deny what you have said," Fleance says, growing defensive. "But my family's lineage is also ancient, and I am related to half the thanes in Scotland, among whom was no more honest man than my father."

"I see I have hit the mark. You *would* bargain your way into a place of power."

"Favor has always been bought and sold," says Fleance sharply. "Do not blame me for the ways of Scotland."

Bitter sadness washes over me at the thought that nothing in this land will ever change. I thought that Macbeth's death would bring peace to Scotland, but now I see that men still clamor for revenge and power over each other.

"And you cannot blame me either, Fleance, if I will not be a pawn in this game, not as Malcolm's wife or yours."

"At least *I* will love you!" he cries.

His declaration hardly fills me with joy. "You will love me—if I marry you?" I ask warily.

"I mean, I do love you. Now."

"But you clearly love Scotland more!" The accusation bursts from me.

"And you do not?" Fleance grows heated. "You sought out Macbeth and brought about his downfall—what was the purpose of that? It was not only revenge, for you showed no delight at his death. Nor was it ambition, for you do not wish to rule. Then what moved you, if not love of Scotland?"

His questions take me aback. What was the purpose of my coming to Dunsinane? I had told Colum that I sought justice for Scotland. But was my desire that simple or pure? Perhaps I hoped to prove myself a better person than the tyrant and his wife who bore me. Yet what did I do but betray my own father, bringing him to his knees in surrender? So that Macduff could slay him. So that my despairing mother could take her life. However deserved their deaths were, I am still guilty. Despite what I said to Fleance, my hands are indeed stained with their blood. Hoping to free myself from violence, I have perpetuated it. And now I am held fast in Dunsinane. All I have learned is that revenge is a lust that is never satisfied, the boar that is never beaten, except in dreams.

"I don't know anymore if it was the love of Scotland that moved me to come here, Fleance," I admit with a weary sigh. "But I know for certain that I love you."

A hopeful smile spreads across his face. "Then you will stay with me."

"No, for I also know that my search is not yet over."

His smile fades. "What do you seek, if not me?"

I spread my hands out before me, palms up, and lift my

shoulders. "I will know when I find it. Please, only help me escape from here."

Fleance presses his hand to his forehead. I know he is weighing the consequences of betraying the powerful Malcolm.

"I will," he says at last.

Before he goes to find my sword and armor, he unlocks Luoch's cell. I wake up my brother and relate my conversation with Fleance. Luoch is anxious to rally warriors against Malcolm, and I tell him to go without waiting for me. The drunken guards are snoring heavily. Luoch grabs their weapons. We squeeze each other's hands in farewell, and he escapes into the night. I am sad to see my brother go, for I fear that it is his fate either to be killed soon or to become Scotland's next king and be killed later. It takes no dream from the Asyet-world to show me this.

I pile straw beneath the blankets to fool the guards into thinking that Luoch and I are asleep. Then I wait for Fleance's return. It saddens me to think that we are parting after yet another disagreement. How long will Scotland's woes separate us? Such somber thoughts fill my mind in the darkness. At every sound I startle, afraid the guards are waking. After what seems like hours, Fleance returns with my sword.

"Here, take this guard's jerkin and helmet so that you may leave Dunsinane without rousing suspicion," he whispers. "I hid your horse at the base of the hill east of where the king was slain."

I am surprised that Nocklavey let Fleance lead him. How did he know he was not being stolen?

While Fleance tugs off the jerkin, the guard opens his eyes and starts to protest, but Fleance makes a fist and strikes him on the head, knocking him out again. I open my mouth to thank him for the risks he is taking, but he cuts off my words.

"Quiet, and hurry. This must be your sword, though it is not the old one I gave you."

I shrug my arms into the guard's too-big jerkin and take the sword from Fleance, examining the bright silvery blade that slew the boar.

"Nay, it is the much finer one you left for me, when you went from Dunbeag for the last time," I remind him.

"I have never seen it before," he insists.

I stare at Fleance, then at the sword. "Then how—?"

"It does not matter," says Fleance urgently. "Go."

I sheathe the sword and buckle the scabbard around my waist. A strange feeling of lightness comes over me, as if I could leap right over the walls of Dunsinane. Again I wonder who left the sword for me, but I am content to live with the mystery.

"Wait, Albia." Fleance touches my sleeve gently. "Where will you go?" Then he holds up his hands. "Nay, it is better if I do not know—if Malcolm finds out what I've done."

My eyes are filled with tears, so that my love's face is only a blur. I step away from Fleance, afraid that if I touch him back, I won't be able to let go of him, ever.

"*I* don't even know where I am going, Fleance. But you can find me, if you will. I wanted to find you, and I did."

As I turn away, Fleance reaches for me, grasping the end of my girdle hanging beneath the jerkin. It passes quickly through his fingers and I feel only a slight tug at my waist.

But it might as well be a rock pulling on me, so hard is it to run from Fleance again.

Chapter 29

Pitdarroch

Albia

Nocklavey bears me away from Birnam Wood and Dunsinane Hill and along the sinuous turnings of the River Spey. This time we stay clear of the steep and snowy Grampian Mountains.

Nothing slows him, not hunger or thirst. Streams part as he splashes through them so that hardly a drop dampens us. Startled animals flee before his thundering hoofs. And I go where he takes me, burying my face in his thick mane and pressing my feet against his flanks until we become like a single creature. I have no destination. I am simply fleeing Dunsinane and a far worse prison: marriage to Malcolm.

Running heedlessly, I do not notice the changes at first. One night the moon no longer lurks behind a scrim of clouds, but shows bright as a silver button pushed halfway through the cloth of night. Then I hear the owlets hooting to each other and the melody of the nightingales. By day I find myself squinting, for the world has again become a place of sunlight and flickering shadows. The warmed wind passes over me. It is a pure pleasure not to be always cold. On the tips of twigs, buds swell and turn green with promise. Slowly, my senses open up to these forgotten things.

I pass through villages where people walk around with dazed looks, as if they have dwelled too long in a cave.

"The tyrant Macbeth is dead!" I cry, spreading the news.

Their bewildered looks turn to smiles of joy. Then they ask, "Who will be the king now?"

Having no sure answer, I only spur Nocklavey harder, leaving the people to wonder. Maybe if I stop long enough and still myself, the Sight will come to me. It has already shown me a line of kings with Banquo's features. Will Fleance one day rule? Only time will reveal if what I saw was truly the As-yet-world or only a glimpse into Macbeth's fearful mind.

No matter how fast and far Nocklavey takes me, I cannot outpace my thoughts. Thoughts of Macbeth's touch, his fearful raving, the lifeblood flowing from his neck, his glassy eyes. He was my father, and I his daughter—the offspring of evil. I can't escape that thought. No, not even by thinking of Banquo as my better father. I run, too, from the thought of my mother's lifeless body on the hilltop. Did anyone bury her when they abandoned Dunsinane? Did she mourn me when she left me to die? Geillis was my truer mother, for she raised me with love. But Geillis is dead. Banquo is dead. Macbeth and Grelach are dead. I am orphaned over and over, and what am I left with? The blood of kings and a queen—all dispatched now to the Under-world, to face the justice of the gods—still flows in my veins and will as long as I am alive.

There is no outrunning the truth.

There is no letting their blood from my veins, without dying myself.

There is only the taming of it. The curbing of cruelty and the nurture of one's better nature. What Geillis told me when I was a child now comes home to roost in me, like a dove to its dovecote.

I am not the prisoner of my past. I am not helpless before the Sight. It was not my visions that drove me to act, but my actions that revealed what those visions meant. I made mistakes because I did not understand what I saw. But I could not understand, until time and my deeds had unfolded the truth. The fact that I share Macbeth's and Grelach's blood does not force me to repeat their evil. My deeds are my own. As Macbeth's deeds were his.

I am no longer clutching Nocklavey's mane in my fists. He slows his gait. I notice bluish flowers among the heather, nodding their tiny blooms in the warm wind. My mind feels lighter, as if a hood has been pushed back from my head.

Did not Geillis and her sisters teach me that the four worlds are interwoven? That gods and other beings travel between them? Their traces are everywhere—in the braided girdle that guarded my virtue; in Nocklavey, my loyal warhorse; in the sword mysteriously left for me. But the boar that threatened my life in the snowstorm? Yes, even it was a gift. For I see now that fighting it was my test. I slew the boar; thus I did not slay the king and like him gild my hands in human blood. I held in my wrath and Macbeth came to his knees, confessing his wrongs. The foul and deadly beast of my own ill nature is what my gifted sword gave death to in the mountains.

And who strengthened my sword-arm but Fleance? He took no delight in my weakness, but trained me to bear arms. By doing so, he taught me to discipline myself. What a prince among men he is! If I were with him now, I would tell him this: *You are suited to be a leader. I would travel to the farthest reaches of Scotland in your company.*

My thoughts of Fleance fill me with hope, even as the distance between us grows with Nocklavey's every stride. I know as firmly as I feel the girdle around my waist that my future will be bound with his. One day, Fleance will find me. But not yet.

Now I am no longer running away from Dunsinane but toward Pitdarroch. The place itself draws me. Of course I should come back to the oak, where the four worlds meet and where my mother lies buried. Colum is nearby, and pale-haired Caora with Helwain in the Wychelm Wood. They tend to Wee Duff, whom I see reunited with his father. Pitdarroch, so far from the field of war, is a place of peace and healing. Here is where I know myself.

I see the great oak tree even in the dark. Behind its tangled branches, the moon glows, a white face crossed with many-fingered hands. The ground is a web of shadows, alive with night creatures who nestle among the roots. In the distance the stones of Stravenock Henge stand against the sky, their surfaces white where the moonlight strikes them.

The night is loud with the chirping, grunting, and

rustling of night creatures. In them the gods rejoices. Ban-righ controls the god of night again. She will make the winds blow, the tides rise and fall, and women's blood flow again, all according to nature. I remember the night on the shieling when she first visited me and the white doe beckoned. Now she lights the stones of Geillis's cairn for me. I remember my sorrow when Geillis died, like a wound that aches even after it heals.

Tonight I will lie here, where the four worlds meet, and wait for the dream that will show me my future.

⁓

A white doe steps between the tangled roots of the oak tree, moonlight and shade stippling her pale fur. I thought of her before I slept, and now she visits my dreams, unmoving, only her dark eyes blinking. I want to follow her, but my feet are as heavy as rocks. The doe fades like an insubstantial mist.

I see a face like my own reflection in water. It is older, lined with care. The lips move in silence. I strain to listen. What are they saying? A coif covers her hair. Tears pool in the blue eyes—*my* eyes. Why am I sad? What grief will come to me? I do not want to know. I will close my inner eye to this Sight.

No, show me Fleance's face! Show me myself with Fleance. Let me feel his arms about me.

Instead I see a round face, with brown hair and greenish eyes—Geillis as she looked before she became ill.

My mind reaches out in yearning for the Under-world.

"Mother," I hear myself murmur.

"How can she know me, even while she sleeps?" comes an unfamiliar voice.

Does she speak to me? Let me come to you, Mother; show me where you are.

"I will always know you," I say, stirring. I feel the hard ground beneath me.

"Albia, wake up."

I open my eyes. Rhuven is kneeling beside me. Her cloak brushes my skin. The sun is a blaze of fire on the horizon, making me blink. I am disappointed to find myself in the Now-world. And why is Rhuven at Pitdarroch?

"I mistook you for Geillis," I say, rubbing my eyes. "Did we both come here to be with her?"

Rhuven does not reply. Her face is a cipher of shifting emotions. She turns her head slowly to the side and I follow her gaze, startled to see a woman standing nearby. Her back is to us and she wears a blue woolen tunic and a silk hood. Her face is buried in her hands and her shoulders are shaking.

"It is your mother," whispers Rhuven.

"Am I still dreaming? Is it Geillis?"

Rhuven shakes her head. "Nay. It is Grelach."

Like a sudden gale, Rhuven's words throw me backward.

"But Grelach took her life at Dunsinane! Is it her spirit from the Under-world?"

"Albia, she is alive. We escaped from the tower before Malcolm captured it. It is your mother—the one who bore you."

I cannot make myself believe her. Yet the desire grips me to know the mother who let me be lost.

"Show me her face," I demand. As soon as the words are out of my mouth, I shake my head. "Nay, go away. I will not see her!"

"Please Albia, only let her behold you," Rhuven pleads.

I hold myself still. I force myself not to turn away. I looked upon the murderous king; I will not fear to look upon his wife.

Then Lady Macbeth turns. Her hood hides her downcast face. Her hands, clasped at her throat, are raw-looking and scabbed. Slowly she pushes back her hood, and a mass of dark hair, threaded with silver, tumbles forward. She lifts her head. Hers is the face I just dreamt, with the blue eyes and pale, lined skin

"Albia, do you know me?" she whispers, her voice barely audible.

She calls me by my name. How dare she use my name without asking? *Do I know her?* She does not look like someone who would cast out her infant daughter, abuse her only son, or conspire to kill a king. But neither did Macbeth look like a murderer. Evil is ashamed to go naked, but hides behind a mask.

This woman, however, seems to be hiding nothing. She gazes at me with her gray-blue eyes—my eyes. I can see that she was once beautiful.

"You are Grelach. My . . . my mother." I intended the words to be an accusation, but they slip harmlessly from my lips.

"Daughter, I pray you, forgive me."

With these words, tears begin to course down her cheeks. She wipes them with her fingertips, then gazes at her wet hands in surprise.

Rhuven gasps. "My lady, you are weeping!"

Grelach nods and looks up again. She seems to be smiling.

"All that I did," she says, letting the tears roll down her cheeks unstopped, "was born from my despair—at losing you, Albia."

Her voice breaks, and her hands flutter to her sides, like birds unable to fly. But she swallows and tries again.

"Now that I have found you, I may hope . . ." She leaves the sentence unfinished.

Rhuven picks up one of her hands. "For peace, my lady?" she prompts.

Grelach nods. "Now that he is dead." Her voice sounds stronger now. She looks at me. "The time is free." She takes her hand from Rhuven and slowly extends it toward me.

I glance at at the long fingers, the palms red and blotched from self-torment. I am afraid to touch her hand. But why?

The time is free.

I feel it, too. All that was bound can be released. With Macbeth's death, nature is reclaiming Scotland, stone by stone, tree by loch by glen. Slowly the land is freed from tyranny. Only my mother is still bound.

Unless I forgive her.

I step outside myself and observe this Lady Macbeth, late queen of Scotland, granddaughter of a king. She stands before me like a once-proud tree, struck by a storm and now broken-limbed. She has nothing and no one. Her infants are all dead. Luoch has renounced her. Only Rhuven loves her. But only I, her daughter, can ease her suffering.

I long to unleash the questions that crowd onto my tongue. *Why did you consent to his evil? Was it from weakness or the strength of your own ambition? Were you my father's victim or his tempter?* But I say nothing. I am not sure the answers even matter anymore.

I begin to reach out my hand, then fold it quickly over my chest, grasping my upper arms. I cannot put aside sixteen years in a single moment. I hear a fresh sob from Grelach and close my eyes against her.

Through my sleeve I feel the jeweled band, like Geillis's hand holding my arm. She had no reason to love me, a crying baby dropped in her lap. But she did. I have no reason to love Grelach and every reason to hate her. We stand close enough so that a breath of wind brings me the scent of her hair and clothes: woodsmoke, and lavender, and peaty earth. Yet the gap between us seems as wide as a chasm in the mountains, as profound as the deepest loch in Scotland.

I force myself to glance at Grelach. Her shoulders are slumped and she is weeping. I realize that I am taller than she is. Just then she draws herself up, as if sensing my gaze. We stand eye to eye. Hers are blue pools of tears.

I remember how I used to be afraid of the loch, of the monsters that lurked in its watery depths. But none of them had ever harmed me. One, Nocklavey, I even tamed and made my servant. As I slew the boar. As I faced my father with a firm arm. What do I have left to fear? This woman can no longer harm me. But I can hurt her terribly. With a word, I can cut every thread of her hope.

I lean forward and touch Grelach's hand. I do not speak.

Her fingers close around mine with such force that her knuckles turn white. I feel her strain toward me as if she would clasp me in her arms, but like a queen she stands erect, holding herself back.

I see myself taking both her wounded hands in my own. The creases around her eyes and mouth, like so many rivers inked on Scotland's map, seem to relax, softening her expression. I glimpse my mother when she was my age. With my fingertips, I stroke the skin of her hands until the bloody spots begin to fade, then disappear.

Author's Note and Acknowledgments

Lady Macbeth's Daughter is a work of fiction inspired by Shakespeare's *Macbeth*, which is based on what passed for history in Shakespeare's time: Raphael Holinshed's *Chronicles*. Holinshed in turn got his material from fourteenth- and fifteenth-century chroniclers. By the time Shakespeare wrote *Macbeth* (sometime after King James came to the throne in 1603), it contained more fiction than fact. He telescoped the action into a very short time span, combined two different royal murders from Holinshed, and made Macbeth inexcusably evil. Shakespeare kept the Weird sisters he found in Holinshed, for they would please not only playgoers but King James, who was an avid witch-hunter. With their predictions about Banquo fathering a line of kings, Shakespeare (following Holinshed) created a mythical ancestry to flatter his sovereign and patron.

When you read Shakespeare's *Macbeth*, also look at the excerpts from Holinshed (reprinted in the Signet Classics and Norton Critical editions, to name but two). It is fun to study how he changed his sources and to ask why. Nick Aitchison's fascinating *Macbeth: Man and Myth* (London: Stroud and Sutton, 1999) asks these questions in a much larger context. As his title suggests, he sorts out the history from the later fictions. With this kind of foundation, you'll be able to see how I, too, altered my sources. I restored some of the history Shakespeare changed, but I also went out on a big limb by creating an entirely new character and putting her at the very center of the story.

What *do* we know about the "real" Macbeth? He indeed killed King Duncan in a dynastic feud but went on to rule Scotland in relative peace for seventeen years (1040–1057). In 1054 Duncan's son Malcolm defeated Macbeth in battle, but Macbeth's kingship survived until Malcolm killed him in 1057. Macbeth had married Gruoch, the granddaughter of a king, after killing her first husband in battle (avenging the death of his own father). Gruoch had a son, Lulach, by her first husband, and he ruled Scotland briefly (1057–1058) until Malcolm killed him in 1058. It was a bloody time. Shakespeare got that right.

There is no record of children being born to Macbeth and Gruoch. But written records were pretty scarce then, so they could have had children. The birth of a daughter especially might have gone unrecorded. Regardless of what *might* have occurred, why did I create Albia?

The quick answer, among others, is that I wanted to give an entirely new perspective on the events of Shakespeare's play, using a protagonist who is outside the main action but crucial to its unfolding. (Whom in the play would you have chosen for this purpose?) I considered having Lady Macbeth tell the story, but she is an accessory to the central crime of the play. Though she is a tragic figure, I didn't think that my younger readers would identify with her. But it was Lady Macbeth who gave me a tip when she tells her husband: "I have given suck, and know / How tender 'tis to love the babe that milks me . . ." (1.7.54–55). Shakespeare's Lady Macbeth admits that she has nursed a baby? Then why do they have no children in the play? When I looked at all the male characters in the play with sons, I asked myself how the lack of a son might make Macbeth so anxious about his legacy that he is driven to commit murder. How might the loss of a child affect Lady Macbeth? So I invented Albia and made her rejection by her father the single event that precipitates all the tragic action of *Macbeth*.

To create a vivid physical setting for my protagonist, I studied a number of books, the best of which were Ann MacSween and Mick Sharp's *Prehistoric Scotland* (London: B. T. Batsford, 1990) with its magnificent photographs of tombs, ritual stones, forts, and henges. Also good is Iain Zaczek and David Lyons's *Ancient Scotland* (London: Collins and Brown, 1998). For details of daily life, two useful resources are I. F. Grant's *Highland Folk Ways* (Edinburgh: Birlinn Ltd., 2007) and Regia Anglorum, a Web site that re-creates in fascinating detail English and Scottish life from 950–1066 (www.regia.org). To help me invent the stories and belief system of Albia and the Wyrd sisters, I dipped into Sir George Douglas's *Scottish Folk and Faery Tales* (London, 1892. Reprinted Bath, U.K.: Lomond Books, 2005) and Arthur Rowan's *Lore of the Bard: A Guide to the Celtic and Druid Mysteries* (Llewellyn, 2003). Another useful Web site with several links is www.medievalscotland.org, covering Scotland from 500–1603.

Actually going to the places you are writing about is a great way to do research, and "I need to research a book" is the best excuse ever for a trip overseas. In the summer of 2007 my son Adam and I visited Scotland, driving on the wrong side of the road from the prehistoric ruins of the Kilmartin Valley, to the stone henges at Callanais, to Cawdor Castle and Dunsinane Hill, eating haggis, neeps, and tatties along the way. Thank you, dear heart, for your company. (On my Web site, www.authorlisaklein.com, you can see photographs of some of the places that inspired the setting of this book.)

But the journey really began more than thirty years ago at a high school in Peoria, Illinois, when I first read *Macbeth* in an English class taught by Judith Burkey, and then with a nutty bunch of classmates wrote and performed a parody, *The Tragedy of Rich Macwood*, surely the silliest homecoming skit in that (now defunct) school's history. Thank you, Julie Bartley, Brian Green, Mike Humkey, Joe Kella, Liz Klise, Cyndi Lakin, Kevin McGowan, Tom Mueller, Beth Newsam, Jerry Novy, Paula Schweickert, Bob Simon, Patty Van Buskirk, Martin Willi, Louise Ziegler, and everyone in that Academy of Our Lady / Spalding Institute class of 1976 who made the Bard roll in his grave, laughing. Wasn't that a blast?

Returning to the Now-world, my gratitude goes out to